M   Raizner, Bernard I.

Insult to injury

$16.46

DATE DUE		
MAY 1 1 1990	NOV. 7 1990	
JUN 4 1990	MAY 7 1991	
JUN 2 1 1990	JUN 1 9 1992	
JUL 5 1990 pd		
AUG 9 1990		
AUG 2 9 1990		
SEP 2 2 1990		
OCT 1 6 1990		

© THE BAKER & TAYLOR CO.

INSULT to INJURY

Insult to Injury

BERNARD I. RAIZNER

E. P. DUTTON  NEW YORK

PUBLISHER'S NOTE: *This novel is a work of fiction. Names, characters,
places, and incidents either are the product of the author's
imagination or are used fictitiously, and any resemblance
to actual persons, living or dead, events, or locales
is entirely coincidental.*

*Published in the United States by E. P. Dutton,
a division of NAL Penguin Inc.,
2 Park Avenue, New York, N.Y. 10016.*

*Published simultaneously in Canada by
Fitzhenry and Whiteside, Limited, Toronto.*

Library of Congress Cataloging-in-Publication Data
Raizner, Bernard I.
Insult to injury.
I. Title.
PS3568.A427I57   1988   813'.54   87-19968
ISBN 0-525-24600-2

COBE

Designed by REM Studios

1 3 5 7 9 10 8 6 4 2

First Edition

I wish to dedicate this novel
to Pamela Walker
and Allen Rosen
in gratitude for
their time and energy,
their ideas and their talents,
and mostly—for their love.

Acknowledgments

For their love and encouragement, I wish to thank my dear mother, Claire; my late father, Nat; my sister Joan; my brother Albie; my sister-in-law Andrea; my nieces and nephews; and my good friend, Dr. Joseph Ingber.

For their assistance and contributions to this project, I wish to thank my tactful and talented editor at E. P. Dutton, Jason Harootunian; my agent, Susan Protter; Sharon Powers; the late William Quinn; Detective Al Marchiselli; former Detective Al Brenner; Ann Borchardt; Herb Lieberman; and Jeanne Danielson.

Finally, I wish to thank Michael Phillips, who told me I could write, and Ben Rapoport, who convinced me.

INSULT to INJURY

The phone rang but the young woman just stared at it. Finally, the persistence of the seventh or eighth ring changed her mind. "Perhaps it's not him, perhaps it's important," she thought. "Besides, I can't go on living like this!" She reached for the phone.

"Now I want you to listen carefully to me," the voice began. "You know who this is." He continued: "I'm downstairs in the corner phone booth. In the last half hour, I've made a dozen bogus calls to the Sixth Precinct. Every available patrol car in the area will be tied up for the next twenty minutes. You can call the cops, but they'll never get there in time."

Her hand was shaking so much the phone receiver made a scratchy noise against her ear. "Why are you doing this to me?" she pleaded. "Why don't—"

He cut her off: "I have your keys and I'm coming up. In a few minutes you'll be dead."

For several seconds she stood there frozen. Finally, the sound of a dial tone snapped her out of it and, taking quick, short breaths, she dialed a number. Busy signal. The busy signal seemed to get louder and louder and louder until it was deafening. She screamed and that set her whole body in motion. She ran from her apartment into the hallway, pounding on every door, yelling, "Help me, help me, please help me!" But there was no response—nothing.

She leaned her back against the wall and stared up at the fluorescent tube on the ceiling. Her legs began to give way and she slowly slid down the wall, until she was seated on the floor, tears rolling down her face. Not one door opened. Not one voice called to her. All she could hear was her own convulsive breathing. All she could feel was the cold sweat that covered her whole body.

"I've got to get out of here," she whispered. Reaching the doorknob above her, she pulled herself up and began to tiptoe down the stairway. At the next landing she heard footsteps from below. She stopped. They were getting louder—they were coming up. They were *his* footsteps, she realized.

She raced back up and into her apartment, slamming the door behind her. She checked to be sure both locks had engaged. The footsteps were getting louder—closer. She had to do something. Suddenly, they stopped. She turned, her eyes riveted upon the door. "Oh my God," she mourned herself, as she heard a key creeping into the lock. She tried to scream but no sound came.

Sylvia Rosen's evening had started poorly. She and her eldest daughter had argued again.

Although they'd quarreled many times before, their spats always upset Sylvia. That night she got a case of heartburn and her right eye began to twitch. To calm her nerves, she reached for her needlepoint basket. Her latest project centered around an adorable wire-haired terrier with only a few flowers in the background. (She'd grown tired of flowers.) By the time she'd completed the dog's pointy ears, Sylvia Rosen was totally relaxed. It will make a lovely throw pillow, she thought. It'll go perfectly with Janis's new sofa.

Suddenly a distant howl, followed a second later by a thud from the backyard, startled Mrs. Rosen. "Ouch," she cried, having pricked her finger. As she sucked on the wound, she got up to investigate the strange noises.

She nudged her bifocals up a bit and peered out the window but it was too dark to see anything. After shutting off the two lamps that lit her living room, she pressed her nose against the pane. Right near the redwood picnic table she spotted a dark object that didn't belong. About the size of a melon, it wasn't moving, but as Mrs. Rosen stared, what appeared to be a tail seemed to wag slowly. Suspecting that an injured animal lay there, she grabbed a sweater, opened the back door and stepped outside.

The outdoor light had been broken for years—the building's superintendent said he'd have to bust up a wall to fix it. The Chinese lanterns that hung between the fire escapes probably still worked. Mrs. Rosen's brother had set them up last summer for a Fourth of July bash and they really lit up the patio. But extension cords had to be connected and Mrs. Rosen didn't want to bother now. Besides, after a few seconds outside, her eyes were adjusting to the darkness and she could see much better. She walked slowly around her small vegetable garden toward the picnic table and then looked down. Lying in a pool of blood, the face of a dark-haired young woman stared up at her. Sylvia Rosen screamed and turned away, only to have her eyes fall upon another horrific sight: near the building line, under a Chinese lantern, lay the headless body.

Mark Cantor boarded the Fifth Avenue bus en route to his apartment in the Greenwich Village section of lower Manhattan. It was a cloudy day but unusually warm for the first week of March. He had taken advantage of the mild temperatures to stroll around the Midtown area.

A little buying spree had failed to cure another mild depression and, with no plans for the evening, he wasn't in any rush to get home. From his living room window he would see Greenwich Avenue with all the couples strolling in and out of the street's many restaurants and boutiques. He would feel as if he were the only person in New York City who was alone on Saturday night.

So Mark didn't mind that the bus crept along in the heavy traffic, stopping every few blocks. At Fifty-eighth Street Mark watched the kids gathering around a mechanical giraffe in the window of FAO Schwarz. One little girl screamed with joy every time the six-foot-high toy moved its head. At Fifty-fourth Street he peered down upon a bored workhorse drawing a buggy, unafraid of the surrounding monsters beeping their horns. At Fifty-second Street, the silver-haired lady who'd been standing next to Mark managed to get herself and two large shopping bags over to the exit door. Her place was taken by a young woman whom Mark did not notice until he accidentally brushed against her when the bus lurched forward at the Forty-ninth Street stop.

No more than five feet two or three, and with a small bump on the bridge of her nose, she lacked cover-girl beauty. But she was, nevertheless, striking. Her unusual amber eyes initially drew his attention. She had thick, long, and lustrous auburn hair, and a ghostly white complexion.

Not wanting to stare, Mark looked out the window, but kept stealing furtive glances at her. She appeared to be in her early twenties and had high cheekbones, Mark noticed, smiling to himself. Mark had always been a sucker for high cheekbones. He tried to watch the shoppers along Fifth Avenue, but was much more concerned with the young lady whose dainty, long fingers wrapped around the overhead pole only inches from his hand. Suddenly his heart was beating so loudly he was certain everyone could hear it.

Finally, she felt his gaze, turned and looked at him. Her eyes had a thin, dark rim around the light golden iris which made them glow. The sight electrified his body. He felt a rush and then became paralyzed until she looked away. He turned casually, giving her his back.

"I've got to talk to her," he thought to himself. Wheels started spinning in his head. He could feel the adrenaline pumping. But like a car left in the garage all winter long, the engine would not turn over. Mark Cantor could not think of anything to say. At one point he actually began to speak but stopped himself before the first word was fully formed. He quickly cleared his throat so that she wouldn't think he was a weirdo making funny noises.

Finding himself at a loss for words was a new experience for Mark Cantor. He had always been quite adept at approaching a woman he didn't know. And the more turned on he was, the easier it was for him to turn on the charm.

His friends marveled at his confidence. He seemed to have absolutely no fear of rejection. Perhaps this was because he never personalized it when a woman didn't respond to him. He knew that no matter what he said or what he did, there would always be those who just weren't interested. Some were preoccupied, some preferred a different type. Thus, to him it was "a sin not to try, but certainly no disgrace to fail."

Not only did Mark have brass balls when it came to approaching women, most times he was effective in securing their lasting interest and this, no doubt, was another reason for his great confidence. Indeed, Mark Cantor was a ladies' man.

People who didn't know Mark were often surprised that women found him so irresistible. He was not rich and sophisticated, and didn't pretend to be either. Physically, he was unimpressive. Only five feet eight inches tall, he looked thin wearing a sweater and scrawny in a bathing suit. His chin receded slightly and his bottom lip drooped a bit.

But while no Adonis, Mark was easy to look at. His large, light brown eyes were highlighted by remarkably long lashes, giving them both warmth and intensity. Thick curls of sandy brown hair draped over his ears like a puppy dog. A full mustache added sex appeal while masking the imperfections of the lower part of his face. He had a small, straight nose and when he smiled crescent-shaped creases curled like parentheses around his mouth. Mark had a face which conveyed a softness that made one feel safe. He had the perfect package for his winning charm.

Witty and clever, Mark knew how to tickle a funny bone, and he was a great raconteur, with an anecdote for every possible subject. He could also be stimulating in serious discussion as well as light-hearted talk. Perhaps most important of all, Mark Cantor knew how to listen. When it served his purpose, he could draw women out and make them feel as scintillating as he was.

With such assets and abilities, it was no wonder that he could sweep a lady off her feet. But there was another reason for his great success.

He had programmed every experience involving the opposite sex into his computerlike brain. By the time he was twenty-five Mark had an enormous store of information and had become an expert on predicting and causing responses in women. By obtaining a body of truths and arranging them systematically, he had turned the art of seduction into a science.

But as Mark took another look at the young woman on the bus, he felt butterflies in his stomach, and a sopping wetness in his armpits. He could not even recall his past successes in similar situations. At that moment, conversing with this total stranger seemed to be an impossible feat.

Mark hoped she'd get off the bus and stop torturing him by her mere presence. But the large, antique, gold-filigree earrings she wore told him that Greenwich Village was probably her destination. If he was correct, with traffic bumper-to-bumper, they had a long way to go.

Unable to initiate conversation in a vacuum, he hoped for some startling event to comment upon or anything that might create a subject for friendly discussion. He had never required a stimulus in the past but now he was out of practice.

Just past the Forty-second Street intersection it happened. The little bald-headed old man carrying a lady's umbrella who'd been seated directly in front of Mark's obsession got up to exit. The young woman started toward the empty seat but stopped in her tracks to read the message neatly stenciled on it: WON'T YOU PLEASE GIVE THIS SEAT TO THE ELDERLY OR HANDICAPPED. She hesitated, looking around as if to see whether anyone in the vicinity fit the description. No one. Mark saw his opportunity, but fear kept the words in his throat. At that instant, he glanced out the window and one of the stone lions guarding the public library seemed to stare right at him.

Where is your courage? he asked himself.

No sooner had he been shamed by the statue than he turned to her and began, "What's the matter—you don't qualify for the seat?"

"No," she smiled. "I guess I don't. But I don't see anyone

around. I was just trying to figure out if you're allowed to sit there until someone comes. . . ."

"Actually, miss, I was a little embarrassed to tell you"—he tried not to be convincing—"but you see I have a bad leg—old war injury . . . Nam!" He tapped his right thigh twice and smiled.

Mark looked like the type who managed to avoid hardships. His smile, as intended, dispelled any doubt she may have had. She didn't believe him and sat down.

"That damn war gets no respect," Cantor muttered to himself, making sure she'd hear it. She smiled as she was supposed to, but looked the other way. After the bus had made two more stops Cantor tried again:

"Are you going to give the seat up if someone *old* gets on the bus?"

"Yes," she said, starting another smile.

"I see, so you do have some reverence for the aged," Mark teased. "It's only the handicapped you don't give a damn about."

She completed her smile and almost went into a laugh, but didn't say anything and completely avoided eye contact with him. Mark had overcome initial resistance countless times. Persistence, that's what was needed—where was that old persistence?

It took him a few more stops to think of something else to say and then he leaned down toward her—close enough so as not to be heard by others, but not so close as to invade her body space. "Let me ask you something," Mark said. "Supposing a man gets on the bus who looks at least sixty-five years old and he's carrying an athletic bag with a tennis racket sticking out; would you get up for him?"

Again the girl smiled, and she responded, "I really don't know," and this time she did look at Mark. But there was a definite impatience in her tone. And immediately after she spoke she abruptly turned away from him.

At Thirty-ninth Street he studied the fashionable women entering and leaving the Lord & Taylor department store. He looked for those who were prettier than the girl on the bus, and he found a few. But she was the one he wanted. He glanced down at her, hoping she'd start talking to him, maybe ask a question or simply comment about the weather—anything. But she was turned in her seat to look out the window. Cantor was upset.

She probably has a boyfriend, he concluded. She might even

be married. Mark had never looked to see if she was wearing a wedding band. In fact, for all he knew she might be dull or dumb, mean or crazy, or for any number of other reasons not desirable, but that possibility had never even occurred to him.

He could have felt proud. After all, it had been a long time, and despite the fact that he wasn't as quick and sharp as in the past, he had talked to her, and had been original and amusing in his approach. But Mark found no comfort in that.

By the time the bus reached Twenty-third Street Cantor was despondent. He could not get her out of his head. There was something so compelling about this young woman that she had awakened him from a long, deep sleep. During Mark's retreat from romance, he hadn't seemed to notice a pretty face. But this girl was different—magical!

Who was she? He wanted to get to know her, and even before he did, he wanted to be with her. But for whatever the reason, it was apparent to him that nothing was going to happen. That was the bottom line and that's why he was so sad.

At about Eighteenth Street, she finally turned forward in her seat. When the bus stopped at Fourteenth Street she looked up: "Do you want to stop at my place before heading home?"

At first Mark was flabbergasted. Had he imagined the invitation? Then he realized that she wasn't talking to him, but to a woman standing to his immediate right. She was at least ten years older than her friend and seemed to have too much of everything: she was considerably overweight, had a long, bulbous nose and a large mouth; her hair—thick, coarse, kinky, and wild, seemed to be taking over not only her head, but the entire front of the bus.

Despite her prominence, Mark had been so engrossed in his new heartthrob that he hadn't noticed her companion. Never once during this long bus ride had he seen them converse. That's strange, he thought.

"I have to go to the Eighth Street Bookshop first, I promised my sister I'd pick up this old novel she wants; it's out of print and that's the only place that has it," the ugly one said. "Wanna come?"

"Sure," replied the other.

Mark laughed at himself for thinking that dreams do come true. He turned around as if to hide his foolishness from the two women. He recognized the small Gothic church on the western side of Fifth Avenue with the heavy wrought-iron fence protecting its trees and garden. He didn't have to look at the street sign to know they'd just passed Eleventh Street. Just after turning left on Eighth Street, the bus stopped, discharging at least a dozen passengers including Mark Cantor.

Instinctively, he walked west, back to the corner—the direction of his apartment. Although the light was in his favor he stood and looked around. He didn't want to go home yet, but where could he go?

As he stood there contemplating his alternatives, none of which particularly appealed to him, he was startled by a familiar stranger.

"Hiya, soldier, you look lost," said the young woman from the bus whom Mark had found so appealing.

He stared at her, dumbfounded by the sudden turn of events. She continued: "I read about you guys coming back from the jungles of Southeast Asia, and having difficulty adjusting." As she spoke, Mark watched her full, sensuous lips. "Or is it that you just don't know your way around this part of town?"

Recovered from his initial surprise, Mark answered, "Well, let me put it this way." He spoke slowly, planning his words: "I know where I want to be, but I don't know how to get there from here."

"If you tell me what you're looking for, I might be able to help you."

"You probably could." Mark arched his brow to look sexy. "I'm looking for your apartment!" he said, letting a devilish grin seep through. She smiled while her eyes studied his.

9

"Wise guy, huh," she said.

Suddenly her friend stepped closer and pretended to clear her throat.

"Oh, I'm sorry," the pretty one said. "My name is Joanna and this is Theresa."

Mark forced a smile for Theresa and introduced himself.

"So which way are you headed?" Joanna asked. "Or are you really lost?"

"No, I'm not lost. I was just trying to decide whether to go home or do some errands first."

"Where do you live?" she asked.

"Over on Greenwich. Where are you two headed?"

"Eighth Street Bookshop."

"Same direction. In that case, I'll walk with you and do my errands some other time. I mean—if you don't mind."

"I don't care when you do your errands," she said with her own wise-guy twinkle in her eyes.

As they browsed in the shop windows along the way, Mark used one of his old, patented techniques: "Did you decide what you're gonna get me for my birthday yet?"

Joanna played right along: "I've got a pretty good idea."

"I don't want you spending a lot of money on me."

Joanna smiled. "Don't you worry about that. I've got something very special in mind for you this year and I don't care how much it costs!"

"And to think—I was afraid you'd forget."

As the three strolled down Eighth Street the sun peeked through the clouds, igniting brilliant reddish highlights in Joanna's hair. "You've got incredibly beautiful hair," Mark told Joanna. "I love the color."

"Thank you. I use henna," Joanna said. "It's a natural tint, from the root of a plant. The ancient Egyptians discovered it."

"You know, Joanna, when we first met I thought you might be a bit too wholesome for me. But now that I know you dye your hair . . ."

"I also smoke and drink."

"Shocking," Mark kidded.

"Actually I only drink on special occasions."

"Listen, I've got a great idea," Mark said, taking hold of Joanna's arm to bring her to a halt. "Since *this* is a special occasion, why don't you let me buy you and your friend a drink right now. There's a pub around the corner called the William Shakespeare—they've got a great ballad singer."

Joanna looked over at her girlfriend, as Mark faced the two of them waiting for an answer.

"Oh, I can't," Theresa said. "I must get that book before the store closes, and then I've got to get home and get ready for tonight."

"What about you?" Mark said, turning to the real object of his desire. "You're not going to let me drink alone, are you?"

As they sat side by side in a cozy booth at Shakespeare's, Joanna told Mark, "I just moved. I was living on the corner of Sullivan and West Third Street, you know, near the park."

A guitar player sang in the background. Mark lit Joanna's cigarette and then took a sip of wine as Joanna explained why she had to get another apartment.

"My place faced out on West Third. If you were going to design a street and you wanted to make it as noisy as possible, what would you put there? Well," she said, answering her own question, "the Carvel store attracts a lot of people who just stand on the corner until they finish their ice cream. But of course, business is a little slow in the winter so West Third has a disco and to make sure people know it's there, a speaker blasts outside. Of course, they don't want it to be too quiet during the day, so they have a motorcycle repair shop! Most of the buildings down there don't have stoops, but of course there's one right outside *my* window. Every derelict in the Village knows my stoop—they hold meetings there! And when the bums aren't using it, it's a stage for street minstrels! Most of them are pretty bad. There was this harmonica player who'd come by every night at one o'clock and play the same goddamn song. He was driving me crazy. So one night I go down and tell the guy where I live and how much I dig his sound. Then I tell him there's a lunatic in my building with a hunting rifle who's been threatening to shoot him because he can't sleep with that noise. 'Listen, I'll really miss you,' I say, 'but you better find another place to play.' "

Joanna took a drag of her cigarette and Cantor noted the absence of any lipstick mark on the filter. He realized then that she wasn't wearing a drop of makeup, and still she looked great.

11

"I never heard that harmonica man again," she added after the pause. After a healthy swig of wine, Joanna resumed:

"Of course, there was a firehouse on the block. No noise award–winning street could be without fire engines. And that's where they made their big mistake. You see, what they failed to realize was that it always takes a few blocks before the siren on a fire truck warms up and gets really loud; so for maximum noise, you put the firehouse a few blocks away, not on the same street!"

Mark grinned from ear to ear, not just amused by her story, but also generally pleased at finding a pretty woman with a lively personality. "You couldn't scare the fire department into moving the station house?" he teased.

Joanna smiled, giving Mark a long look as if she'd just discovered something else she liked about him.

Mark got funnier as the evening progressed. At one point, Joanna, her sides splitting, begged him to stop.

"Did you know that your eyes close when you laugh," he told her. "That could be a problem: when you're really having a good time, you don't even see who you're with."

"I know who I'm with now," she said as she took his hand in hers, "and I'm having a great time."

"Me, too." Mark smiled at Joanna and the smile remained on his face as his eyes roamed the framed book jackets that decorated the walls in a continuous, colorful chain like an old gypsy's necklace.

When the singer concluded his third set, Joanna was starting a fifth glass of wine without apparent effect, while Mark was still nursing his second.

"I know you're not a native New Yorker—where you from?" Cantor inquired—the first mundane question either had asked.

"I'm from Grosse Pointe, a suburb of Detroit."

Mark recognized it as one of the wealthiest communities in the country and this new information pleased him. He liked women with class.

"I came to New York to study acting, when I was seventeen," she continued.

"How'd your parents feel about that?"

"Well, my father died when I was ten. Mother wanted me to go to college and was very upset about the whole thing."

12

Joanna stared up at the wrought-iron chandelier that hung above the bar. "She stayed angry, too. I'd phone her and she was always 'on her way out.' I'd write and she wouldn't answer. I went home for Thanksgiving a year later and she wouldn't talk to me. Every once in a while I'd try again—a letter, a phone call—finally, I gave up.

"A few years ago, she remarried," Joanna's voice was cracking, her eyes fixed on the chandelier. "I found out about it afterward."

Mark had on his sympathetic face, but this time he really felt it. Joanna squeezed his hand. "She still lives in the old house. They probably turned my room into a gym—I heard her husband's an exercise fanatic."

Fighting back tears, Joanna abruptly changed the subject: "So how come a sharp guy like you doesn't have a date on a Saturday night?" She turned to Mark. "Your girlfriend out of town for the weekend?"

"No girlfriend," Cantor spoke softly, looking deeply into Joanna's eyes. "Matter of fact," he added in a somber tone, "I haven't had a date in a long time."

Such an admission was totally out of character for Mark Cantor, but the computer was down and it felt good.

"Your ex give you a rough time?" Joanna waited for a response.

"No, I'm afraid I gave her a rough time . . ." his voice trailed off, as he pushed away the butt-filled ashtray. "Not really. The relationship just didn't work out . . . and I've had a bad taste in my mouth."

"How long ago did it end?" Joanna probed, gently stroking Mark's hand.

Mark thought for a moment and seemed surprised by his answer: "About a year now."

"That's a pretty long time to be recovering." Joanna patted Mark's thigh. "Now come on, drink up—you don't age wine in a glass!"

As the guitar player did his rendition of Rod McKuen's romantic ballad, "Jean," Joanna and Mark looked at each other without speaking. Gas lamps on the wall provided the pub's only illumination and in the dim light, Joanna's eyes now looked green.

"What color are your eyes?" Mark broke the silence.

"They're hazel," she answered, her hand on his knee.

"They're beautiful," Mark said, taking a closer look. Specks of yellow, green and brown danced in the flickering light.

Mark felt Joanna's hand stroking his thigh and his jeans were getting painfully tight in the crotch. He snuck his hand down the front of his pants and placed his member in a more comfortable position. Joanna caught him and smiled. "I was bent," Mark grinned sheepishly, as he pulled his hand out.

"Well, why didn't you let *me* fix it?" Joanna said in a breathy voice as she stared at the bulge. "I would have helped. Besides, you didn't do a very good job."

The next thing Cantor knew, Joanna's fingers were gently tracing the outline of his erect penis along the stretched denim. Mark's eyelids fell. It had been a long time since he'd been touched by a woman.

As Joanna rubbed harder, Mark's pleasure became more intense. Then suddenly her hand was gone. He opened his eyes to find the waiter standing before him: "Can I get you folks anything else?"

Mark looked at Joanna. "Are you hungry?" he stammered. "Would you like something to eat?"

Joanna's provocative smile answered his question. "Just the check," Cantor told the waiter. "As soon as you can, please," he added after clearing his throat.

When the waiter left, Mark shook his head. Joanna put her arm around him, and her tongue came out to moisten her lips. "So, do you still think I'm 'too wholesome' for you?"

Joanna Voorhees's new apartment was on the top floor of a five-story townhouse on Tenth Street just off Broadway. Built before World War II, the building had been converted into an apartment house more than fifteen years ago, and had not been renovated since. The outside had been painted a dull gray, which was starting to peel, and a jungle of ivy decorated the side facing the street, making the rusty fire escapes barely noticeable. With only fifteen units, the building was too small for a concierge, or a doorman, although apparently the rents were more than moderate. Instead, like many Manhattan apartment buildings, it required a key to the outer door or a buzz from the intercom to gain entry. However, when Joanna couldn't find her keys immediately, she opened the outer door by simply slipping a hair comb on the side of the door to disengage the lock.

"Tight security," Mark commented facetiously.

"What do you want for three hundred a month," Joanna remarked in the same spirit. "A friend of mine had the apartment for years and never had any trouble. It's a pretty good block."

Inside, fine mahogany paneling lined the hallways almost halfway up the wall, but not high enough to distract the eye from the rather gaudy floral paper above it. The building didn't have an elevator, but though Mark and Joanna were a little drunk, they were strongly motivated and climbed the four flights quickly. When they reached her floor, Joanna sat on the top step to perform the awesome task of finding the apartment keys in her large, junk-laden shoulder bag. "I hope I didn't leave them inside," she muttered to herself, "I hate to bother that poor super again."

Emptying the contents of her bag on the landing, she finally located the keys. She then put her things back in the bag, including an empty box of Chiclets and two ancient Hershey bar wrappers. Her door had two locks and when she was unable to turn the second key, Mark assisted and the door opened.

Her apartment, although sparsely furnished, wasn't much neater than her purse. Dirty dishes covered the café table just off the kitchenette and the wooden floor was cluttered with cardboard boxes.

"When did you move in?" Mark asked.

"Two weeks ago, but I've been so busy, I haven't had a chance to get the place in shape."

Joanna took Mark's jacket and hung it up, while he maneuvered through the maze of boxes to check the view. Her windows were bare but a metal gate covered one and the other was practically opaque with streaks of fresh paint. He raised the sash and stuck his head outside. It was a back apartment: he could see the small yards below and the rear of a larger apartment building too close across the way.

"Not exactly the New York skyline," Joanna yelled to him, "but at least it's quiet."

Mark left the window open and navigated his way back to a caned rocking chair in the center of the room, while Joanna

15

put a Rolling Stones album on a modest stereo that sat on a stack of boxes. Noticing a hand-painted oriental vase atop a small wicker table a few feet away, Mark got up to admire it.

"That's a beautiful piece," he said, thankful he'd found something to compliment.

"Yes, isn't it lovely? My next-door neighbor gave it to me as a housewarming gift. He was going to throw it out—said it was too feminine for his apartment."

"Did it come with the roses?"

"Those were a present from myself," Joanna stammered as she lit a cigarette and some incense on the same match.

"You didn't take much furniture from your other apartment."

"Well, I'll tell you, Mark, some friends helped me move. They were supposed to borrow a truck, but they showed up in a station wagon. We were going to do it in two trips, but after we packed up the wagon for the first load, I saw what was left, and decided not to come back. Most of my stuff was junk, and it was time for a change."

Joanna put out her hardly-smoked cigarette and moved closer to him. He could reach out and touch her but delayed for a moment to savor the thrill of anticipation.

The sweet smell of incense mixed with her own gentle fragrance to delight Mark's senses. When he put his hands on her shoulders, it was like a gun going off to start a race. They kissed frantically. Their hands explored, fondling, sometimes grabbing, moving quickly from one discovery to another. After a few minutes, they were both dizzy and standing suddenly became difficult. Joanna gently pushed him away. Heading toward the bathroom, she looked over her shoulder. That thick, radiant hair swept across her face, covering one eye. "Why don't you wait for me over there?" she said low and raspy, pointing with a glance to a sleeping alcove where a huge cedar chest towered high above a mattress on the floor. She swiveled her hips. "I'll be right back."

"Save the sexy nightgown for the next time," Mark told her, "it might be too much."

"Should I save the diaphragm for the next time?" she asked facetiously, holding back a grin.

"I'll wait," Mark said, not embarrassed by his error. It hardly mattered—basically, they were still on the same wavelength.

Joanna didn't take long. Her clothing had not lied; she was, in fact, more exquisite nude than she was dressed. Although she was not tall, her legs were long and shapely. Her breasts, just large enough to fill a champagne glass, were rounded and firm with nipples swelled and beckoning. As Joanna walked toward the bed, her boyish hips gently swayed. Mark noticed that her armpits were unshaven, and although he was not accustomed to the European look, he found the resemblance to a pubic bush arousing.

She lay down on her side next to him, but stayed several feet away, propping her head up with her hand. The tenderness in her eyes quickly changed to desire. But even as she pulled down the sheet covering Mark, he sensed that she didn't want him any closer just yet. She surveyed his lean but well-toned arms and then his hairy chest. She studied the boxes formed by his abdominal muscles and the line of curls that began at his navel and pointed straight down to where her eyes now lingered. Mark couldn't feel his hard-on and didn't dare look but the pleased smile crossing Joanna's face confirmed that all systems were go.

He moved closer and reached for her slim waist. In an instant their bodies were locked in embrace. Their lips met and their mouths opened wide, fitting perfectly, as they took turns probing with their tongues. They bathed each other in soft, wet kisses. Joanna's fingers spread through Mark's hair as he nibbled the smoothness at the nape of her neck. She buried her tongue deep inside his ear and then it all became a dream.

Mark drifted into a strange euphoria similar to a drug-induced high, a partially numbing spell, as if to shield him from the madness such intense pleasure would surely bring. For the first time in his life lovemaking was completely instinctual, with no thought process involved—no decision to touch her here or there, hard or soft, fast or slow. And like a dream, the experience was somewhat blurred so that afterward he could not recall all that had happened or the sequence of events, being left only with flashes of magic moments without order: her fingers squeezing his balls hard enough to cause a strangely pleasing ache deep inside his gut, then gently stroking his penis; her eyes rolling back into her head when he sucked and licked her clitoris; her vagina—warm and soft—enveloping him so snugly that even when they paused between pelvic gyrations he could feel it twitch;

17

his tongue gliding down the crack of her luscious ass and then, with utter abandon, delving deep inside her anus. Was he so beside himself that he'd really done *that?*

He remembered the sounds of pleasure: her moans becoming screams, so loud they could've been mistaken for cries of pain. And although a whimper was usually the loudest noise he made during sex, he had a distinct recollection of matching her decibel level. Yet so dreamlike was the experience, that Mark only vaguely recalled having intercourse in the missionary position and he wasn't completely certain of that.

Afterward, with the smell of sex permeating the air, Mark lay on his back looking up at the shadows on the ceiling. "When I was in the fourth grade," he told Joanna, "I said the word *nice* in class and my teacher scolded me: 'You're too bright to use words like that,' she said, 'it has no real meaning!' Well, I guess Mrs. Ross had never had great sex, because *that* was *nice.*" Mark said the word softly this time, elongating the single syllable so that it floated.

"Well, I think your teacher was right," Joanna responded, lighting a cigarette. "*That,* my dear, was *wonderful!*"

As soon as she finished smoking, Joanna started kissing Mark's chest and then his stomach. She nibbled at his hip and began softly licking the inside of his thigh.

"Hey, slow down," Mark implored, "I'm not nineteen. I need a little time to get a second wind—if you know what I mean."

"That's okay," Joanna whispered, "you can rest. *We'll* just go on without you!" Mark looked down at her and suddenly realized that he was already hard again, as Joanna began circling the head of his penis with her tongue.

They spent almost the entire night making love. For Mark, each successive experience was less ethereal, but more intense than the last. As he gained greater control, Joanna began enjoying explosive orgasms, during which her entire body would go into convulsive trembling.

At dawn, Mark lay there exhausted but too excited to sleep. He watched Joanna dream. He hoped it was a pleasant dream and that he was in it.

The next morning, Joanna rushed Mark out, explaining that her aunt was due shortly for brunch.

"Remember," she told him, "I really didn't plan on you."

"Can I call you?"

"Well, I don't have a phone yet—it's supposed to be installed on Wednesday. Why don't you give me your number and I'll call you next week."

"I'll tell you what," Mark proposed, anxious to make definite plans, "next Friday, can we have dinner then?"

"Sure," Joanna said.

Then Mark did his efficiency routine. "I'll give you my number anyway in case something comes up, you can call me."

"Fine," Joanna agreed.

Mark jotted down the two numbers on a piece of paper, and, pointing to them, he concluded the arrangements. "This is my office, this is my home. If I don't hear from you, I'll pick you up here Friday night at eight, okay?"

"Fine," Joanna repeated.

Mark nodded. God was in heaven and all was right with the world!

Mark Cantor stood tall before the jury in Bronx Supreme Court and without the aid of any notes delivered his final argument, as always, in a relaxed and confident manner. While summarizing the evidence presented in the most damning way, he held the jury's complete attention, varying the volume and inflection in his voice, looking from side to side to catch each juror's eye. As was his practice, he saved his most crushing blows for last:

"On the night of his arrest, Frank Ramos told Sergeant Montanez that he'd dated the complainant a few times, and that when she was told that he had a girlfriend, she became furious, assaulted him and started screaming rape.

"The very next morning he had a different story. He told Assistant DA Shapiro that he and Miss Garcia had met for the first time that evening at the Xanadu discotheque in Yonkers, and after having sex in his car, she demanded money, and when he refused to pay, they argued and fought.

"Before the grand jury, he testified that they'd met at the Cat Club in New Rochelle, dancing for hours before they left.

"And yesterday, in this courtroom, his story slightly different once again, he told you they spent only an hour together drinking at the bar there, before he invited her to leave with him.

"Each time he gives his version of the facts they change. Why does the defendant have so much trouble getting his story straight? I'll tell you why: because that's what it is—a story—a total fabrication!"

As he concluded, Cantor's voice grew progressively louder and angrier: "He lied to Sergeant Montanez, and then he lied to Assistant DA Shapiro; he lied to the grand jury and he took the stand here and lied again! He lied to them and he lied to you. He lied before and he lies now!"

Having worked himself into a frenzy, Mark stopped and walked toward Ramos, staring into the eyes of the young Hispanic. Slowly he raised his arm without bending his elbow and pointed his index finger at the accused. He spoke deliberately and didn't raise his voice this time, but there was even more anger in his tone.

"Frank Ramos is a liar . . . he's a liar and a rapist!" While he spoke, his arm remained extended, without the slightest movement, the index finger straight like the barrel of a gun as if he were taking aim and, if he pulled the trigger, Ramos would topple from his chair.

Mark paused and then brought his arm down as slowly as he had raised it, his eyes still fixed on the defendant. A few more silent seconds passed before he turned away from Ramos and walked toward the jury to complete his summation.

Cantor did the routine—pointing that finger at the accused like a one-man firing squad—in all his cases. It had become Mark's trademark. Lawyers in the Bronx courthouse called it his "*j'accuse* position." It was the final word, somehow making all his previous arguments seem irrefutable.

* * *

20

In 1971, a year out of law school, Mark Cantor was appointed an assistant district attorney in Bronx County. In only four years, he'd built a reputation as one of New York City's finest prosecutors. Although he had tried all kinds of cases, he now specialized in crimes of violence, particularly rape—"as violent a crime as murder itself," he'd tell the jury, "because it ravages the body, twists the mind, and cripples the spirit."

Although he'd never expressed a preference for sex prosecutions, Cantor's surprising victory in the 1973 Saint Mary's Park rape case led his boss, DA Paul Capellini, to give him a string of such assignments. Mark did not object, finding them a challenge because of the difficulty of getting convictions in that type of case. And the crime particularly suited Cantor's style. He was an emotional prosecutor, alternately working himself into tears of sympathy for the unfortunate victim, and then into rage against her evil assailant. His impassioned pleas would have been comical in a simple burglary or grand larceny prosecution, but they were appropriate and extremely effective in cases involving the trauma of rape.

Over the past three years, Mark Cantor had successfully prosecuted more than one hundred sex offenders. His stirring summations were famous for salvaging weak cases. As one court observer put it: "He makes the jury forget about such legal trivialities as reasonable doubt." Defendants who were foolish enough to assert the right to testify in their own behalf met with another Cantor weapon: a brilliant cross-examiner, he could make anyone sound like a liar. Judges, as well as juries, were caught up by his ability to evoke outrage, and imposed uncharacteristically severe sentences after Cantor convictions.

It was no wonder then that for every defendant who chose to battle this Goliath of the courtroom, almost twice their number threw in the towel before a witness was sworn. Despite the fact that Cantor's plea bargains were definitely no bargains at all, for many it was easier to plead guilty and do time, than to go to trial and be ripped apart and publicly humiliated only to wind up behind bars anyway.

The statistics were indeed impressive. In the two-year period from January 1, 1974 to December 31, 1975, Cantor had personally put more sex offenders behind bars than *all* the other prosecutors in the City of New York, *put together.*

21

Although he was by no means "famous," Mark Cantor was becoming well-known. He never made *The New York Times,* but his name appeared often in crime-oriented newspapers like the *Daily News.* In the local press, like the *Bronx Press Review,* Mark got as much copy as his boss, the district attorney. Capellini didn't mind—Mark was making his office look good. But for the DA's in New York's other counties, Cantor had become a source of embarrassment: women's organizations around the city wanted to know why the conviction rate for sex offenders was so low in the other boroughs. If these cases were so "difficult," how come that guy Cantor from the Bronx always wins?

Sergeant William Montanez was swiveling around in Mark's desk chair when Cantor returned to his office.

"Guilty on all counts," Mark announced matter-of-factly.

Montanez got up to let Cantor sit. "My man, you are the Muhammad Ali of the courtroom: you dance like a butterfly and sting like a bee."

Mark smiled. "It's easy when I've got a guy like you in my corner. He put the Ramos folder in a file drawer marked KAPUT. Like all the furniture in Mark's small office, the file cabinet was metal, old, and ugly. "You did an excellent job, Willie; congratulations," he told the officer.

Mark Cantor didn't like most of the cops he worked with. He found them lazy, sloppy, and stupid. They often failed to voucher evidence, get the names and addresses of witnesses, or give the proper constitutional warnings to defendants. Invariably they made mistakes in their reports that created problems for Cantor when a case went to trial, and clever defense attorneys tried to turn their errors into reasonable doubts. Some cops embellished upon the facts, without being clever enough to get away with it under cross-examination. But William Montanez was a straight shooter. Smart and thorough, when *he* made an arrest, it stuck. Furthermore, Mark liked him as a person. The feelings were mutual.

"The jury was out for only a few hours," Mark informed the officer. "If all cops were like you, my job would be a lot easier."

"Thanks, I appreciate the compliment. But I didn't come here for praise or to find out the jury's verdict. I just came from your boss's office and guess what?" Montanez had a devilish grin on his coffee-colored face. "The Jenkins case is scheduled to begin the week after next, and Capellini's got to be in Albany at that time."

"So?"

"The defense has been demanding a speedy trial and with the press always lookin' over his shoulder on this one, Capellini doesn't want to ask for another adjournment."

Mark stopped rearranging the papers on his desk. "The chief is going to let someone else try Jenkins?"

"Well, not just anyone—he's assigning the Muhammad Ali of the courtroom."

This time Mark didn't smile. "Are you putting me on?"

"Nope. Looks like we're gonna be workin' together again real soon."

Just then the phone rang. "Yeah, chief," Mark answered. "I'll be right up."

Montanez grinned: "Now you'll be cool when he tells you."

"Yeah, thanks."

Thomas Jenkins had been charged with robbing, raping, and beating an eighty-two-year-old woman in the supposedly safe Parkchester community. The case received a lot of publicity when the seventeen-year-old defendant skipped town after an error was made in setting his bail too low. Jenkins's capture two months later in Atlanta, Georgia, made the front page of New York's tabloids, and at each scheduled court appearance, busloads of outraged citizens came "to make sure justice is done."

Capellini briefed Cantor on the case that Friday afternoon, the meeting lasting almost two hours. Mark didn't get home until 6:30 and immediately he began preparations for his date with Joanna.

He called his favorite French restaurant and made a reservation for two. Then he began to doubt his choice. The food's excellent, he thought, but the atmosphere isn't very romantic . . . besides, maybe she doesn't like French food.

Quickly, he called Ye Waverly Inn, an out-of-the-way, one-hundred-year-old restaurant that featured a fireplace and cozy corners. That's a good choice, he thought. Joanna's probably never been there and it's an interesting place . . . of course the food isn't class A . . . Oh well, I'll decide later . . .

Mark rarely wore a suit on a date, but tonight he wanted to look his best. He'd pretend he was coming directly from work so he wouldn't appear anxious to impress. Standing tall in front of the full-length mirror on his closet door, Mark examined the navy pinstripe suit he'd worn that day and decided he wasn't too crazy about the paisley necktie. He reached for his favorite tie— a Liberty of London floral pattern, with dabs of subdued green, orange, and yellow, lively without being loud. Unfortunately it didn't match his suit, so he changed into a solid midnight-green Givenchy, a bit older than the Cardin he'd had on, but just as fashionable. As he changed his shoes and socks to conform to the new color scheme, the phone rang.

It was Rick Marley, with whom Mark occasionally played tennis. Rick was reputedly one of the Upper East Side's great ladies' men. Without mentioning the arrangements he'd already made, Mark asked Rick if he could recommend a restaurant for a special date. "I've got the perfect spot for yuh," Marley responded immediately. "The Red Lantern." Mark had never heard of the place. "Where is it?" he asked.

"It's on Third Avenue in the Twenties . . . My batting average must be around seven fifty going there—it's fuckin' magic. You could take a nun there and get laid. Ask for the table in the left rear corner . . . up a few steps."

Mark cut the conversation short after getting the phone number and Rick's assurance that the food was excellent: ". . . Hey, I wouldn't send you to a restaurant if the food wasn't great!"

Mark made a reservation for two, politely insisting on the table "in the left rear corner, up a few steps." He'd decide later which restaurant would best suit the occasion.

En route to the front door Mark stopped at the parsons table in the hallway for his keys. They were not there. After a frantic search of the apartment, he discovered that the keys were already in his trousers pocket. Mark smiled. It had been a long time since a date had generated such excitement in him. For one week he had been thinking about Joanna Voorhees. It was as if their first meeting had been a fairy tale. Despite the fact that he had relived each second, each word, each touch a hundred times in the last six days, he couldn't believe it had ever happened at all. Tonight, Mark would pinch himself to make sure.

It was Friday night in Greenwich Village. The streets were beginning to stir. Mark crossed Sixth Avenue hardly noticing the six-foot-four transvestite, or the man who played a rubber band attached to a bobby pin with a range of sound almost comparable to a mandolin, or the sale at Balducci's where oranges the size of grapefruits were "only" eighty-nine cents each. He still had not decided on the restaurant and for a block wrestled with the alternatives. As a trial lawyer, Mark was accustomed to making important decisions quickly, but when he reached Fifth Avenue, the problem was still unresolved. A block later his solution was to describe each to Joanna and let her make the decision.

Nor was the remainder of the evening planned. No strategy was mapped out. It was uncommon for Mark to play it by ear. Spontaneity, for him, was usually just another act. But tonight, the computer wasn't necessary.

Suddenly Mark was on Tenth Street, and gazing up at Joanna Voorhees's apartment building. Somehow it looked different. Mark checked the number on the house against the notation he'd made in his address book. He was still confused until he entered the vestibule and through the glass inner door recognized the tacky wallpaper above the wood paneling in the hallway. The J. VOORHEES label on the mailbox for apartment 5-B brought him total relief. Mark found the 5-B button on the intercom and pressed it firmly. There was no answer. He pressed again. No answer.

There must be some explanation, a misunderstanding, perhaps. But the sick feeling in his gut told him there was no mistake.

It couldn't be, he thought, remembering how she had practically consumed his tongue when they kissed, how her body had writhed in ecstasy when they were making love. And she'd been so open with him, even discussing her problems with her mother. There had to be an explanation.

He checked his watch, though he already knew the time: he was five minutes late. She's in the shower, he surmised. He pressed the intercom button four more times, each time holding his finger down for several seconds. No response. His dream was shattered. Joanna was bright and beautiful, clever and funny, sensuous and sexy. She was perfect except for one thing—she was not there.

Suddenly it dawned on Mark that Joanna's intercom might

not be working. Those things were always breaking down. Unaware of the problem, she was probably sitting up there waiting for him. He noticed a phone booth across the street and ran to it, inserting a dime while keeping his eyes fixed on the entrance to her building.

"Information, I'd like the number in Manhattan for Joanna Voorhees, V-O-O-R-H-E-E-S . . . it's a new listing, she got her phone this week . . . the address is Sixty-nine East Tenth Street."

"One moment please," she told him. The "moment" lasted several minutes. Mark tapped nervously on the glass door.

"Checking under the name Voorhees, V-O-O-R . . . ," she began, very slowly. Mark knew that when the operator started repeating the spelling of the name it meant she hadn't found the number. He was impatient and cut her off, "Did you check new listings—brand new listings?" he inquired, the urgency apparent in his voice.

"Yes sir, I did," she replied, "and I do not show a Joanna Voorhees at that address spelled V-O-O . . . ," and she began again enunciating the letters carefully and pausing between each. Although it was painful, Mark let her finish and then requested she check under a spelling of the name omitting the *H*. He was fairly certain the version he'd originally given her was correct, and wasn't surprised when she again came up blank.

"Are you sure that it's a new listing?" the operator asked, trying to be helpful. "I have not checked the regular listings."

"She just got a phone this week, if she got it at all," said Mark, realizing that perhaps it had not yet been installed.

"Well sir, then it would be a new listing and we might not have it yet. Why don't you check in a few days?"

"Thank you," Mark said, hanging up.

Remembering how easily Joanna had gained entrance to the building without a key, Mark ran back across the street and tried the same trick with a credit card. He was not as adept as she, but after a few minutes he caught it right, heard a click, and was in. He glanced at his watch. "I'm fifteen minutes late. She's probably starting to worry," he thought, reassuring himself.

Mark dashed up the four flights as if they were two, caught his breath and knocked on the door.

There was no answer. He knocked again—harder now, almost in panic. Still no answer. He stared at the door. There

26

wasn't a sound inside the apartment. He opened his suede coat, which was making him very warm, and looked at his suit and his favorite tie. He laughed at himself.

He walked down the stairs slowly and glanced in the lobby mirror on his way out the door. He looked good. It's a shame to waste this get-up, he thought. He'd call an old girlfriend . . . but who? It was getting late. He could go down to Soho and check out one of the bars, but he wasn't really dressed for Soho. Perhaps the East Side. But he hated bars. Maybe dinner with a friend . . . Tom's probably home . . . no, he wasn't really hungry any more. Besides, he wanted to be alone.

When Mark got back to his apartment, he telephoned his office since he'd given Joanna the twenty-four-hour number, but there were no messages. Maybe she'd call later. He put away his suit and returned his favorite tie to its own hook. Trudging to the kitchen in his underwear and stocking feet, Mark reached into the freezer where he kept a small stash of marijuana. He took it to the living room and rolled a joint. For the first time in his life, he got stoned alone. Instead of stopping when he was high, he smoked a second joint. His head was swimming and his body was numb. He couldn't think and he couldn't feel, and that's just the way he wanted it. An hour later, he was sound asleep.

Mark couldn't get Joanna out of his head. He couldn't believe that she'd deliberately stood him up without good reason. He convinced himself that Joanna must have lost the piece of paper on which he'd written his phone numbers. Not knowing his last name or where he worked, there'd be no way for her to reach him.

Each day he called Information to see if she'd gotten her

telephone. On Wednesday he met with success, but although he kept trying the number, it wasn't until Friday evening that Joanna finally answered:

"Hello."

"Joanna?"

"Yes."

"This is Mark . . . remember me?"

"Oh, hi," she greeted in a subdued tone. "Of course, I remember you."

He waited for an apology to follow but got only an uncomfortable silence. Not knowing what to say, he groped, "So . . . you finally got your phone, huh?"

"How'd you guess?"

Her sarcasm told Mark what he didn't want to know, but just to make sure, he asked: "So what happened to you last Friday?"

"Oh, yeah, I couldn't make it," she said casually.

Mark didn't raise his voice but anger punctuated each word of his next question: "Couldn't you at least have called and let me know?"

"I did call you. There was no answer."

"Which number did you call? I gave you two numbers," he cross-examined.

"Yes, I tried them all," she insisted.

"What time did you try me?"

"Seven o'clock—and then I phoned you again a little later," she said defensively, before suddenly getting angry herself: "Hey, what is this—the third degree?"

Knowing he had definitely been home at seven, Mark just shook his head. After another long awkward pause, Mark let go: "I don't understand you, Joanna. That night . . . I thought we both had a great time—I thought we really shared something!"

"Listen, Mark," she said curtly, "I was high and horny—don't make a big deal out of it!"

Although he generally slept late on Saturdays, Mark woke early the next day to meet Tom Bastone.

"Hey, this is great," Mark congratulated, pretending enthusiasm, as he entered the large, vacant office. "Lotta space."

28

He peered out one of two large windows in the room and his face lit up. "Tom, this is spectacular—what a view!" he exclaimed, gazing out on the skyline of lower Manhattan. "The rent must be a fortune. Are you going to be able to afford this place?"

Tom smiled, as if amused by his friend's almost parental concern, then proclaimed: "You gotta spend money to make money!"

"So why didn't you spend a little more money on a couple of painters, instead of ruining my weekend, you cheap fuck?"

Tom laughed. "A little menial labor will do you good. Besides, I don't have much choice—we kinda overextended ourselves on the construction and furnishings . . . but wait till you see my desk—ebony. You can see your face in that shine—real class."

"You're crazy," Mark said, shaking his head, though by no means surprised. Tom Bastone had always been given to extravagance. He was the type of guy who'd rent a stretch limo for a special date, even though the evening would leave him flat broke.

"It'll be all right," he responded. "We've already got so much business lined up, I figure we'll be in the black within six months."

Even wearing stained overalls, Tom Bastone was handsome, although the attire did seem totally incongruous. With every jet black hair sprayed permanently in place, Bastone, as always, looked like he'd just come from the barber shop. Broad shoulders and chest gave the impression of a big man, but Tom Bastone was only a few inches taller than Mark. His very masculine face featured a Roman nose to match an authoritative square jaw, and a small scar in the left eyebrow added ruggedness to his look.

"You can't make a decent living as a private detective working for someone else," he said. "Five years slaving for Parnelli taught me what I need to know. Might as well take the shot while I'm still young. You know what I mean?"

"You'll do fine," Mark assured.

Bastone gave Mark a heavy-duty paint scraper and assigned him to a peeling window frame.

As they worked, Mark remained unusually quiet, while Tom chatted away:

29

"So I smile at her and, I swear, she smiles back. Then every once in a while for the next hour, we're exchanging these looks. Her date is sitting there chomping away and doesn't notice anything." Tom paused to take a position higher on the ladder. "When she's finished eating, she gets up from the table—she's going to the ladies' room or something—and as she walks by, gives me the eye again, like I should follow her."

"You didn't, did you?" Mark guessed, mild disappointment in his voice but confident that he was right.

Bastone laughed. "You know me too well. I almost did . . . but my heart was pounding like a fuckin' drum. I didn't know what I'd say to her. This chick was gorgeous," Tom sighed, as he turned a dull gray wall bright white with his roller.

"Sounds like all you had to do was say hello! She was making it easy for you. What the hell were you waiting for? Did you think she'd send the waiter over with her phone number?"

"It's happened."

"I know that's how you met Sally," Mark said, "but you can't expect all women to be so aggressive."

"You know I'm not good at that stuff. If you were there pushing me . . . maybe." All of a sudden, Tom stopped painting and turned his head toward Mark. "Hey, speaking about aggressive women, how'd your date with that chick Joanna go?"

"There was no date," Mark said sullenly. "She stood me up."

Bastone came down from the ladder and walked over to Mark: "Are you kidding?"

Cantor just shook his head. Flakes of old paint flew from the window frame, as he recounted the disappointing evening and his conversation with Joanna a week later. "I don't understand people like her. How could she do that?"

Surprised by Mark's naïveté, Bastone asked, "Haven't you ever been stood up before?"

Mark stopped working. "I don't know," he said, searching his memory. "I guess I have . . . I must have, but I really don't recall specifically." He sharpened the scraper blade with a stone then looked up at Tom. "Look, I'm sure getting stood up is always unpleasant, but this is different." His eyes narrowed. "What she did . . . was fuckin' mean!"

"What are you talking about? How many times have you pulled shit like that in your illustrious career!"

"Wait a minute," Mark protested. "I never did anything like this."

At first, Tom didn't respond. He poured some more paint in the tray and resumed working on the bottom part of the wall. But after a few silent minutes, he sensed Cantor still stewing and resumed the discussion: "Mark, what *really* bothers you? Is it that she stood you up? That she didn't bother to call? Or is it that she played with you—made you think she dug you when she really didn't give a damn?!"

Cantor continued to work, then a moment later muttered, "She didn't even bother to give me an excuse—I wasn't worth the energy of a lie." He held the scraper so tightly, the veins were popping out of his forearm. " 'I couldn't make it,' that's what she said. Shit, I knew she 'couldn't make it.' That's an explanation?"

Instead of just stripping the paint, Cantor was gouging out chunks of wood from the window frame.

Trying to capture the casualness in the tone and inflection of her voice, he quoted Joanna again: " 'I was high and horny, don't make a big deal out of it.' " Then, in his own angry, incredulous tone he repeated, " 'Don't make a big deal out of it!' "

Tom gently took the scraper from Mark's hand. "So what's really upsetting you, is that it was just a one-night stand. You've had a hundred of those, only this time you're on the wrong end—*you* were the one-night stand! That's the problem." Mark's frown made Tom angry: "Well, isn't it? Admit it! And to make matters worse, you really liked this girl. You didn't want her to be a one-nighter. But how about that blonde from Joel's Christmas party, or the waitress at the Riviera Lounge, the Bolivian girl you met in the supermarket? I could make a list ten pages long and I'm sure it would still be incomplete. How do you think *they* felt?"

The pensive look on Mark's face told Bastone that his friend was beginning to listen. Tom continued: "Think about it, man. You charm them, flatter them, make them laugh and do whatever you do to get into their pants. You think they go to bed with you because they know you're just horny? Bullshit. Maybe sometimes they're just out for fun, but don't you think some of them really liked you and expected to see you again because they thought you liked them too?"

Stunned by his best friend's denunciation, Mark stared at him with open mouth. Then, recovering, he nodded, "I can give it, but I can't take it—is that it?"

"Seems that way to me."

"Being punished for past sins," Mark muttered to the floor, then turned back to Bastone and smiled. "Anyway, she didn't know I was a fuck!" They both laughed out loud.

"If there's anything left of that window frame, why don't you start painting it," Bastone said, giving Mark a brush and a fresh can of paint.

As he stirred it with a screwdriver, Cantor asked, "Was I really that bad?"

"No," Tom reassured him, "minor league, compared to your lovely Joanna."

Bastone was feeling guilty for being so rough on Mark. In an overly compassionate tone, he asked: "How'd your conversation with Joanna end?"

"I said, 'One of these days, somebody is going to teach you a lesson!' and then hung up."

"What'd you mean by that?"

Mark shrugged. "I don't know—I was just mad. . . . It's like a kid when he's angry at someone and he says, 'God's going to punish you!' " After a pause, he smiled and said, "Can you imagine if I'd told her 'God's going to punish you'?"

Again they laughed, but Mark quickly got serious again: "You know, I think you're wrong about something," he began. "It's not being a one-night stand that bothers me. I mean, sure it's a disappointment: you meet a girl you like, you think it's mutual, and it's not. That hurts but I can deal with it. What really ticked me off was that she didn't call. I gave her both numbers. She never called to cancel and she didn't even call afterward to apologize. That's an insult! It's like I don't exist. That's what makes me furious."

"Look, Mark, the girl's screwed up and obviously a coward. She did a shitty thing and didn't have the guts to face you. That's why she didn't call. You can bet this wasn't the first time she pulled something like this. It's her problem, not yours, so why don't you forget about it?" Mark nodded and it seemed Tom's little speech had cooled him down.

When Mark finished painting the window frame, he picked

up a roller and a tray of paint and began doing the wall around it. After several long strokes, the roller grew too dry and applied the paint unevenly, leaving a pattern of streaks and blotches like a Rorschach test picture. Vaguely resembling a woman's face, the image seized Mark's attention. Then suddenly it turned into the vision that had haunted him for a year: the long, matted hair in complete disarray; the sallow complexion and trembling lips; black rings around sunken, zombie eyes.

The roller fell from his hand, landing in the tray and splattering paint all around. Still Cantor remained transfixed by the frightening sight until Bastone, hearing the noise, called out, "Mark, are you all right?"

His friend's voice broke the trance. "Yeah, I'm okay." Mark paused. "I still keep seeing Carol's face—just the way she looked the last time I saw her. I can't seem to get it out of my head."

"How many times have I told you not to blame yourself for what happened. She had her problems way before she ever met you."

Mark shook his head. "I led her on. . . . I was never going to marry that girl—I should've ended it much sooner."

Tom thought before speaking: "Dying relationships often drag on. But you never promised her anything and she always knew you weren't ready to settle down." Bastone started cleaning up the splattered paint and soon Cantor joined the effort. Tom sighed: "You've got to stop torturing yourself over this."

Using a screwdriver, Mark picked up the roller from the tray and wiped off the handle with a rag. "I just wish there was some way I could tell Carol I'm sorry."

They continued painting, and for the next ten or fifteen minutes, neither spoke, until Tom broke the silence. "I read about that Jenkins case. Capellini's trying it himself, huh?"

"He was going to, but now he wants me to handle it," Mark said with obvious displeasure.

"Mark, that's great," Bastone got very excited. "What a feather in your cap. That case will get lots of publicity—you're gonna be famous."

"Terrific," Cantor uttered in a monotone.

"You don't sound very happy about this."

"I'm not! That kid belongs in a hospital—not a jail. The

state psychiatrists say he's not crazy. Well, was it uncontrollable *lust* that drove a teenager to rape an eighty-two-year-old woman? Was *larceny* in his heart when he beat her almost to death for seven bucks?"

Unable to believe his ears, Bastone stopped working while Mark kept painting away as he continued: "There's something awfully primitive about our system. This kid has been screaming out for help since he was twelve—in and out of reform schools that just made him worse. Now we're shocked and want to put him away forever. The whole thing stinks, and I really don't want to be part of it. I may just have to turn down this assignment."

After a few silent seconds of shocked disbelief, Bastone composed himself: "I don't understand. What's come over you? You've handled all kinds of cases. The only time I ever heard you complain about an assignment was that marijuana bust. You felt like a hypocrite but you still tried him."

"That was years ago . . . and I recommended probation," Mark defended.

"But how could you have any conflict here? This guy is a vicious animal who attacked a poor, defenseless old woman. Jenkins's own mother was quoted in the *Post* as saying, 'He should be put behind bars for the rest of his life!' If you don't have the heart to prosecute this bastard, you might as well quit your job!"

"I'm thinking about that too," Mark snapped back.

Mabel Moore, the victim, was the first witness at the Jenkins trial. Several times during her questioning she became confused about details, some of which related to her ability to get a good look at her assailant. Her advanced age and the traumatic ordeal she'd endured was certain to engender sympathy from the jury, but the problems with her testimony made Sergeant William Montanez a very important witness.

His direct examination went smoothly with Cantor asking short, open-ended questions that permitted the witness to relate the story in a narrative fashion:

"He was hiding in the closet. I saw his sneakers sticking out. When I pulled the clothes away, he waved a six-inch switchblade at me, so I drew my gun." Montanez paused and turned his luminous eyes from Cantor to the jury. "After seeing that poor ole lady all bruised and bleeding, I was tempted to blow that kid away." The witness gave the defendant a quick sneer. "Of course, I didn't. I just aimed my service revolver and said to him, 'Put down that nail file before I make a hole in your face.' " Several jurors smiled, pleased more than amused, by Montanez's tough-cop style.

Knowing he couldn't make a dent in the witness's testimony about the incident itself, defense attorney Michael Cordero focused his cross-examination on other arrests the officer had made years before. In two cases, he'd been accused of police brutality, and in another, a narcotics dealer claimed his twenty-five thousand in cash had disappeared on the way to the precinct. Since all these charges were ultimately dismissed, Cordero's questions were all impermissible. Montanez kept glancing over at Mark expecting him to intercede, but Cantor remained silent. Finally, the judge grew impatient and yelled "Sustained!" though Mark hadn't even objected. Spectators whispered, debating whether his passivity was a deliberate strategy or lack of concentration. The latter seemed more likely, when Montanez gave Cantor a quizzical look as he stepped down from the witness stand.

Indeed, in the midst of his most important trial as a young prosecutor, Mark Cantor had something else on his mind.

As soon as he arrived home from court, Mark took off his three-piece suit and changed into chinos and his college sweatshirt which he always wore inside-out. Pacing from room to room in his railroad flat, he decided this would be the night.

Mark stood at the foot of his bed. He'd once imagined Joanna lying there, a contented smile on her face. On the nightstand stood a candlestick encrusted with a mountain of multi-colored wax drippings, evidencing many nights of passion, the

way a tree's rings reveal its age. Mark glanced at the red candle—
one he'd put there for Joanna—its wick still white. Only a few
inches away, the telephone seemed to grow larger and larger as
he stared at it.

Mark knew the number by heart, but instead of reaching
for the phone he walked away. He circled the suede sofa in the
living room a couple of times and decided to make the call from
the extension phone in the study, the room where he prepared
his brilliant summations, where he read, studied, deliberated,
and decided. He marched in determined, but when his eyes met
the row of law books on the wall, he began to lose his nerve.
"This is crazy," he thought as he sat in the old oak desk chair.
"I should just forget her." Then his mind wandered back to that
last conversation with Joanna:

"What happened to you last Friday?"

"Oh, yeah, I couldn't make it."

No apology, no explanation.

"Couldn't you at least have called and let me know?"

"I did call you. There was no answer."

"Which number did you call? I gave you two numbers."

"Yes, I tried them both."

Lies, every word a lie.

"I thought we shared something the other night."

"Look, I was high and horny—don't make a big deal out
of it!"

The words kept ringing in his ears until he realized his
right hand had clenched into a tight fist. He tried to relax. She's
not worth it, he said to himself. Feeling a twitch in his eye, he
got up to look in the bathroom mirror, but it wasn't visible. His
palms were sweaty, so he rinsed his hands in cold water. En route
back to the study, Mark turned off all the lights in the apartment,
except for his desk lamp. I must forget her, he decided.

But swiveling his old oak desk chair around, he reached
for the telephone and dialed the number. He hoped she'd be
home and at the same time wished there'd be no answer. Four
rings seemed like ten. Just as he started to hang up, he heard
her voice on the line. "Hello?"

Tucking in his chin, he answered, "You're going to pay."

That was all he said before depressing the cradle button
with his finger. With the receiver still in hand, Cantor sat mo-
tionless for several minutes.

His next call was to Tom Bastone. He never bothered to identify himself and now he spoke in such a high-pitched tone that, at first, Bastone didn't recognize his voice: "You're not going to believe this. I must be crazy, I must be fuckin' bananas. Do you know what I just did? I committed a misdemeanor . . . no, it's a felony—I think it's a felony. Hell, what's the difference— it's a crime. I just committed a crime. Me—a lawyer, a goddamn assistant DA . . ."

By this time Tom had realized it was Mark but he was talking so fast Bastone could barely understand him. "Calm down," Bastone ordered, but Cantor kept ranting, "I'm worse than Rosenthal. You remember Jerry Rosenthal—the guy in my office who propositioned a complaining witness? That was embarrassing, very unethical, and maybe even illegal, but shit, that was red-blooded. This is fuckin' sick!"

"Hold on, Mark," Tom said firmly, "just take it easy and listen to me. I want you to calm down, relax for a minute. Where are you now?"

"I'm home," Cantor told him.

"Okay. Now I can't follow you when you talk a mile a minute, so slow down and tell me what you did."

"I just made a threatening call," Mark informed, beginning to compose himself. Bastone was surprised but at the same time relieved. The way Cantor had been carrying on, Tom was afraid it was something really serious. "Why don't you start at the beginning, Mark, and tell me exactly what happened?"

After giving him a detailed account of his call to Joanna Voorhees, Mark asked sincerely: "Well, Tom, what do you think, have I totally flipped out? Am I crazy, or what?"

"Crazy people don't ask if they're crazy. They don't even suspect it's a possibility," Bastone reassured him. "You're just angry. Maybe this will be good. If you'd called and started telling her off, she would have hung up in your face and then you'd be even angrier. This way you let it out."

"Well this is a healthy way of dealing with anger, don't you think?" Mark asked sarcastically. "Scaring the hell out of someone!"

"Listen, you probably didn't scare her so much," Tom said, still trying to console his friend. "She'll think it was a prankster or a wrong number, and she'll forget about it. And you should do the same thing."

"Then you don't think I'm crazy?" Mark asked one more time.

"Come on, will you stop that!" Tom said, getting impatient. "I'll tell you what I think. I think you've been spending too much time alone. If you were dating other women, the number Joanna pulled wouldn't have gotten to you so much. Start going out and meeting people. That's what I think. Matter of fact, Tony Siclari said something about a party this weekend. I'm going to find out more about it and we're going. Okay?"

"I don't know," Mark began to hedge. "If Jenkins decides to testify, we'll probably sum up on Monday. I'll need the weekend to prepare."

"Bullshit! You won't be working day and night the whole weekend. You'll make some time for this party, and that's that!"

"Okay," Mark acquiesced.

As Mark lay in bed, he recalled when he had been the victim of crank calls. Several times a week the phone would ring and as soon as he said, "Hello," the caller would hang up. They began when his relationship with Carol Dimas had become strained and he suspected she was checking up on him. When Mark finally confronted her, she denied it, but her inability to look him in the eye made it obvious he'd found the culprit. Carol had never been very good at lying.

He spotted her walking west on Eighth Street. When she stopped to window shop, the illumination from the shoe store framed her graceful silhouette. Across the street, Mark paid homage in hypnotic trance. The hard rock blaring from the record shop, the cries of street vendors, and the futile honking of car horns, were only a muted hum. The Hare Krishnas with their peach-colored robes and shaven heads, the gang of drunken Villanova students visiting from Philadelphia, and the normal array of hirsute hippies, were all just a blur that night. Even when she joined a crowd four deep to listen to a street minstrel, Mark never lost sight of her. She exuded a sensuality, a radiance, that eclipsed all others.

Although fifty feet and an endless flow of activity separated the two, the young woman looked in Mark's direction for a second as if she sensed his studied vigil. Mark turned away quickly. But when she continued her stroll, he followed. I will have to be more careful, Mark thought.

Still on the opposite side of the street, he remained fifteen to twenty feet behind her at all times. Walking leisurely, he made a concerted effort to look in other directions in order to conceal his singlemindedness. When she stopped again to browse in the window of a dress boutique, he pretended interest in the jeweler's wares across the way.

At the corner of Sixth Avenue, he lost her amidst a waiting herd. But when the light changed and the crowd diffused she emerged like the sun breaking through a gray clouded sky.

By this time, the gap between them had widened and Mark broke into a semi-trot crossing the large intersection as the Don't Walk sign began to flash. Now on Greenwich Avenue, so close to home, Mark felt a sudden dryness in his throat. He thought of withdrawing from the entire affair to the recesses of his cozy apartment, the padded oak chair, and a good book—someone else's thriller. But he never really gave that idea any serious consideration and the chase continued.

Upon reaching Seventh Avenue, she turned right and Mark did the same; this put him directly behind her on the eastern side of the street. Even from a distance of two car lengths, he could see her shoulder-length hair glisten beneath the city lights. But it was difficult for him to keep his eyes above her waist. Her hips swayed gently, naturally, but suggestively. Mark wondered whether it was an instinct, or a practiced art like the tango or samba. He narrowed the distance between them for a better look. The tight white pants she wore left little to the imagination, clinging to each exquisite curve of an obviously firm and shapely derriere. He wanted her and he wanted her bad. But there were still so many people around . . .

Again seeming to sense his stare, she peered over her shoulder. Although their eyes never met, to dispel any possible suspicions she might have he crossed to the other side of Seventh Avenue and continued following her from there. After another two blocks she diagonally traversed Seventh Avenue, winding up just ten feet in front of him. He smiled and became even more pleased when she turned into Twelfth Street—a dark, quiet street, with not a soul around. Perfect. His heart started beating faster and louder, and his palms began to sweat. He knew the time was now.

Just as Mark was getting set to zero in, there was a change in her gait. She was taking much longer strides, and that marvelous swing in her hips suddenly disappeared. "She knows she's being followed," Mark deduced as the gap between them widened considerably.

He had to move quickly. His legs pushed off the pavement, propelling him at a jogger's clip. As he glanced down the sidewalk sped by, the squares of cement became one continuous band, and the glittering specks, fine straight lines of light. When only a few yards separated the two of them, Mark slowed down a bit. As the girl passed under a streetlamp, his elongated shadow began forebodingly to overlap hers. Creeping up from her legs, it swept through her body and emerged beyond. He had walked right past her.

Mark now moved almost in slow motion so that she would catch up to him, but she remained several feet behind. They proceeded in this fashion for almost half a block, before he turned around and spoke. "Are you following me?" Mark asked her with a straight face. She stopped in her tracks.

"Am I following you?" she began in shocked disbelief, and then, outraged, she screeched, "You're following me!"

She'd taken him seriously; in fact, she thought he was crazy. Of course, he could have simply told her he was kidding, but instead, Mark lighted his face with that patented Boy Scout smile, and continued the farce: "Now how could *I* be following *you*, if I am in front of you, and you are behind me!"

"Well, you are, and you have been . . . ," she began, trying to make her soft, tender voice sound firm. Mark was disappointed that she still hadn't caught on, but he was willing to make allowances for anyone who looked as good as she did. Even from a distance, he'd been able to see that she was lovely. But now, up close, Mark realized that this girl was something special.

Every feature on her face was perfect. Her lips were rich and full, symmetrical and sensual. She had high cheekbones, a delicate nose, and a sharply defined jawline leading to a strong but feminine chin. Dark-complected, her skin was clear and smooth. Luxuriously thick and shiny hair, light, golden brown in color, framed the masterpiece. But it was her eyes which arrested Mark's attention. Very dark and very large, they were sensitive, but striking; innocent, yet seductive. And they had a limpid tranquility which remained undisturbed even when she raised her voice to warn: ". . . and if you don't stop following me, I'm going to scream for help!"

She walked off continuing on her way, leaving Mark standing there mesmerized. But he recovered quickly, ran after her and loping alongside continued his pitch. "Listen, did it ever occur to you that I might be going in the same direction?" She ignored him and accelerated the pace. Mark decided to try a different approach: "Well did it ever occur to you that . . . that you're the most beautiful girl I've ever seen, and if I didn't try to meet you, I'd be angry with myself for weeks!"

She said nothing in response to his compliment. In fact, she didn't even look at him. But she did slow to a more leisurely gait and that wonderful wiggle returned—all the encouragement Mark needed. "You know it's really not easy going up to a stranger on the street," he said, "especially a gorgeous stranger . . . so it took me a couple of blocks to get my courage up—are you gonna hold *that* against me?"

Her lips began to move slowly toward the start of a smile. But she still offered no verbal response, so Mark answered his own question, the twinkle in his eyes belying the serious tone in his voice, "Well that's really nice—you do hold it against me!" He paused for a moment and, doing a deliberately bad job of pretending defeat, said: "Just because it took me a few blocks . . . just because I'm shy . . ."

She could no longer restrain herself. She smiled—a full-fledged, glorious, broad, and beautiful smile. For the first time, her eyes lingered on his after he'd finished speaking. Mark Cantor had struck again.

"Do you know where the Riviera Café is?" he asked, and when she nodded Mark told her: "Meet me there this Friday night at nine."

"But I don't even know you," she protested mildly.

In a gentle, reassuring voice, Mark answered, "And I don't know you—that's why we're getting together."

More than two years had passed since Mark first met Carol, but he remembered all the details of that evening, aided, no doubt, by the many times he'd heard her tell the story. The reminiscence had temporarily taken Cantor's mind off his crank call to Joanna Voorhees, but had hardly tranquilized him. Still upset, he lay in bed unable to sleep.

Mark forced his eyes closed, but his thoughts soon raced back to Carol again and another night when he was battling insomnia.

They'd quarreled earlier in the evening, but she returned for a surprise visit. As Mark sat propped up by two big pillows, Carol stood before him and immediately shed her trenchcoat, revealing that voluptuous body adorned only by a bra, garter belt, and panties—all of black lace—and a pair of fishnet stockings and stiletto heels. Mark's eyes popped out of his head. "Where'd you get that outfit?" he asked.

"You don't like it?" Carol worried.

"Like it? I love it! You look dynamite." He shook his head in amazement at how incredibly sexy she was.

Carol smiled, happy she'd pleased him. "Would you like me to dance for you?" she asked seductively.

Although sex with Carol had always been terrific, this was the first time Mark had fantasized about her since their breakup. Recalling that very special night made his penis hard.

After turning on the stereo and finding a disco station, Carol began to gyrate her full, round hips. The fishnet stockings stretched tightly around her long muscular legs, and her shiny, golden hair swayed gently as she moved.

She unhooked her bra and let it fall, revealing a pair of large, luscious breasts that defied gravity. They bounced joyfully as she danced to the pulsating beat. She licked her finger and circled her nipple with it, then held both breasts and began kneading them.

Mark kept his eyes shut tight, afraid she'd disappear if they opened. Reliving the incident, just as it had happened, he pulled his rigid cock back and forth in rhythm to the imaginary music.

Next Carol began to slide her panties down ever so slowly, a tiny bit at a time, and when the top of her pubic bush was revealed, she brought them up again. Then, looking down at his throbbing cock, she pursed her lips and sucked in air as if she were taking it all in her mouth.

About to burst, Mark stopped stroking to prolong his pleasure. But the sensation barely subsided as Carol turned around and played the same peek-a-boo game, giving him titillating glimpses of her round, tight ass.

But when she peered over her shoulder to watch him, her face had suddenly changed. Pale and drawn, with black circles around her eyes, Carol looked just as she did the last time Mark had seen her—only hours before she swallowed a fatal dose of Valium.

The sudden sight of his recurring nightmare immediately caused his penis to go limp. He opened his eyes, hoping she'd be gone, but Carol's apparition stood at the foot of his bed— the same grotesque face atop the beautiful, scantily clad body. Mark's head bounced up from the pillow.

Her lips trembling, she spoke: "I don't care if you don't love me any more—just let me love you."

"I can't," Mark yelled.

"You can date other women," Carol begged. "Let me see you . . . just once in a while. Please—I can't live without you."

Mark reached for the candlestick on the nightstand and hurled it through her, shattering the glass of a Modigliani print that hung on the wall.

"Leave me alone," he screamed at Carol.

But she was gone.

Mark threw a volley of punches into a pillow until he'd exhausted himself. "Why?" he cried. "Why did you have to do this to me?"

Thomas Jenkins testified in his own behalf and told an imaginative tale about being in the building to commit a burglary in another apartment when he heard the old lady screaming. He went to help her and saw a young black man running out. He testified that the woman was in shock and so when the police came, he was afraid he'd be blamed and hid in the closet.

Not a bad story under the circumstances, but listening to that bald-faced lie snapped Mark out of his slump and during cross-examination he ripped Jenkins apart. To no one's surprise, the jury found the defendant guilty of all charges.

Mark customarily took a day off after a trial. His superiors tolerated this self-granted privilege. His superiors tolerated it perhaps because he put so much energy into his cases, but probably because he always won. After the Jenkins trial, however, Cantor stayed out for a week. "I'm not feeling well," he told his bureau chief.

For the next month, Mark didn't try any cases, devoting his time, instead, to answering motions and other paperwork. On the day he was to begin the Orchard Beach rape case, Cantor phoned in sick and was in bed for a week.

The flu had left him tired and weak, but when Mark returned to work, Judge Burton ordered him to begin the trial. During that case, while lunching at his desk, Cantor received a call from Doris Williams—the DA's personal secretary. "The boss wants to see you right away." The uneasiness in Doris's voice troubled him. The heavyset black woman had been with Capellini for years. She'd worked for him when he was a city councilman and he had taken her along when he became DA.

Nothing went on in his office that she didn't know about. If Doris Williams was upset, it must be bad news, Mark reasoned as he headed upstairs. Maybe the chief is pissed at me for not trying any cases last month. Perhaps he doesn't know I'm on trial now. That should cool him off.

But Mark became more concerned when he arrived at the reception area, and sensed the serious business that awaited him. Doris Williams never looked up from her desk as she told Cantor, "Go right in!" She had a special affection for Mark, whom she jocularly called Clarence after the famous trial lawyer, Clarence Darrow; even when she was busy, she always gave him a warm greeting. More significantly, the door to Capellini's office was closed. As he knocked, Mark began to worry. His boss usually kept the door open to suggest accessibility to both his staff and constituents, though the fact was the threshold could not be crossed without assent from the armed cop at the front desk, as well as the critical nod from Doris Williams. A moment later, Mark recognized the stentorian tone, "Come in!"

Paul Capellini's office was impressively large—at least thirty feet long and almost twenty feet wide. And it had a wonderful view of Yankee Stadium right down into the playing field. But with dark wood-paneled walls and a worn, dull green carpet, it was a dreary room which looked even more dismal that cloudy day. As Mark entered, he noticed two stern faces turn toward him. Seated at the far end of the baroque conference table that formed the base of a T with Capellini's cluttered desk, were a young, fair-skinned, typically Irish woman in a police uniform and a much older, white-haired man with bushy white eyebrows, who would have looked very distinguished but for the outdated polyester suit he wore.

Seated in his high-backed leather chair Paul Capellini's light green eyes appeared gray and lifeless; even the waves of his longish red hair seemed to lack their customary fire. Over the last few years, Mark had seen his boss angry, happy, preoccupied, and occasionally tired, but this was the first time Cantor had ever seen him sad. Though only a few feet away, Mark could barely hear him when he said, "Sit down, Mark. This is Sergeant Judith Larsen and Inspector William Langhorst. They're from New York County and they'd like to talk to you."

Mark turned to the inspector but it was the lady sergeant

who spoke first: "With your permission, Mr. Capellini, as unnecessary as it may seem under the circumstances, I think I should begin by advising Mr. Cantor of his constitutional rights." Focusing her attention on Mark, and sounding like a recorded message, she read from a small card: "You have a right to remain silent. . . . Anything you do say may be held against you in a court of law. . . . You have a right to a lawyer. . . . If you can't afford one, the court will provide one free of charge. . . . Do you understand?"

Mark couldn't figure out what was going on. Practical jokes were not uncommon in the DA's office, but would Capellini himself be a party to such a thing?

"Of course I understand," Cantor said, smiling weakly. "What is this, a gag?"

"I'm afraid it's no gag," the inspector interjected, glaring at Mark with his button eyes. "Sergeant Larsen would like to ask you a few questions."

Mark studied the man for a few seconds and realized this was no prank. Inspector Langhorst just wasn't the type. Cantor glanced over at Capellini but the DA had swiveled his chair around to the side, and was staring blankly at the wall.

"Do you know a young woman named Joanna Voorhees?" Larsen asked.

"I met a Joanna Voorhees," Mark answered hesitatingly, "but I don't really *know* her very well."

"Did you ever call her on the telephone?" was the sergeant's next question.

"Yes . . . ," Mark replied, wondering if he should expound or wait until he knew where this was leading. Larsen didn't give him much time to decide before firing the next question: "Did you ever threaten her over the telephone?"

Without thinking, Mark blurted out: "Wait a minute, that was a joke . . . it was just a joke."

"I'm afraid Miss Voorhees didn't find it very funny," Larsen responded.

All of a sudden, Capellini turned his chair forward again and, facing the others, interrupted: "Wait a minute, Miss Larsen . . . excuse me, *Sergeant* Larsen, it occurs to me that by conducting this interrogation in my office, despite the fact that you've given Mr. Cantor the *Miranda* warnings, this young man may

46

feel pressured to waive his constitutional rights, and I think it fair to tell him that if he wants to talk to a lawyer before answering any more questions . . . that's not going to jeopardize his position as an assistant DA."

The inspector gave Capellini a dirty look, but Mark had gotten the hint and told everyone that he would like to talk to a lawyer.

Moments later, Cantor was placed under arrest. Oddly enough he was not told, nor did he ever ask, what the charges against him were.

Mark Cantor had been to detective squad rooms before. As an assistant DA, he was sometimes assigned to interrogate persons accused of very serious crimes immediately after their arrests. Some appeared to be scared, most looked grubby, and even the well-dressed ones usually smelled from sweat. On their fingers all had black stains that told they'd been fingerprinted. No matter how well they'd washed, they never got all the ink off.

The detectives' office at the Sixth Precinct in Manhattan reminded Cantor of many Bronx station houses—dingy, paint-peeling walls, crowded with steel desks and gray file cabinets. Yet he felt uncomfortable and disoriented in this squadroom—*his* hands had the black stains.

The place bustled with activity: some officers speaking on the telephones, a few typing quickly with two fingers, files being pulled, chatter at the coffee machine. Cantor knew many city detectives, but none of these people.

Sergeant Larsen asked Mark some pedigree questions—home address, date of birth, etc.—and after filling out the arrest report, inquired in a sympathetic tone, "Have you reached your lawyer yet?"

"I left a message with his secretary," Cantor muttered.

"So you don't know when he'll be here?"

"No, not exactly."

Larsen sat forward in her chair and with her voice still soft, began: "Look, I know that in Mr. Capellini's office you declined to answer any more questions . . . and, as you well know, you still have that right." The paper clip she was bending out of shape belied her calmness. "But if you could answer a couple of questions now, we might be able to put a quick end to this whole mess."

Mark grinned. He knew Larsen was trying to get him to talk and it amused him that a dumb cop—indeed, a dumb *lady* cop—thought she could trick him. He felt challenged and, therefore, compelled to answer.

Larsen merely asked him about his whereabouts on a certain date. Ultimately, Cantor remembered being home alone that night. But he couldn't imagine what relevance an alibi might have in a case involving a harassing phone call.

Almost two hours later Phil Roselli finally barreled into the Sixth Precinct, his vest popping out of his jacket and a big cigar sticking out of his mouth.

Cantor had been a law student when he'd first met Roselli. Mark had worked one summer for the probation department at the Bronx Criminal Court, where he became intrigued by a stocky, old man with a bald head, who always wore a carnation in his lapel. Baggy trousers and gaudy, wide ties made him look Runyonesque, but Mark had heard that he was one of the best criminal lawyers in the city. One day he followed Roselli into a courtroom and watched him argue a legal motion on behalf of a man accused of burglary. The prosecutor, a diligent fellow, had come armed with a lengthy brief in support of his position. After reading it, Roselli countered by citing just one case—*Lawrence* v. *Fox,* a landmark decision which every lawyer knew involved a contract dispute with no possible relevance to a criminal matter. Apparently familiar with Roselli's reputation both as a skilled practitioner and a man with a sense of humor, the judge knew not to take him seriously, but didn't quite get the joke. Readying himself for a good laugh, he understated the problem.

48

"But, Mr. Roselli, I don't believe the *Lawrence* case is quite on all fours with our situation."

Roselli leaned over the defense table and explained: "Well, Judge, let me put it this way: *Lawrence* v. *Fox* has about as much to do with our case, as the decisions this young man put in his little book here," Roselli said, holding up the prosecutor's brief. "Now I know how bright this assistant is and if there was any legal precedent on this issue, you can be sure he'd have found it!" As the judge grinned, Roselli tossed the brief onto the counsel table and continued. "The truth is there are no cases directly on point—no legal precedent. It's a case of first impression and the decision must be based on fairness . . . fundamental fairness. This court is famous for that, so I have every confidence Your Honor will reach the right decision." After a bit more colloquy, the judge ruled in favor of the defense.

Upon leaving the courtroom, Roselli retrieved the half-smoked cigar he'd left on top of the door lintel, and Mark offered a light. "I was just listening to that motion you made. I'm only a law student but it sounded like you won one that you should have lost," Mark said, trying to strike up a conversation.

"Let's just say it coulda gone either way," Roselli responded modestly. Then he put his arm around Mark. "You wanna know the secret of this business, young man?" Answering his own question, Roselli said, "Put a little fun in their day. Oh, sometimes it's inappropriate, but most of the time it's okay. Judges, juries—they're all just people. Life's tough, the job gets boring . . . Make 'em smile, and they'll like you. If they like you, they'll reward your client."

"That's encouraging," Mark muttered sarcastically. Then, changing the subject, he pointed to the carnation in Roselli's lapel and asked, "That flower real?"

"Of course it's real! Know what I do? Beginning of the week I buy five of these. Keep 'em in the refrigerator so they stay fresh. Each day I wear one, then throw it away. The whole deal costs me two bucks a week and it makes me look classy! Looks classy, doesn't it?"

"Yeah, but if you really want to be funny," Mark suggested, "you ought to get one of those plastic flowers that squirt water!"

"Hey," Roselli shot back, "I ain't no fuckin' clown!"

During that summer Mark got to see Roselli in action a

number of times. And in his last year of law school, he'd call Roselli's office to find out if the attorney was engaged in a trial, and run up to the Bronx courthouse after class, to supplement his education. Even as an assistant DA, Mark snuck away whenever he could to observe the master. He saw Roselli cross-examine witnesses until black became white and two plus two equaled five. He watched him make cops look like criminals and experts look like fools. Indeed, Phil Roselli was no clown. Oh, he could bring a jury to laughter, but when it served his purpose, he could also enrage them or put tears in their eyes. With his Bronx accent and bargain-basement clothes, forever mispronouncing the names of witnesses, Phil Roselli didn't *impress* jurors—but they trusted him. As a result, he consistently won acquittals for defendants against whom the evidence had at one time seemed overwhelming.

After Cantor had been a prosecutor for several years with a substantial number of trials under his belt, he and "the Bald Beagle" finally met as adversaries. (One of the assistant DAs had affectionately given Roselli that nickname—a takeoff on the phrases *bald eagle* and *legal eagle*—because of his sad, hound-dog eyes and stubby legs.) Familiar with his tricks, Mark was well prepared and made certain his witnesses were, too. When Roselli tried to amuse, Cantor interrupted him before the punchline. When the Bald Beagle used his intimidation technique of standing right on top of the witness, Cantor complained that his view was blocked and the judge ordered Roselli to step back. And best of all, summing up last, Mark compared the defense to his opponent's carnation: "From far away it looks real, but up close you can see it's plastic!"

Roselli may have underestimated his less experienced adversary, but Cantor did have a very strong case to begin with, so when he won a conviction, it was hardly an upset. "You know my flowers ain't plastic," Roselli muttered to Mark as they left the courtroom after the verdict.

When they next opposed each other, Roselli was more careful and Cantor more confident. The return match was a case that could have "gone either way" on the facts, so lawyer skills would be decisive. The classic battle pitting the bright young sharpy against the shrewd old pro attracted a large audience, including many attorneys. When the jury found the defendant guilty of all charges, Mark had won a significant victory over the man who for years had been his idol.

But despite the outcome, Mark had been humbled by the experience: "It's hard to describe," he later told one of his colleagues. "Against Roselli you've got to stay on your toes every second, and still you're a step behind. . . . I just got lucky this time."

One day Mark bumped into Roselli at the kosher delicatessen near the Bronx courthouse. "You're a good lawyer, Cantor," the defense attorney said in response to a simple hello. Though the remark lacked glittering superlatives, coming from Phil Roselli, Mark took it as a great compliment. It left him speechless.

One year later, when Cantor was arrested, he returned the compliment. Mark knew many criminal lawyers. Choosing Roselli to represent him in this hour of personal need was the finest accolade one attorney could pay another.

As soon as he'd gotten Mark's message, Roselli had rushed over to the Sixth Precinct, a fresh carnation in his lapel. After conferring privately with Judith Larsen for about fifteen minutes, he joined Mark on the wooden bench near the window.

"How ya doin'?" asked Roselli, chomping on the cigar.

"Okay . . . I suppose. It's a little embarrassing."

Mark's choice of words confused the defense lawyer. "A little *embarrassing*?" he asked, raising his almost hairless eyebrows.

"Yeah . . . well, a *lot* embarrassing, actually," Mark corrected himself.

Although still confused, Roselli let it slide and changed the subject. "So, if you needed a lawyer, how come you called me? You've pinned my ears back twice already."

"Well, you're still the *second* best lawyer I know," Mark kidded. "Besides, you know what they say: An attorney who represents himself has a fool for a client!"

Roselli smiled politely, surprised by Mark's jocular attitude. "That lady detective tells me you made a statement after being advised of your rights. That true?"

"Well," Mark hesitated, "I told her I phoned the girl . . ."

"And you admitted threatening her?"

"Sort of," Mark nodded.

"Sort of?" Roselli repeated, straining to keep his voice down. "You told Larsen you did it as a joke. Is that right?"

"Yeah," Mark said softly as he nervously twirled the end of his mustache.

Roselli shook his head. "Brilliant, just brilliant. If a guy like you doesn't know enough to keep his mouth shut . . ."

"Oh, what's the big deal?" Mark shot back, holding both palms up. "I can't believe the way everybody's treating this thing. They had an inspector up at Capellini's office when I was questioned. I've been booked and printed and one of these goons wanted to put handcuffs on me. And you . . . you talk like I just confessed to robbing a bank! Hell, it's only an aggravated harassment."

Stunned by Cantor's apparent ignorance, Roselli let some cigar ash drop in his lap. Before he could speak Mark ranted on, "Look, I realize that I'll have to resign as an Assistant DA, but can't we work out some kind of deal where I can plead to a bullshit violation that won't affect my license to practice law?"

Roselli hadn't even heard the question. "Did you say aggravated harassment, is that what you think you're being charged with?" he asked.

"Isn't that the charge?" Mark replied.

"Well, I guess it may be *one* of them, but it certainly isn't the main charge."

Cantor squinted. "What is the main charge?"

Roselli looked Mark square in the eyes. "Murder," he informed him. "You're charged with murder!"

"Murder?" Mark shouted in shocked disbelief. "Whose murder?"

"The girl you threatened—Joanna Voorhees."

Dumbfounded, Mark's jaw dropped and his mouth stayed open until finally he whispered, "She's dead?" When Roselli nodded Mark turned away and, staring out the window, muttered, "And they think I killed her?"

When Sylvia Rosen discovered the severed head and body of a woman in her backyard, she ran into her apartment and dialed 911. "A woman's been murdered," she told the police operator. She broke down into tears after giving her name and address. Within ten minutes uniformed Patrolmen Gilmore and Yukovich responded to the five-story apartment building. Tall and lanky, Yukovich had a bony Neanderthal forehead and a long chin. Gilmore was a head shorter, with a baby face and a peach-fuzz mustache. Nicknamed Mutt and Jeff by the guys at the Sixth Precinct, both had been on the force for only a couple of years and neither had ever seen a dead body outside a funeral parlor. Their first homicide was a decapitation. Yukovich immediately called their command for assistance.

"Did you recognize the victim?" Gilmore asked Sylvia Rosen as she sat on her living room sofa.

"No. I didn't look so closely," she said.

The young man seated next to her interjected, "It's that new girl. She just moved in a few months ago." Phillip Klagsbrun lived right above Mrs. Rosen and she'd called him right after phoning the police. "I don't know her name," he continued, "but I think she lived on the fifth floor. If I looked at the mailboxes, I could probably figure it out."

Accompanied by Gilmore, Klagsbrun walked into the small vestibule in the front of the building and studied the names on the mailboxes. "It's Voorhees in 5-B," he deduced. "I recognize the other names—they've all lived here a while. She's gotta be the one."

Moments later, two more uniformed cops arrived. Leaving them with the severed corpse, Gilmore and Yukovich walked up the stairs to the fifth floor—the building didn't have an elevator—and Klagsbrun followed right behind. Gilmore knocked on the door to 5-B and, getting no answer, tried turning the doorknob. "It's locked," he told his partner.

"You shouldn't've done that," Yukovich said in a monotone. "There might've been a fingerprint on that knob."

"No signs of forced entry," Gilmore noted, ignoring the reprimand.

Klagsbrun whispered to them from the staircase: "The super lives on the first floor. He's got keys to most of the apartments."

"Oh, yeah," said Gilmore. "You better wait here," he told Yukovich. "I'll go with him to get the keys."

After hustling down the stairs, Klagsbrun pointed to the door across from Mrs. Rosen's and Gilmore knocked on it.

"Who's eet?" came a groggy voice with an accent.

"Police!" Gilmore announced.

A Puerto Rican man with curly hair, in an undershirt, opened the door, hiding behind it from the waist down.

"You the super of this building?" Gilmore asked.

"Yessir."

"Have you got the key to apartment 5-B?"

"Yessir, I do," the super said. But moments later he returned to report: "I'n sorry. I cannot find dose keys."

"Ah, shit," Gilmore muttered, then he turned to Klagsbrun. "I once dislocated my shoulder breaking down one of those fuckin' doors. Do me a favor: I want to get back upstairs. Tell one of the officers in Mrs. Rosen's apartment to call Emergency Services right away and when they get here, send them up to 5-B." Then Gilmore looked at the super: "Is there a fire escape going to that apartment?"

"Yessir, dee door to dee roof ees open—just poosh eet."

Gilmore climbed back up the four flights where Yukovich greeted him, "Nothing doing here."

"I'm gonna try to get in by going down the fire escape. Stay right where you are." Gilmore continued up a metal staircase leading to a steel door. He pushed the bar that ran across it and when the lock didn't release, he pushed again with more force. The door opened and he walked over the roof toward the rear of the building. He climbed down the ladder to the first fire escape. This is it, he thought, but a metal gate on the inside of the window barred entry. Another window—no gate and wide open—led to the same apartment, but more than a yard separated it from the end of the fire escape. "They don't pay me enough to try something like that," Gilmore said to himself. He remained for a few minutes to see if anyone was inside apartment 5-B, then he made his way back up to the roof and down the stairs to the fifth-floor landing where two other police officers had joined Yukovich. One held a battering ram, so Gilmore knew they were from Emergency Services.

"They say we gotta wait for Homicide," Yukovich told his partner. "The guy's downstairs now."

Detective Fred Harrison had been with the police department for ten years, assigned to the homicide squad for the last three. He'd seen lots of dead bodies; he'd seen a heart popping out of a stiletto-carved chest and a face blown away with a shotgun. But the sight of a decapitated woman—her eyes open—shocked even Detective Harrison.

After Sylvia Rosen had described for him the sounds which brought her out to the backyard, Harrison spoke with Patricia Nolan, another tenant. She'd seen all the police cars in front of 69 East Tenth and had come downstairs to see what was going on. Wearing a red satin robe, her platinum hair in curlers, Mrs. Nolan entered the open door to the Rosen apartment, introduced herself to Detective Harrison as "the occupant of apartment 4-A," and told the detective:

"About an hour ago, I heard a lot of noise comin' from the hallway, so I open my door a little—you know, to find out what it's all about. Well, there's this woman up on the fifth floor banging on all the doors yelling 'Help!' or 'Help me!'—somethin' like that. Then she stops and all I hear is her sobbin' up there."

Harrison, who'd been taking notes on a small pad, stopped writing to ask, "Did this woman live in the building?"

"I don't know," Mrs. Nolan answered, raising her eyebrows, which had been plucked clean and were defined now by a thin penciled line. "I couldn't see her face and I didn't recognize the voice!"

The detective apologized for the interruption and asked her to continue.

"Well, then she starts walkin' down the stairs, but she stops on the landin' between the fourth and fifth floors. That's when I heard footsteps—sounded like a *man's* footsteps, walkin' kinda slow. She probably heard him, too, 'cause she suddenly ran back upstairs into one of the apartments—I heard the door slam."

The chatter of other officers in the room made it difficult to hear, so Harrison moved as close to Mrs. Nolan as his enormous girth would permit. "Do you know *which* apartment she went into?" he asked.

"One of the apartments at the end of the hallway—5-B or 5-C—the doors are close together and I really couldn't say which it was," she said, crooking her neck to look up at him. Fred Harrison was tall as well as wide, measuring almost six feet three in height.

"What happened next?" he said.

"Well, when she went into the apartment, I closed my door, but after maybe a minute, I opened it again—just a crack. There was a man on the stairway only a few steps from the fifth floor—I couldn't see his face—and he went up and into one of the apartments."

"Which one, do you know? Was it the same apartment the girl went into?"

"Again, I can't say for sure 'cause I couldn't see him go in, but it *sounded* that way."

"Well, what exactly did you hear?" The detective pressed, his dark eyes bulging.

"First I heard keys jingling, then the door squeaked open and slammed shut. There was some noise . . ." Mrs. Nolan played with the top button of her robe. "I waited and then heard a muffled cry. I knew something terrible had happened."

"What did you do after the muffled cry?" Harrison asked.

"I shut my door and just stood there. I couldn't move, you know what I mean?"

"You stayed by the door?"

"For five or ten minutes. I was paralyzed."

"Did you hear anything?"

"Nothing."

Harrison rubbed his stubbled chin. "Did you hear anybody going *down* the stairs?"

"Nobody went down the stairs," Mrs. Nolan declared, her voice firm.

56

"You would have heard that?"

"Definitely. My door is right near the stairs. You couldn't tiptoe down without my hearing it—not the way those old wooden stairs creak!"

A man in a blue blazer interrupted: "They're waiting for us upstairs, Fred. The girl lived in apartment 5-B."

"I'll be up there in a minute," Harrison said. Then, regarding Mrs. Nolan again, he asked: "The man going up—could you describe him?"

"Like I said, I just seen his legs. He was wearing dark trousers. That's all I know."

"And you saw just the lower part of the girl, too?"

"From the waist down," Mrs. Nolan answered. "She was wearing a white skirt—one of those peasant skirts the hippies wear." Harrison tucked the memo pad into his back pocket. "Is the dead girl in the backyard wearing a white skirt?" Nolan asked.

"Looks like it *was* white," Harrison said softly. "Well, thank you for your help." He took a few steps toward the door, then turned back to Mrs. Nolan: "By the way, when you heard her yelling for help, did you call the police?"

Patricia Nolan just bowed her head.

"At any time this evening, did you call police?" Harrison asked in an accusatory tone.

Mrs. Nolan straightened up and, patting down her hair as if it weren't already stuck to her head by the curlers, she shot back, "Listen, Officer, this building is full of weirdos. If I called the police every time something strange happened around here . . . I just mind my own business."

Harrison lumbered up the stairs to the fifth floor where Patrolmen Gilmore and Yukovich and the two men from Emergency Services waited. He introduced himself and then the gray-haired man in the blazer who stood behind him carrying a black leather bag: "This is Detective Luzinski from the Crime Scenes Unit."

Luzinski remained on the staircase as Harrison stepped over to the door marked 5-B. From his tan golf jacket, he removed a flashlight and shone it up and down between the door and its frame. "Okay, fellas," he said, turning to the men with the battering ram. "There's two locks; the top's a dead-bolt." They went to work, and after only two thrusts, the door opened, part of the frame pulling from the wall. They stepped back as Harrison kicked the door open further so his wide body could pass through. He examined the locks again then turned toward Yukovich: "See if anybody's home in the other apartments on this floor," he ordered, "and don't let anyone leave this building until I get a chance to talk to them."

Detective Fred Harrison entered apartment 5-B with gun drawn just in case the murderer was still there. To his left—a small, round table with a full cup of coffee, an open magazine, and a set of keys. Behind a beaded curtain, a tiny kitchen, dirty dishes piled high in the sink. In the living area, a rocking chair facing the wall. On the peach-colored sofa, a large handbag, its contents half-emptied. A ten-dollar bill peeked out of the red wallet. "He wasn't after her money," Harrison concluded. At his feet, a mess of cigarette butts and an upside-down ashtray. Near the wall opposite the entry door, between two windows, a white, wicker table turned over on its side. A few feet away, shards of painted porcelain and a few wilted flowers in a puddle of water on the wooden floor.

Harrison stepped slowly into the alcove—a large chest, mattress, and a shelf with a small TV, a stereo, and two speakers. He opened the chest and slid the hanging clothes from one side to the other. "No one hiding there." Then he kicked open a door that led to the bathroom, stared at the shower curtain, and pulled it open just to make sure.

Returning his gun to its shoulder holster, the detective looked out the window barricaded with a metal gate. It led to a fire escape. The other window was wide open, the bottom sash raised as high as it could go. Careful not to rub against the frame or sill, he stuck his head outside and peered down. Almost directly below he could see the white tablecloth that covered the victim's body, and, a few feet away, the towel that covered her head. Twisting his upper body, Harrison looked up to the roof. Then he pulled his head inside and his eyes roamed around the L-shaped room. The walls were bare, freshly painted, white and clean. The puzzled detective ran his hand through his hair.

When Fred Harrison entered the Voorhees apartment he'd expected to find a gory scene: blood splattered around, that sickening crimson puddle on the floor, perhaps even chunks of flesh. But there wasn't a trace of blood anywhere. Had the killer cleaned up? That would be very unusual, the detective thought. Maybe he took the girl to the roof after Mrs. Nolan shut her door. Maybe it happened up there.

As Harrison trudged out of the apartment he told Luzinski, "You can start dusting this place. Cover every inch around the open window," he instructed him, and, pointing to the floor, "See if you can get a print off that broken vase."

Flashlight in hand, Harrison searched the rooftop of 69 East Tenth and its adjoining buildings: no murder weapon, no clues, and no blood. He'd check it again when daylight came, and returned to the apartment still shaking his head.

"Hey, Fred, did you see this?" Luzinski yelled from the sleeping alcove. When Harrison walked over, Luzinski was kneeling in the corner near a milk crate being used as a nightstand. On the top of it sat an alarm clock and a telephone with an empty cradle. The receiver was on the floor. Luzinski turned the crate around for Harrison to get a better look at the recording device inside. The numbers and letters stenciled in yellow signaled the officers. "I think you'd better make a few calls," Luzinski said. "For some reason, this girl had taping equipment issued by PD."

"It comes back. It all comes back. That's Karma. Good or bad, it all comes back." Click.

Following along from a typed transcript, Cantor listened to the tape. Almost every conversation began with a woman answering the phone, with a simple hello. She was identified in the transcript as J. V., and the man was Unk. M., for unknown male.

His next message was less philosophical than the first:

> *"What is that smell?*
> *It's a horrible smell . . .*
> *it smells like a rotten*
> *cunt. Someone's got to*
> *get rid of that smell." Click.*

Incredulous, Mark shook his head and looked at Roselli, who was poking around with a letter opener in an effort to free a jammed desk drawer. He'd already heard the tape a few times and didn't appear to be listening.

> *"Hello, you sweet thing."*

The male voice began the next "relevant" conversation. She sounded groggy, disoriented, half asleep:

> *"Who is this . . . what time is it?"*

As it was in all the calls, his voice was unnaturally deep, audible but slightly muffled, as if a handkerchief had been placed over his telephone's mouthpiece:

> *"I'm sorry. I didn't mean to wake you.*
> *I feel terrible, just terrible. . . . How do*
> *you feel? It's nice that you are still*
> *able to sleep at night." Click.*

Cantor glanced over to the recording machine, watching the reels spin slowly around. The old Webcor model, probably made in the fifties, wasn't fancy, but looked solid and played well.

Mark was out on bail, and he'd been summoned to his lawyer's office to hear the tape, which the DA's office had provided, along with a typed transcript, as part of pretrial discovery.

Phil Roselli practiced law out of the same storefront, one block from the Bronx courthouse, where he'd first hung his shingle almost forty years ago. Seated behind an L-shaped metal desk, his young secretary had greeted Mark. She was a heavyset Puerto Rican girl, who doubled as an interpreter, a necessity in the last few years, since half of the clientele had become Hispanic. A black vinyl-covered chrome-frame sofa and matching chair took up the rest of the small anteroom, providing a waiting area for no more than five persons.

Roselli's office was almost twice the size of the front room, but it was so cluttered and crowded that it looked small. Files and law books were strewn everywhere, despite a long row of five-drawer steel cabinets lining one wall, and a mountain of glass-front bookcases on another. Since there was not one inch of clear surface in the room, Roselli had set up the tape recorder atop the mess on his badly scratched mahogany desk.

There was a total of twenty-eight calls on the tape, but only six were from the anonymous caller. A notation in the margin of the transcript denoted these six as "relevant." Most of the others—the legitimate calls—were not recorded in their entirety because of a "defeat switch" which permitted Joanna Voorhees to shut off the recording mechanism to allow her privacy.

The typed transcript not only gave a verbatim account of the recorded conversations, but also noted the date and the exact time each call began and ended. Roselli had explained that this was accomplished by the use of a special device called a pen register connected to her telephone line along with the tape recorder.

The first anonymous call on the tape was received on April 14th, the second, only two days later, on the 16th. The transcript indicated that the third call, the one that apparently woke Joanna Voorhees, was received on April 19th at 2:36 A.M.

"Hah!" Roselli shouted as the desk drawer finally came unstuck. Sliding it back and forth, he introduced the next "relevant call" with a sarcastic twang in his voice. "You're really gonna enjoy this one."

> *"This is your doctor. I just got the results of your tests back from the lab. I'm afraid it doesn't look good for you."*

But this time there was no immediate click sound—neither party had hung up—and a frustrated Joanna Voorhees screamed out to her tormentor:

> *"Why are you doing this? I know it's you, Mark. Why don't you leave me alone already!"*

His response, after a sinister cackle:

> *"Because, my dear, the best is yet to come."* Click.

61

Although there was still more tape to be played, Roselli shut off the recorder. Mark's face was ashen, and his mouth wide open.

"I can't believe it," he finally said, "she thought that was me." After a pause, Mark said: "Well, thank God that part's not admissible."

"I'm not so sure," Roselli replied softly, as if he were almost afraid to upset Mark with a contrary opinion. "Of course I'll move to suppress that portion, but . . . I don't know . . ."

"Are you kidding?" Mark fumed. "It's hearsay, and you can't get more prejudicial!"

"Well, I'm glad it's so clear to you. It's a shame you're not the judge," Roselli quipped as he began to pace.

"Not even a close question," Mark insisted. "It's basic."

Roselli stopped and ran his hand over his smooth, shiny head. "Look, counselor, I'm not going to argue with you." His eyes narrowed. "I said I'll make the motion and I hope you're correct. But right now I'd like you to hear the rest of this."

He switched the machine back on. After Joanna said hello the tape ran silently for at least fifteen or twenty seconds before they heard only a few words in that same weird voice:

"Toward my hand."

Mark gave his lawyer a quizzical look. Roselli shrugged. "She must have pressed the defeat switch by mistake and then turned it back on, or maybe there was some trouble with the equipment. I don't know," he said as the tape continued to play several of the legitimate calls.

Roselli removed his already unbuttoned vest and threw it over a chair. Then he tilted his head, putting an ear close to the machine. On the tape, Joanna could be heard telling a woman that she had just got out of the shower and would call her back in a few minutes.

"Sounds like she didn't bother hitting the defeat switch that time," Mark commented.

Roselli raised his hand to request silence as he announced, "This is it."

"Now I want you to listen carefully to
me—you know who this is. I'm downstairs,

*in the corner phone booth. In the last half
hour, I've made a dozen bogus calls to the
Sixth Precinct. Every available patrol car in the
area will be tied up for at least the next twenty
minutes. You can try the cops but they'll never
get there in time."*

Joanna Voorhees interrupted him, her voice trembling:

"Why are you doing this to me? Why don't—"

He didn't let her finish:

*"I have your keys and I'm coming up.
In a few minutes you'll be dead."*

That was the last call on the tape—the last call Joanna
Voorhees ever received.

Roselli didn't bother to turn off the machine and it hummed
as he stared at Mark with his droopy, bloodshot eyes. "Well?"
he finally said, breaking a long, tense silence.

"Well, what?" Cantor barked. "It's not my voice! I told you:
I made one lousy call, and it's not on that tape! Does it sound
to you like my voice?"

"No, not really . . . no, it doesn't, but . . ." Roselli searched
his desk until, in an ashtray buried under some papers, he found
a cigar butt.

As he paused to light it, Mark offered a suggestion: "We'll
make a tape of my voice using the same equipment, saying the
same things, and let them compare it. Simple."

"Not so simple," Roselli said, puffing away. "Unfortunately,
it's rather obvious that the caller is disguising his voice—*no one*
sounds like that. If we make a tape with your voice, it won't
prove a damn thing"—Roselli finally shut off the recorder—
"except that this isn't your *natural* voice!"

Mark nodded. "You're right," he said, rubbing his chin. His
eyes suddenly opened wide. "What about a voice print?"

"Voice prints aren't admissible—you know that!" Roselli
said, flicking ashes on a floor strewn with them.

"Of course I know that!" Mark replied indignantly, "but
maybe we could use it to convince them not to prosecute. Lie
detector results aren't admissible either, but my office . . . er, my
ex-office dismissed plenty of cases based on them."

The voice print was a scientific method that had been developed to identify a person by his voice. According to proponents of this technique, everyone's voice has certain characteristics, which are as unique to the individual as fingerprints. An electronic device, the sound spectrograph, is used to produce a graphic display of speech called a "bar voice print," which remains distinctive even if the person attempts to disguise his voice. By comparing the bar voice prints made from the recording of a questioned voice with those from a recording of known origin, a voice can be identified. Application to Mark's case was obvious.

Announced in 1962 by its developer, Lawrence G. Kersta of Bell Laboratories, voice-print identification had a checkered history. Although many law enforcement agencies raved about its usefulness, by 1976 the courts in most states, including New York, had decided it was not reliable enough to be acceptable as evidence in a criminal case.

Although lie detector tests had suffered a similar fate, their use as an investigatorial tool was becoming more and more widespread among prosecutors. In certain cases some DAs would even enter into agreements with defendants and their lawyers whereby the charges would be dismissed if the accused passed a lie detector test administered by the state's polygraphist. The defendant's part of the bargain was to waive his objection to the admissibility of the test results, in the event he was found untruthful. As an Assistant DA, Cantor himself had often entered into such stipulations in troublesome cases where he thought the defendant might be innocent, but lacked substantial evidence to support his suspicions. Mark had great confidence in lie detector tests, and his willingness to use them had won him a reputation for being fair, despite his toughness.

Roselli was almost certain that the Manhattan DA didn't believe in voice-print identification, and would never dismiss a case based on it. "I'm sure they don't even have the equipment," he told Cantor. "But they might go along with a polygraph." Leaning over the desk, he stared into Mark's eyes as if he were looking right through him. "Would you be willing to take a lie detector test?"

This was the moment of truth. Mark hesitated for only a second. "Of course," he said without flinching, then added: "If they agree to dismiss all charges when I pass it."

Roselli sat down, relaxed, the suspicious glare gone from his eyes. "Good . . . that's good," he said, "I'll ask Quinn about the voice print and if he turns me down on that, I'm sure he'll go along with a polygraph." Roselli's optimism was reassuring. The nightmare, Mark assumed, would soon be over.

But when the news came, it wasn't good: "They won't do it," Roselli reported to his client. "Not the voice print, not even the lie detector test. When the assistant—this fella Quinn—turned me down, I went over his head to DA Krieger himself. . . . I couldn't budge him."

Mark was irate: "But why? You said they use polygraphs in New York County. This is a proper case for it—it's the perfect case for a lie detector test! Something fishy is going on here. It's political, I tell yuh—they want to ruin me!"

Roselli, more reserved in his disappointment, was also surprised by the refusal. "I don't know . . . I don't know. Krieger told me that because you're an Assistant DA, they'd be subject to criticism—accused of a whitewash—if they did anything to circumvent a jury."

"What?" Mark screamed, outraged. "You mean to tell me I'm being discriminated against because I've devoted my career to prosecuting criminals!"

"Well, that's what he *said*, but I think they were just jerking me off. At one point I told Krieger, 'Forget the dismissal. Just give him the test, consent to have the results—whichever way it comes out—admitted into evidence and leave it up to the jury.' "

"Wait a minute," Mark interrupted, "I told you—"

But before he could chastise Roselli for altering the terms of the deal *he'd* offered, the Bald Beagle cut him off:

"Relax. He wouldn't go for that either. I just wanted to see if they were being straight."

"And they weren't?" Mark asked, though he already knew the answer.

"And they weren't," Roselli confirmed. "I don't know why they turned us down." He shook his head, then stared at the ceiling for a few seconds before returning his attention to Cantor. "I think it's time we hired an investigator," Roselli offered. "For a case like this, I'd recommend Frank White. He's expensive, but he's good."

"White's a fat cat. He doesn't give a shit any more," Mark

countered. "In fact, his men do all the legwork now—you don't even get White when you hire him."

Roselli didn't argue the point. "You got another suggestion?"

"Yeah," Mark announced firmly. "Tom Bastone!"

"Tom Bastone. Who the hell is Tom Bastone?"

"He's a guy I know personally—used to work for Vince Parnelli. He's sharp . . . knows his business and he'll put his all into this case."

Despite the glowing appraisal, Roselli was not pleased. "Are you sure? There's a lotta good private detectives in this town. I never heard of this guy."

"And I know prosecutors in Brooklyn and Queens who've never heard of you! What's that mean?"

"Where's Bastone work outa?"

"He just opened his own agency in Manhattan." When Roselli frowned, Mark added: "He was Parnelli's top man for years."

Roselli shook his head.

In an earnest tone, Cantor had the final word: "Phil, Tom's a close friend and an excellent investigator." He paused. "I'd trust him with my life."

"Good, 'cause that's what you'll be doin'!"

Just as Roselli had promised, he made a motion before the trial to bar the entry into evidence of that part of the fourth conversation in which Joanna Voorhees referred to "Mark" as the caller. He argued that this amounted to an identification of the defendant by a witness (i.e. Joanna Voorhees), who the defense could not cross-examine. "Maybe she was talking about another Mark; maybe she meant Mark Cantor, but was just taking a wild guess. Unfortunately, I can't ask her how certain she was; I can't ask her anything," he told Judge Warren. "That's the very reason for the rule against hearsay and we got it here in its most glaring and dangerous form."

The prosecutor, Kevin Quinn, contended the hearsay rule was inapplicable. Quoting an authoritative treatise on the law of evidence, he presented the definition of hearsay as "an out-of-court statement offered to prove the truth of the matter asserted in that statement." He then attempted to demonstrate that the remark at issue did not fall within this definition: "We are not offering her statement to prove that Mark Cantor was, in fact, the caller, or even to prove that Joanna Voorhees thought he was. The statement is part of an entire conversation and these conversations cannot be edited for the convenience of the defendant."

At times heated, the debate lasted more than two hours. Both sides cited and discussed precedent cases which supported their own positions.

On the following day, Judge Warren announced his decision: "In this case, the recorded conversations constitute a part of the crimes charged, and as such, what *both* parties said during those conversations, is admissible," he ruled. "It is what happened," and falls within what he called the *res gestae,* a Latin term, which is literally translated as "things done." "The statement by Joanna Voorhees, at issue here, is no different than a remark made by a victim during the course of a robbery. I cannot exclude a portion of the facts constituting a crime merely because it may implicate the defendant. It is what happened.

"I am, however, fully cognizant of the problem raised by Mr. Roselli. I will therefore instruct the jury that they are *not* to consider Miss Voorhees's reference to a Mark as any evidence that the calls were made by the defendant, or even that *she thought* they were made by the defendant. In short, I will charge the jury, both when the tape is played and again at the end of the case, that her use of the name Mark is not to be considered by them as any evidence whatsoever of the defendant's guilt."

Shaking his head, a despondent Phil Roselli listened. When certain the judge had finished, he rose from his chair and, with his head down, walked slowly around the counsel table, down the center of the courtroom toward the bench. Though uninvited, he did not stop until he was no more than five feet away— so close he had to bend his neck in order to look up at Judge Warren. There was no jury present and few spectators, but the Bald Beagle put on quite a show anyway:

"With all due respect, Your Honor," he began, a certain sign that harsh criticism was to follow, "the instruction you intend to give this jury does, indeed, address the problem squarely. And I appreciate that the court is so concerned as to give that instruction, not once, but twice. But you could give it to 'em *twice a day, every day,* throughout the trial and you and I both know that it won't be followed. No matter how hard they may try, no matter how diligent they may be . . . in effect you're letting them hear something and then telling 'em to ignore it. But they're only human. Consciously, subconsciously . . . unconsciously, one way or the other, they can't ignore it! You can let it in for some *limited* legal purpose, but once it's in, who's kidding who, Judge— it's in for every purpose."

Despite Roselli's dramatic appeal, Judge Warren adhered to his ruling. Although a major setback, it came as no surprise to the defense lawyer.

Phil Roselli wasn't the only one unhappy with Mark's choice of an investigator. Tom Bastone wasn't exactly thrilled either.

"It's a bad idea," he said when Mark first asked him over a drink at the White Horse tavern. "It's just a bad idea," he repeated, shaking his head. "You should have the best—Coch-ran, or White, even Parnelli—a top-notch guy, not me! I'm not experienced enough."

"When we were painting your office, you told me Parnelli taught you everything you have to know."

"I meant . . . to open my own agency . . ." He shook his head again. "I've never handled a case like this."

"You think those 'top-notch' guys have either?" Cantor asked rhetorically. "Besides, I can't afford the kind of fees they get."

"Come on, Mark, when it comes to something like this, you can't worry about money."

"You can if you don't have it," Cantor shot back. "Roselli's pretty expensive—even with professional courtesy. I don't have much money left."

"Couldn't you borrow from your mother?"

"She doesn't know about this and I don't want her to."

"Oh, Mark, you can't keep something like this secret for-ever. She's bound to find out. Florida's not in another universe."

"She never reads the paper or listens to the news. I don't want to tell her unless I have to—unless I'm forced to."

Bastone shook his head. "Your choice, but I think you're making a mistake." After a pause, his face suddenly brightened. "Listen, Parnelli owes me a favor. I'm sure I can get him to take your case for no more than half his regular fee. Let me talk to him."

"I don't want Parnelli—I want you!" Mark insisted so loudly that people at the surrounding tables stopped to look. Then he pulled his chair closer and lowered his voice. "When I first got arrested you told me, 'If you need anything, just ask.' Well, I'm askin'! And don't worry: I'll pay your normal rate—no favors. I may just need a little extra time . . ."

Bastone's face became red with anger. "It isn't the money, you idiot," he said, "it's the responsibility. What if I don't deliver?"

Mark leaned forward and put his hand on Tom's shoulder. "You'll do the best you can—that's all I want. No guarantees."

In a somber tone, Bastone pleaded, "Mark, if I miss something, if I fuck up in any way, I'll never be able to live with myself!"

Cantor grinned, "So don't fuck up!" Then quickly the grin vanished. "Listen, Tom, I'm putting you in a tough spot, but I'm in a tough spot, too. I think you're just as good as those big-name private eyes, and I'll feel a lot better knowing the investigation is being handled by someone who really cares." Mark put his hand on the back of his friend's neck and pulled him closer. "I need you."

That was all he had to say. Bastone closed his eyes and nodded.

Tom Bastone knew that his best friend could not have killed Joanna Voorhees, so it came as no surprise that the voice on the tape of threatening calls didn't sound at all like Mark Cantor. He played it over and over again, not sure what he was listening for, hoping there'd be a clue, making certain not to overlook anything.

He also spent many hours studying all the police records

about the case. In their efforts to reconstruct the murder, homicide detectives had interviewed the residents of 69 East Tenth Street, and their statements, along with Crime Scene Unit reports and autopsy forms made up a stack of papers four inches thick.

The preliminaries done, Bastone then began the real work. Conducting his own independent investigation, he personally questioned Joanna's neighbors, while his partner Brian Downey tried to find out all he could about the victim herself. After more than a month, Phil Roselli requested a progress report and a meeting was arranged.

As promised, Bastone's new office was smartly decorated. Plush carpeting made Roselli's knees bend. Ultramodern track lights circled the ceiling and lit up the colorful, abstract paintings decorating the walls. Roselli's quick sneer made it clear that he didn't share the detective's taste in art, and he never seemed to notice the impressive view.

Although they'd spoken many times on the telephone in the last few weeks, the two had never met before. Having been told he'd worked with Parnelli "for years," Roselli was expecting a somewhat older man, but hid his displeasure when Cantor introduced him to the youthful Bastone.

Mark and his lawyer took seats in the two suede chairs positioned in front of the large, black ebony desk. Behind it, Bastone sat majestically in a richly padded executive's chair, impeccably dressed in a custom-tailored gray sharkskin suit. His white-on-white shirt, burgundy tie, and matching handkerchief were all of silk, giving him a slick, prosperous look. Wasting no time on pleasantries, Bastone pulled a folder from the matching ebony credenza and, speaking quickly in a gruff voice, got right down to business: "The building's got fifteen units: five floors, three apartments on each. The A line is a one-bedroom floor-through. The B and C lines are studios—the B's face the back and the C's face Tenth Street."

Bastone removed a neat packet of typed papers from the file. He wore a gold bracelet with his initials TVB emblazoned in diamond chips. His nails were short but polished. "There's a separate page for each apartment. On it, you'll find the occupant's name, the date and time of the interview, a detailed account of our conversation, and in some cases, my own impressions. I'll go over them now, and I've got copies you can take with you.

"It's an old building but well-kept and it's got quite a mixture. You got your Greenwich Village types—gays, students, a musician, but there's also some middle-class, middle-aged people and a few old-timers, who've been there for years."

Roselli removed a clean legal pad from his beat-up attaché case and placed it on his lap just as Bastone started going into detail: "The one who provides the most information is this Patricia Nolan," he said, looking down at his notes. "She's a waitress in a local coffee shop. Divorcée in her early forties. Lives in 4-A. A busybody type. Detective Harrison took a statement from her right away. She told me the same thing she told him."

Tom Bastone then related what Mrs. Nolan had seen and heard the night of the murder as Roselli leaned forward, his big belly squashing against his chest. When the investigator had concluded his report on Nolan, Mark's lawyer leaned back in his chair, tapping his Bic pen on the pad: "So the first time Voorhees screams in the hall, when she's banging on doors—that must have been right after she got the phone call, and obviously no one's there yet." The investigator nodded and so did Mark. "A few minutes later a man goes up," Roselli continued, raising his pen in the air. "There's a brief struggle . . . she screams—but only once." Roselli let go of the pen and it bounced on the pad.

"Is that what you think happened?" Mark asked.

"I don't know, but that's the state's scenario," Roselli said. "You can bet on that!"

But it didn't quite make sense to Bastone. "The way Nolan describes it, there was a delay between the man entering and the scream," he said. "Why didn't she scream right away—as soon as he came in the door?"

Roselli shrugged. "Who knows? There are many possibilities. Maybe he told her he wouldn't hurt her. Or she was frozen—frozen with fear. They could say that." He paused before adding, "Yeah, Mrs. Nolan'll make a good witness."

"Quinn's already talked to her," Bastone informed. "He told her she'd have to testify."

"Of course," said Roselli, his jowls bouncing. "What about the other people who lived on the fifth floor?"

Bastone flipped the page: "There's an elderly woman in 5-A—a Mrs. Rio." The detective glanced down at his notes but continued without reading from them: "She heard someone in the hall yelling for help and banging on her door. The old lady didn't answer or do anything. Said she was afraid. This woman has to be close to eighty. I don't know how she makes it up those stairs every day. . . . I asked her if there was any screaming or commotion coming from *inside* 5-B shortly after that. She didn't re-mem-ber."

Patting his neat, blow-dried hair, Bastone flipped another page: "Right next door to Voorhees, in 5-C is a musician—name of Cleveland Johnson." The investigator leaned his head against the high-backed chair and spoke slowly for the first time: "I never got to speak to him. I've been to the building at least a half dozen times. The guy's never home and his phone's unlisted. I left a note in his mailbox asking him to call me. Anyway, Harrison questioned him later that night. He'd just returned from New Orleans—two-week engagement at some Dixieland club in the French Quarter. He told Harrison that he didn't hear anything unusual."

"Was he home when it happened?" Roselli asked.

"Seems he was. Mrs. Nolan heard the screaming and every-thing sometime between 10:00 and 10:30. That transcript you gave me says Voorhees received the phone call—the one that threatened death 'in a few minutes'—at 22:14—that's 10:14. Sylvia Rosen, the lady in 1-B who found the body, told me she called 911 right away and the computer printout indicates police received her call at 22:27—"

"That's 10:27," Roselli interrupted. "So?"

"Well, Johnson told the police he got home at *9:20!*"

Bastone paused as if to give Mark and his lawyer time to digest the apparent inconsistency in Johnson's story. For several moments they all just looked at each other before Roselli broke the silence with a possible explanation: "Well, if he didn't hear anything, maybe he's mistaken about the time."

"Not according to this," said Bastone, glancing at the report and handing it to Roselli. "Harrison questioned him about it in detail, but the guy was positive it was 9:20 when he got home. Third or fourth paragraph down: says he checked his watch as soon as he walked in the door. Seems he had plans to meet a group of friends for dinner that night, but his flight had been delayed. He wanted to see if he still had time to join them. His friends were meeting at 8:30 and he figured they'd still be there. He was exhausted so he jumped in the shower, but it made him more tired and he went right to sleep. Woke up when the police broke down the door to the girl's apartment. It's right next to his."

"But he didn't wake up when Joanna was banging on his door?" Mark asked, his eyebrows raised.

"What time did Emergency Services get there?" Roselli interrupted.

"They waited for Harrison and broke down the door at . . . 11:45," Bastone answered after finding the relevant police report.

His lips clenched, Roselli nodded, then spoke to no one in particular: "The police probably made more noise then she did. Maybe he's a heavy sleeper. . . . It's possible, but I'd still like to meet Mr. Johnson." Then he turned to Bastone. "I want you to keep trying, Tom."

"You think he's lying?" the detective asked.

"Wait a minute," Mark interrupted. "Joanna had this beautiful vase in her apartment. She told me the guy next door gave it to her—'a housewarming present,' she said. Filled with roses. It had to be this fella Johnson. He must've had a crush on her. Maybe she fucked him over, too." Cantor's eyes were popping out of his head. "And that would explain why Nolan didn't hear anybody going down the stairs afterward!"

Roselli grinned and told Mark, "Relax, Mr. DA, I don't think we got enough evidence for a conviction." Then he regarded Bastone. "I'll send Mr. Johnson a letter myself . . . on the good stationery—it's very impressive. In the meantime, you see what you can do. And ask around—find out if he was involved with the Voorhees girl." Bastone nodded and Roselli changed the subject: "Now what about the other tenants in that building?"

"In the apartment directly below Voorhees—that's 4-B—you got Howard Weiss—staff writer for the *Village Voice*," Bastone answered, returning to the quick tempo he'd maintained earlier. "Wasn't home until midnight. At first, police wouldn't let him in the building—I understand he made quite a fuss. Type of guy who would have done something if he heard trouble."

Bastone turned to his next page: "Unlike Jeremy Pakula, who was home and did hear cries for help. Lives on the third floor, in 3-C. A fag. Designs window displays for one of the big department stores.

"He was 'entertaining that evening.' Said the friend he had over was a married man and wouldn't let him investigate or call the police. When I asked Pakula about any other screams later on, he said they'd been smoking hash." Bastone mimicked Pakula's effeminate voice: "I was very wrecked and feeling so guilty for ignoring that poor girl, I kept hearing her screams all night. But I think they were just in my crazy head!"

Roselli and Cantor smiled at the investigator's imitation and, with a page in either hand, Bastone continued: "The guy in 2-C—grad student at NYU—says he heard a 'ruckus' upstairs lasting a minute or two, but nothing unusual after that. Yet next door to him a fella by the name of Phillip Klagsbrun didn't hear anything but *one* scream at about 10:30." Bastone paused to study the report. "He estimates the time 'cause he was watching *Streets of San Francisco* on TV. It started at ten and he heard the scream— described it as a shriek—during the second batch of commercials. Couldn't tell where the sound was coming from. A few minutes later, Mrs. Rosen phoned and told him what had happened, so he ran down to keep her company until the police arrived. He made the initial identification of the body." Bastone waited for Roselli to finish writing, then added, "Klagsbrun is an art director for a small ad agency."

"Which apartment is he in?" Mark's lawyer asked.

"2-B," Bastone answered, glancing down. "I've made a chart of the building for you, so you can see the layout easily and who lives where."

The investigator raced through the rest of his file. The remaining tenants either weren't home that night or couldn't provide any additional information. And no one heard any footsteps coming down the stairs after the scream or at about that time. Nor could any of them provide much information about Joanna Voorhees. "My partner's still checking her out—hasn't turned up much yet," Bastone told Roselli. "She worked as a waitress in a cabaret—studied acting at HB Studios—kept pretty much to herself, no steady boyfriend. We'll keep trying."

When the detective had finished, Roselli returned his pen

to his pocket, and the yellow pad on which he'd scrawled some notes to his attaché case. Bastone handed him the promised copy of the reports and Roselli stuffed that in the case, too. "What's our next step?" he asked, testing the young investigator.

Bastone didn't hesitate: "There are two apartment houses on Eleventh Street that face the back of 69 East Tenth. Somebody in those buildings may have seen something. Might take some time, but I'd like to look into it."

"Good idea," Roselli approved, standing up to signal the end of the meeting.

As he and Cantor waited for the elevator, Mark proudly asked, "So what do you think of Tom?"

"Flashy dresser," Roselli said, removing a cigar from his breast pocket.

"You don't think he's good?" Cantor said, surprised and getting angry.

"Oh, he's good all right," Roselli growled. "I just don't like the way he dresses."

Despite Roselli's "impressive" stationery, there'd been no word from Cleveland Johnson, so Bastone paid a few more visits to 69 East Tenth but failed to find the jazz musician at home. Then about two weeks before the trial was scheduled to begin, the investigator reported: "Johnson doesn't live there any more. Son of a bitch moved. Left no forwarding. Even his union doesn't have his new address."

Roselli immediately contacted Kevin Quinn. "So what!" the prosecutor replied. "The man's not a suspect. He's free to move and he doesn't have to tell you where."

"Does that mean *you* know where he is?"

"I didn't say that, did I?"

"Well, do you?" Roselli persisted.

When Quinn refused to answer, Roselli made a formal demand in court for Johnson's current address. "Absent a showing of suspicious circumstances," the judge ruled, "the prosecution is not under any duty to aid the defense."

Afterward, Tom Bastone met Roselli and Cantor on the courthouse steps and got the bad news. The investigator shook his head in disappointment: "Well, we got ahold of Johnson's photo—a publicity shot—and I know he plays the sax," he said.

"We've checked every jazz club in New York. If the man's working, it's not in this town. But I've got other ideas . . ."

Roselli grabbed the investigator's arm and squeezed: "I want that nigger."

"We'll find him," Bastone vowed.

The People of the State of New York v. *Mark Cantor* had been scheduled for trial on October 12, 1976. On that date, the defense, not expecting any opposition, requested a one-month postponement: "We haven't completed our investigation," Roselli told Judge Warren.

"Is the prosecution ready?" the judge asked Quinn.

"We are, Your Honor," he answered quickly.

As if he were giving the matter careful consideration, Judge Warren paused before declaring, "One week—that's all!" Glancing down at the court record, he justified his decision: "The DA has been ready for two months now. Mr. Roselli, this is your fourth postponement. Be ready to select a jury next Tuesday."

Cantor and Roselli looked at each other, shocked by the court's ruling. The Manhattan trial calendar was backlogged with cases. Why was the judge pushing this one?

Quinn couldn't hide a smile as he tucked the case folder under his arm.

Kevin Quinn came to the New York County DA's office directly out of Yale Law School. Working his way up the hierarchy, after ten years he'd become one of the most effective prosecutors in the Homicide Bureau. From his blond crew cut to his wing-tip shoes, Quinn was a staunch conservative in appearance as well as philosophy. Tall and broad-shouldered, he carried himself like a Marine drill sergeant, his uniform a navy blue Ivy League suit, white button-down shirt, and a rep tie.

Displeasure shone easily on Quinn's sharp-jawed, angular face, and he was obviously perturbed when his first witness took the stand to begin the trial of Mark Cantor. Wearing faded blue jeans and an iridescent Jefferson Airplane T-shirt, she'd disregarded his insistence that she dress "appropriately" for court.

A woman in her early thirties, Theresa Severini was the girlfriend with Joanna on the day she'd met Mark. Using both hands, she swept back the ragged mane of dark, coarse hair from her face as she swore to tell the truth.

Quinn began the questioning by establishing that despite Miss Severini's sloppy appearance, she was a solid citizen. Three years ago, she'd opened a health-food restaurant, and it had become one of the most popular and successful in the Village.

After having the witness acknowledge a friendship of several years with Joanna Voorhees, the prosecutor then proceeded to the heart of the testimony, by asking Severini if she'd ever met the defendant.

Fixing the date as the "first Saturday in March," she began the story on the Fifth Avenue bus, telling the jury that she and Joanna Voorhees were on their way down to Greenwich Village after shopping uptown: ". . . and for a good ten or fifteen minutes, this guy kept staring at her. He gave me the creeps.

"Finally, he started talkin' to Joanna. I don't remember what he said—somethin' about being a Vietnam veteran. She gave him the brush-off and two stops later, he was staring again."

The witness's masculine deep voice, unaided by a microphone, bellowed through the packed courtroom. With its massively high ceiling, the acoustics were generally poor, yet those in the back of the room had no difficulty hearing her.

"He got off the bus at the same stop we did. As we walked to the corner Joanna said to me, 'Hey, that guy is kinda cute. He's got a cute rear, too'—only that's not the exact word she used. It was strange because she'd been so cool to him on the bus when he tried to start a conversation. Now suddenly she's interested! But that's Joanna—you could never figure her out. Sometimes a guy would try to pick her up and she'd be unfriendly . . . she wanted them to try a little harder, to show they had confidence. But if they tried *too* hard, that turned her off. It was all too complicated for me!"

Theresa Severini leaned forward in the chair. "When the guy got to the corner he stopped and stood there lookin' around like he was lost or somethin'. Joanna walked over and started talkin' to him. I didn't hear what she said, but he seemed pretty surprised. She had this seductive grin on her face and after a while he got over his initial shock and smiled back. But she continued to do most of the talkin'.

"When Joanna finally introduced us, he glanced at me for maybe a second—he couldn't take his eyes off her. Said his name was Mark. And he mentioned that he lived around there—I forget the street," Severini testified, pulling at her lower lip.

"Oh, no . . . before that, when we still thought he was lost, Joanna asked him, 'What are you lookin' for?' and he goes: 'Your apartment!' I remember that. The next thing I know, he's walkin' with us. Invited himself.

"I mean, this dude was too much! At first I thought he was shy, but then the guy became so aggressive—like gangbusters. Too slick. He gave me bad vibes."

That brought Roselli to his feet with a loud "Objection!" Before the judge ruled, Quinn instructed his witness to "eliminate editorializations." She scowled at him and a few people in the audience laughed.

After making Cantor sound vulgar, or at least fresh, Severini's next answer made him seem strange:

"Did he tell you or Miss Voorhees what type of work he did?" Quinn asked.

"No," she said, shaking her head. "It wasn't the normal kind of conversation people have when they first meet. He didn't say very much about himself or ask Joanna basic questions like, 'What do you do for a living?' He was weird . . ." Her voice trailed off and, unable to explain what she meant, her horsey face took on a look of frustration. But she perked up when she suddenly thought of an example: "For instance, we're just walking along and from out of the blue he asks her: 'Did you decide what to get me for my birthday?'—as if they were old friends or somethin'!"

Severini conveniently omitted Joanna's responses, which would have revealed that she knew Mark was kidding. Roselli would have to bring this to light when his turn came to cross-examine. But Quinn wasn't yet finished with the witness. Standing behind the counsel table, he leaned over and began to thumb nervously through notes on a yellow legal pad; then, straightening up to his full height, over six feet, posed his next question: "What else did they talk about on the way to the bookstore?"

"I don't know—that's all I remember."

"What about the deaf mute?" Quinn prompted. "Did they have a conversation about a deaf mute?"

"Oh, yeah . . . we passed by this man moving his fingers like he was doing sign language, only . . . there was no one with him— he was alone! Mark couldn't get over how bizarre it looked. And Joanna says, 'Why? Don't you ever talk to yourself?'

"Well, he was very impressed with that comment: he said somethin' like"—Severini squinted trying to recall his words— " 'I wish you weren't so clever. Now it'll kill me if you don't fall in love with me!' At the time neither me or Joanna took it very seriously. . . . I mean, he was smiling when he said it. Of course, now . . ."

Fearing the witness might get melodramatic and say something he didn't want the jury to hear, Roselli jumped up again: "Objection, Your Honor, if the witness could be cautioned about *commenting* on the facts . . ."

Judge Warren sustained the objection and, in a gentle but authoritative tone, he admonished, "Please, Miss Severini, just tell us what you saw and what you heard."

Quinn had a shit-eating grin on his face as he watched the defense attorney drop into his seat. But an austere countenance returned when he asked the witness to relate the conversation that took place in front of the bookstore.

"Okay," Severini began after picking at her lip again. "I wanted to get that book before the store closed. Besides, I felt like a third wheel. So I look at Joanna and I say, 'Listen, I'm going in; are you coming?' She nodded, but then *he* invites her for a drink at this pub around the corner, and before she could say anything, he tells me to join them there when I'm finished. I told him that I couldn't—I had plans for the evening. That really broke his heart," Severini said, her wide mouth turning up in a smile. "He was waiting for Joanna's answer and wasn't even listening to me. She seemed reluctant but she was just being coy. 'I don't think so,' she said. Then he got real serious all of a sudden and looked at her straight in the eyes and said, 'Please!' "

Quinn let the word hang in the air for a few seconds until it settled on every ear. Walking slowly around the counsel table toward the witness stand, he did not pose his next question until he was only ten feet in front of Severini: "Would you characterize, as best you can, the way he said 'Please'?"

Roselli objected to the question but was overruled. Theresa Severini answered: "Like I said, he was very serious, very intense—he seemed almost to be pleading with her. Well, maybe that's too strong. It was just one word, and he wasn't really begging, but he said it in a way—like it was very important to him."

Throughout the questioning, Severini had looked at Cantor just once, so Quinn confirmed the identification: "And this man you've been talking about . . . was the same person now seated over there?" he asked, pointing at Mark.

She glanced over and answered without equivocation, "Yeah, that's the guy."

"By the way," Quinn concluded as if it were an afterthought, "to your knowledge, did Joanna Voorhees know anyone else named Mark?"

The significance of Quinn's final question would not be realized by the jury until later, but Roselli caught on right away. He objected and, when overruled, asked to approach the bench to explain his position. But Judge Warren, getting impatient now, didn't want to be enlightened. He instructed the witness to answer and she responded in the negative.

The next day the courtroom looked like the stage for a rock concert. Three large metal stands had been wheeled in, loaded with audio equipment, including a set of huge Altec speakers placed on either side of the jury, to present Joanna Voorhees's nightmare in stereophonic sound.

Detective Stewart Feldstein, the police electronics expert, introduced the show.

A tall, thin man with kinky brown hair and oversized aviator glasses, Feldstein testified that, at Sergeant Larsen's request, he'd installed "apparatus" in the Voorhees apartment to record *incoming* calls. He explained the pen register device and the defeat switch, demonstrating how they worked. After Quinn distributed a copy of the typed transcript to all the jurors, Detective Feldstein played the tape.

Some of the jurors stared at the recorder or the speakers, others had their heads buried in the transcript as they followed along. There were some raised eyebrows when, during the fourth call, the female voice uttered the name Mark, but no one in that courtroom made a sound until the last call brought gasps from the gallery of spectators. The jurors remained silent, but a few glanced over toward Mark as if looking could tell them if the deep voice belonged to him.

Afterward Feldstein accounted for the long period of silence on the fifth call: while making copies of the tape for the DA and defense counsel, he'd accidentally erased part of that conversation. He explained that the two tape recorders he used were almost identical and that after being interrupted by an emergency phone call, he had turned the machines back on and mistakenly reversed the settings, pressing the play button on the unit which was supposed to record, and the record button on the machine which had the original tape. Pulling at his earlobe, Feldstein told the court that "only seconds passed" before he realized his mistake and corrected it. He further testified that he'd listened once to the original tape before making copies, but couldn't recall the text of the missing segment.

The typed transcript, which the detective admitted he personally prepared, made no reference to any erasure. It described the fifth call as follows:

> April 26, 1976
> beginning 9:31 P.M.
> terminating 9:32 P.M.

J. V.: "Hello?"
Unk. M.: (inaudible) ". . . toward my hand."

Phil Roselli began his cross-examination, "As a police electronics expert, you've prepared many wiretap or electronic surveillance transcripts, have you not, sir?"

"I have," Feldstein answered. "Hundreds."

Glancing at some papers on the defense table, Roselli continued, "Now in the transcript for the April twenty-sixth call, the term *inaudible* appears. You've used that term before in other transcripts?"

"Sure," the witness said, peering down at the copy on his lap.

"Many times?"

"Quite a few."

"And would I be correct in saying that the term *inaudible* usually refers to a situation where the transmission isn't clear enough to transcribe?"

When Feldstein nodded, Roselli moved around the defense table and, with both hands stretching out his jacket pockets, he charged toward the witness stand. "*Inaudible* means you can't make it out, you're unable to hear it; isn't that right, Mr. Expert?"

"Yeah," the detective said faintly, again pulling at his earlobe.

Roselli crouched over, but never took his bloodhound eyes off the witness. "Well, when you heard the original tape before making copies, were any parts of that April twenty-sixth call inau-dible?"

"No, counselor," Feldstein stared back, "but it's inaudible now."

"Yeah, it sure is!" Roselli shouted, his face bright red.

Unshaken, the witness leaned forward in his chair and in a firm, sincere tone, offered, "I used the wrong word in this transcript. I tried to simplify things rather than go into a long explanation." Then Feldstein sat back relaxed as if he'd set the matter to rest.

But the defense attorney wasn't satisfied. "You could have written 'erased'—that's pretty simple, isn't it?"

"I guess."

Roselli wanted the jury to suspect that the erased portion of the tape had contained something exculpatory to the defense and Feldstein had used the term *inaudible* intending to cover up the dirty deed. Then the defense attorney attempted to involve Quinn in the conspiracy. Looking over toward the prosecutor, he asked Feldstein, "When did you first tell Mr. Quinn that part of a call had been erased?"

"Some time ago."

"Had you already made up the transcript and given it to him?"

"I think so."

"Did he tell you to correct that transcript—to change the word *inaudible*?"

"He probably didn't even notice it. You're making a big deal about it now, counselor, but it didn't seem so important at the time."

Roselli responded with a quick smile, then started back toward the defense table but stopped before he got there. "By the way, was Mr. Quinn present when you heard the tape in its entirety—before you erased part of that call?"

"No, he wasn't," Feldstein answered. "It was just me and Sergeant Larsen."

During the luncheon recess, Cantor phoned Bastone to report the morning's events. "But you know, I really don't believe it was a cover-up," Mark concluded. "I think Feldstein did make a mistake and was just too embarrassed to admit it when he prepared the transcript."

"You always were good at defending cops," Bastone replied, "but you're not the assistant DA on this case!"

"Yeah, but I know how these guys think . . . how they operate. I believe Feldstein, and I'm afraid the jury does too. Phil was great, but it just didn't work."

"You never know, Mark, if only one juror bought it—"

Just then the operator interrupted demanding more money. Bastone asked Mark for the number at the phone booth, but Cantor deposited another nickel.

"Wanna meet us for lunch, Tom?"

"I'd love to, but I'm expecting an important call in the next hour. I'll speak to you later."

Bastone's "important call" came a few minutes after he'd hung up with Mark, and he decided to get a quick bite himself. Knowing Roselli liked the Delmar Kitchen, a coffee shop near the courthouse, Bastone thought he might catch up with them there.

The Delmar looked like hundreds of other Greek-owned restaurants: artificial plants, artificial wood paneling, and artificial stained-glass lights. Behind the counter was an array of luscious-looking desserts. The cakes, almost a foot high, were meals in themselves, but like the decor, they were "artificial" too—they all tasted the same: the chocolate fudge cake had the same nondescript flavor as the devil's food cake, which was virtually indistinguishable from the cheesecake. Manufactured by an artist rather than a baker, they were distributed to all the Greek coffee shops in the city.

Bastone entered the noisy, packed restaurant and looked around for Mark and Roselli. He walked through checking every table, but he'd guessed wrong—they weren't there. He was hungry and grabbed the only empty seat at the counter.

The dark, mustachioed waiters at the Delmar understood only terms from the menu and maybe *mayonnaise, ketchup, check,* and *bathroom.* Bastone knew that if he kept his order simple, there was a fifty-fifty chance they'd get it right. "Ham and cheese, french fries, and a lemon Tab," he told the man. Tom kept glancing at the door in case Mark and Roselli came in, and it wasn't until the waiter brought his food that Bastone noticed the young lady seated to his left. Chicly dressed in a well-tailored pinstriped suit, she seemed, at first, out of place on a luncheonette stool. Looking closer at her freckled face, pug nose, and fine-spun blond hair in an old-fashioned ponytail, Bastone was reminded of a tomboy in a party dress.

"Ham-cheese, burger deluxe, Tab, Coke," the waiter announced as plates slid off his arm onto the counter. While the hamburger was put before the woman and the sandwich before Tom, the two cola-colored sodas had been left midway between them, and it was impossible to tell which was which. Of course, the waiter disappeared immediately. Noticing a lemon floating on top of one of the drinks, Bastone reached for it, explaining, "This must be mine. I ordered lemon."

"So did I," the young lady replied, pointing to another lemon buried under ice in the other glass.

"Well, it doesn't really matter to me," Tom said, trying to be amicable. "I'm watching my weight but it's not crucial."

"But I'm afraid it does matter to me," she said apologetically. "I can't stand diet soda." Though soft and distinctly feminine, her voice was full and firm.

"Why don't we give it the taste test," Tom suggested, mild surprise registering on her face. "I can't tell the difference until I drink half the glass, so why don't you try it? You don't look like you have any communicable diseases."

"None that I know about," she smiled. But all she could manage was a look at the glass until he urged, "Go ahead." Still she hesitated before finally reaching for it. She took a sip and made a grotesquely pained face as if she'd swallowed vinegar. "This one's yours," she declared, pushing the glass toward him.

"I had a feeling." Tom held back laughter but was unable to keep a smile from slipping through. He took the Tab and started eating. Bastone was ravenous and by the time the waiter delivered the french fries, he'd already devoured the whole sandwich.

The well-dressed lady with the ponytail renewed the conversation. "Don't you love it when they bring the french fries for dessert?"

"Yeah, that's one of my pet peeves, too," Tom agreed, "but in this case, I didn't give him much time."

Her eyes moved from her less than half-eaten hamburger to the crumbs on his plate. "Pretty hungry, huh?"

"Very. I didn't have breakfast."

"You should always have breakfast—most important meal of the day," she said earnestly.

"So I've heard. Trouble is I can't get up in the morning. So I'm always late and never have time for breakfast."

"Go to bed earlier," she politely suggested.

After trying a greasy french fry, Tom returned his attention to the more appealing sight sitting next to him. "I bet you're one of these people who wake up refreshed and raring to go," he said with feigned contempt.

Placing her hamburger on the plate, she replied, "I don't have trouble getting up . . . but I'm always late for work, too."

"What kind of work do you do?"

"For the city," she answered allusively, then quickly fired back "What do you do?" giving Tom the impression that she wasn't particularly proud of her occupation.

"I'm a private investigator."

"Are you kidding?" she said in disbelief.

Most women became curious or interested when Bastone gave his occupation, but this response was novel and somewhat disturbing. "What's the matter," he said, turning toward her and sitting straight up in the stool, "don't I look like a private eye?"

"Well, you certainly don't look like Mike Hammer or Sam

Spade." She carefully inspected his double-breasted silk suit. "You look more like a . . ." Tom's eyes were glued on hers as he waited for the verdict. "Like a salesman!" He squinted as if in pain. "A *top* salesman," she added, causing his face to relax. "Anyway, my other guess was a mafioso," she grinned, "and I gave you the benefit of the doubt!"

"Well, thanks, that was kind of you," Tom said.

"I just meant that you look too successful to be a private detective. I didn't think they made a lot of money."

"Some do, but I don't," Tom grinned.

All of a sudden, she looked at her watch and gasped, "Oh, Christ, it's five minutes to two! See, I told you I'm always late. But this time it's your fault," she teased, her deepset blue eyes twinkling. Then she grabbed her check from the counter and rushed off with a quick but sincere "Nice talkin' to you."

Bastone waved good-bye and watched her walk briskly to the cashier. She had a pretty good figure, he noticed. He sat there thinking that it really was nice talking to her. She was so friendly—why didn't he ask for her telephone number?

True, she really wasn't his type—Tom Bastone preferred flashier women. Of course, had he been strongly attracted to her, conversation would never have been so easy for him. And she had gotten prettier as they spoke. "What a jerk!" he berated himself for not following through. Then again, it had all ended so abruptly—her hasty departure had made it impossible to get her phone number, he rationalized. But, having watched Mark Cantor so many times, he knew that wasn't true.

Richard Moriarty, a big burly ex-cop with a wrestler's neck and tiny ears, was the prosecution's next witness. After getting seriously wounded during a drug raid, Moriarty had left the police force; he had gone to work for New York Telephone and was now their head of security. Acting as the liaison between the phone company and law enforcement agencies, Moriarty was in charge of releasing unpublished telephone numbers to the authorities when "good cause" was shown. That phrase, he explained to the jury, merely meant "when properly requested."

Moriarty testified as to the procedure: "It's requisitioned. Say you're a New York City detective and you want this person's phone number and you call and the operator tells you he's got a phone, but at the person's request, it ain't listed. Okay. The detective sends a letter on official stationery. Actually, we got a form, and they're supposed to fill out our form, but if they send us a letter, that's okay. Anyway, he puts down the information— name, address, the reason he needs the phone number, etc.— and we send it to him. Usually they don't really give us the exact reason . . . I mean, they try to be real vague. We give it to them anyway . . . you know, if it looks official."

"Do you ever get requests from any of the district attorneys' offices?" asked prosecutor Kevin Quinn, standing behind the state's table.

"Oh sure," Moriarty nodded his big blond head. "DAs call on us a lot," he began proudly, sitting up tall and pulling his shoulders back so his powder blue polyester shirt strained across his huge chest. "See, they're always looking for people . . . you know, like witnesses."

"And is the procedure the same?"

"Yeah, it's the same. They usually use our form. They must keep a stack of 'em there."

Having laid the foundation, Quinn moved on to the specifics:

"Mr. Moriarty, prior to your coming to court today, did you have occasion to check the official records of the New York Telephone Company with regard to a telephone instrument at 69 East Tenth Street in Manhattan, Apartment 5-B?"

"Yes, I did," Moriarty said as he leaned his elbow but missed the arm of his chair. "Yes," he repeated.

"Can we have a time period here, Judge?" Roselli interrupted.

87

Without moving his head, which was buried in papers, Judge Warren peered over his bifocals toward Quinn. In repose the jurist's light brown face was without a wrinkle, white-gray hair and tired eyes the only clues to his advanced age. But to demonstrate concern he'd furrow his brow, as he did when he told the prosecutor, "You will clarify that, Mr. Quinn."

"Very next question," Quinn answered with an assuring nod. Then he turned to the witness stand. "And for what time period did you check?"

Moriarty responded, "Well it all happened in March," then waited for the next question without further amplification.

Quinn's lips tightened. "What do you mean *it* all happened in March?" he asked, pinching each word.

Moriarty read from an index card on his lap:

"A new instrument was installed in that premises on March the fifteenth, 1976. It was supposed to go in March tenth, but it didn't . . . it went in on the fifteenth."

After establishing that the index card was an official record of the telephone company, Quinn asked that it be admitted to evidence and Moriarty remained to interpret it.

"In whose name was that telephone registered?" Quinn led.

"Joanna Voorhees," came the crisp reply.

"And that was an unpublished number?" asked Quinn.

"No," Moriarty corrected, "originally the customer's number was listed—"

"You're speaking now of Joanna Voorhees," Quinn interrupted, "is that right?"

"Yeah, Joanna Voorhees," Moriarty continued. "Then, apparently the customer requested a change in her phone number and didn't want the new one listed."

"And when did Joanna Voorhees get her phone number changed to an unpublished number?" Quinn asked, clarifying Moriarty's last answer at the same time.

"Well, according to the record, it would be March twenty-ninth."

"Can you tell the jury what the unpublished number was?"

Moriarty looked down at the card and read from it: "555-5912."

"And that number was unpublished," Quinn repeated.

"That's right," said Moriarty.

A few of the jurors were shifting restlessly in their seats and one or two even yawned, but just as boredom was setting in, Quinn asked, "Can you tell us exactly what the term *unpublished* means, that is, what are the consequences of having an unpublished number?" Moriarty misinterpreted the question and answered, "I think you pay more!" There was some laughter, and then he proceeded to give the response Quinn was looking for: "It means it ain't in no directory, and if you call Information, or what they now call Directory Assistance, you'd be told the party has a phone, but they can't give out the number. Actually, they don't even have it in their books—they just got the name and address." Then he proudly added, "Only my office has the number."

Quinn paused for a few seconds and stepped around the counsel table to let the jury know he was coming to the important part.

"Now, Mr. Moriarty, you've told us that there is a procedure whereby the telephone company can release an unpublished number to a law enforcement body." Quinn paused again and, slowing the pace, asked, "Can you tell me whether the number 555-5912, registered as an unpublished number to Joanna Voorhees, at 69 East Tenth Street, was ever requisitioned by any law enforcement agency?"

"Yes it was," said Moriarty, surveying the courtroom with an air of confidence while he awaited his next cue. His manner suggested that this part of his examination had been well rehearsed.

"And what agency was that?" asked Quinn, as he moved slowly toward the witness.

"It was the Bronx District Attorney's office," Moriarty said, trying to put a touch of drama in his voice.

"Can you tell me when you received this requisition?"

Moriarty glanced down at a paper in his hand, different from the card he had been reading from earlier.

"According to the requisition sheet, it was April, April fourth to be exact. That's the date it was requested and we sent out the information on the same day."

"The fourth of April, 1976," Quinn repeated for emphasis. Then, turning to the jury, with his back to the witness, the prosecutor continued in a raised voice: "Can you tell me specifically *who,* in the Bronx District Attorney's office, requisitioned Joanna Voorhees's number?"

The answer came back from Moriarty without hesitation, and in an even more dramatic tone: "Assistant District Attorney Mark Cantor."

"Thank you, Mr. Moriarty," Quinn said in a cocky sort of way, as if the telephone company man was an eyewitness and he'd just buried Cantor. But his testimony, though not devastating, was damaging. The telephone company records proved that Mark knew Joanna's number at the time she was receiving the threatening calls. They also showed the lengths to which he'd gone to obtain that number.

As Quinn strutted back to the prosecution table, he scanned the jury with a smirk on his face to underscore the victory. And perhaps to see their reaction. Then, from a manila folder on his table, Quinn removed a piece of paper and had Moriarty identify it as the original of the requisition document. Introduced into evidence as People's Exhibit Number 2, it was read to the jury. The telephone company form noted as the "reason for request" the fact that Joanna Voorhees was a witness who could not be reached. The "name of the case" for which she was supposed to be a witness was listed as *People* v. *Thomas Jenkins.* At the bottom appeared the signature of Mark Cantor.

Quinn's announcement that he had "no further questions of the witness" was the cue for the defense to cross-examine Moriarty. But Phil Roselli casually declined: "I have no questions of this gentleman."

The next witness was Sergeant William Montanez. He entered the courtroom, walking briskly to the witness stand, his head bent over. He was a large, well-built man but he slouched in his chair and spoke so softly that several times Quinn had to ask him to speak up. Montanez testified that Joanna Voorhees was neither a witness, nor a possible witness, and indeed had no connection whatsoever with the Thomas Jenkins case.

Throughout his direct examination, Montanez never once looked in Mark's direction. Roselli again declined to cross-examine, and when excused, the sergeant fled the courtroom as if it were on fire.

As he did at the close of every day, Judge Warren instructed the jury not to discuss the case with anyone. Cantor followed his lawyer into the elevator, out of the building, and two blocks south along Centre Street. Roselli took long, powerful strides, surprising for a man pushing seventy with short, stubby legs, and Mark strained to keep up. When they reached a small, triangular park, he sat down on an empty bench. Mark joined him. In this urban oasis, with its patch of worn grass and several trees providing some visual escape but no insulation from the sounds of the city, Roselli finally spoke. He kept his voice low, but his face was red with anger.

"Why didn't you tell me about that phony requisition sheet!" The bright day lit up all his wrinkles, caused in part, no doubt, by other clients who had not told him all.

"I forgot," Mark said softly. "I just forgot."

"How could you forget when you went to all that trouble to get the number?" Roselli asked incredulously, his soft brown eyes bulging.

Mark shook his head from side to side, like the victim of a pickpocket who suddenly realizes he's been robbed though he felt nothing. Then he tried to explain: "First of all, I never spoke to her using the unlisted number. Second of all, getting it was no big deal—it was easy—"

"It was also *illegal,* or at the very least, a misuse of your authority!" Roselli interrupted. "Was that such an *unimportant* event, that you couldn't remember it!"

"Yes, it was 'unimportant,' " Mark shouted back, "and that wasn't the only time I did it either." Mark lowered his voice but he still seemed angry: "You know, you make it sound like some kind of corruption." Then he turned away and muttered, "I was one of the honest prosecutors."

"I know you were honest. . . . Why do you think I never tried to bribe you!" Roselli said, all too seriously. "Every defense lawyer in the Bronx knows you were an 'untouchable,' but the jury doesn't." He got up from the bench and started pacing. "This crap makes you look lousy—a public official who uses his power for personal gain."

"Phil, a lot of guys in the office did it," Mark defended, his eyes following Roselli from side to side. "It was like a 'fringe benefit' of being an assistant DA."

Roselli stopped in his tracks and yelled: "Sounds great. You gonna tell that to the jury?" He stepped closer to Mark and stood over him. "More importantly, you think that jury is gonna believe you put in a phony requisition to get her unlisted number and then never dialed it?"

Judge Warren's refusal to postpone the trial put enormous pressure on Tom Bastone, forcing him to work day and night on the Cantor case. Hoping to find someone who'd witnessed the murder of Joanna Voorhees, he and his partner—Brian Downey—had canvassed the two buildings on Eleventh Street that faced the rear of 69 East Tenth. Each was eight stories high with six units on a floor, but the detectives focused their attention on those tenants in the back apartments. While the list hadn't been completely exhausted, they'd interviewed a few dozen people without any success. Nor were they able to learn much about Joanna Voorhees: her neighbors didn't know much, and her close friends wouldn't talk to anyone trying to help the accused killer.

Tom Bastone's fear of being unable to come up with anything helpful was quickly being realized, when progress was finally made in another area. A fifty-dollar bill he'd given to a secretary at Cleveland Johnson's union had paid off: she'd just received the jazz musician's union dues. "It came in an envelope with a San Francisco postmark," she told Bastone.

Although the field of his search for the missing neighbor had now been substantially narrowed, the detective still hadn't found him. Nevertheless, Bastone was extremely excited by the breakthrough and anxious to report it to Cantor and Roselli. He rushed over to the courthouse, hoping to see them before the day's proceedings began. However, when Bastone arrived, Sergeant Judith Larsen had just taken the witness stand, so he quietly slipped into an empty seat in the rear of the large courtroom.

Leaning against the wooden rail that separated the participants from the spectators, prosecutor Quinn asked, "And what is your specific assignment at the Sixth Precinct?"

"I head the Sex Crime Unit there," the young woman answered. On the petite side and wearing a ruffled silk blouse, she didn't look like a lady cop.

"How long have you held that post?"

"Since the department initiated the program—that would be a little more than a year ago," she said in a sweet, clear voice that sounded familiar to Tom Bastone. He leaned forward and took a better look at her delicately pretty face, but couldn't quite place it.

The witness testified that on March 26, 1976, the Voorhees girl came to the Sixth Precinct station house to lodge a complaint. Emotionally upset when she arrived, the desk officer referred her to Sergeant Larsen. "She wasn't crying," Larsen told the jury, "but she kept ranting: 'You've got to help me.' I asked her to calm down and suggested she take a few deep breaths. Then I gave her a glass of water."

When the witness faced the jury, Bastone got a profile view and realized who she was. Wearing her golden hair in a French knot and with more makeup on her face, she looked almost sophisticated, but she was definitely the same young woman he'd met a few days before at the Delmar Kitchen. Although she'd been vague that day, she'd not been inaccurate—indeed, she did "work for the city."

Bastone's eyes were opened wide as the witness continued to relate her conversation with Joanna Voorhees: "When she finally became composed, I asked her what the problem was. I don't remember her exact words but she said she'd received a couple of threatening phone calls. It seems about a week or so before she'd met a man on the street and given him her phone number. When he called she'd had a change of heart and refused to see him. He got angry and hostile, so she hung up." Larsen glanced down at some notes and added, "This was on March eighteenth or nineteenth—she wasn't sure." Larsen paused, then looked up again. "After that, he called two more times, she told me. In both of these instances, he didn't identify himself, but she recognized his voice." Larsen peeked down at her notes again. "When he called on Wednesday, March 24th, all he said was, 'You're going to pay,' and then hung up."

Roselli rose from his seat behind the defense table. "I object. Your Honor, all of this testimony is hearsay and, furthermore, there's been no showing of connection to . . ." But Judge Warren cut him off abruptly. "Your objection is noted," he said, peering over his bifocals. "Please make your objections without speeches." Then he motioned Roselli to sit down by merely extending his hand over the bench and bringing it down slowly. "Proceed."

Larsen continued: "In the early evening of March 26th— just before she came to the precinct—he phoned again. This time he tried to disguise his voice by speaking in a deep tone. It was also a little muffled, she said. He began by calling her sweetie, and this time he didn't threaten her directly, but started talking about death. He ignored her when she asked who it was and then she hung up.

"At this point I asked her the name of the man she'd met on the street and she said, Mark—he'd told her his name was Mark—but he never gave his last name. I asked her some more questions, but other than a physical description, she couldn't tell me anything about him."

Quinn moved away from the rail and took a few steps toward the witness stand. "And what was the physical description Miss Voorhees gave you?" he asked, glancing over toward the jury.

Looking down at her lap, Larsen began: "Five foot nine, slim, in his late twenties, brown—"

Roselli stood up again, and drowning out the witness he said, "Your Honor, she's reading from something which isn't in evidence and—"

"I offer it in evidence," Quinn shouted over Roselli, "and ask that . . ."

With everyone speaking at the same time, the court stenographer, a little gray-haired woman with rhinestone-studded eyeglasses, threw up her hands in frustration and told the judge, "I'm not getting any of this."

"Hold it, hold everything," exclaimed Judge Warren, restoring order. He regarded the witness. "Sergeant, are you reading from something?"

"Yes, from the complaint report—the UF 61."

"Is that an official record kept in the regular course of the business of the police department?" he asked, using the technical words necessary to qualify it as admissible.

"It is," the witness replied.

Warren turned then to the prosecutor. "You're offering it in evidence, Mr. Quinn?"

Taking the hint, the assistant DA responded, "Yessir."

"Show it to Mr. Roselli," the judge ordered, and a court officer carried the piece of paper from Larsen to the defense counsel, who glanced at it and as soon as he looked up, Judge Warren asked him, "You have an objection, sir, to its introduction into evidence?"

Roselli started to rise. "I do and would like to state my reasons," he said softly before straightening up.

"You can make your record later, Mr. Roselli. We've got to move along. Your objection is overruled. The UF 61 is admitted in evidence as People's Exhibit Number . . . I think we're up to . . . Three."

Starting over, Judith Larsen read the description from the police record: "Five foot nine, slim build, in late twenties, brown curly hair, brown eyes, mustache." With Theresa Severini having already identified Cantor as the Mark Joanna Voorhees met on the street in early March, the description in the UF 61 merely corroborated that testimony. But its impact seemed greater on the heels of Joanna Voorhees's claim that the one who made these two anonymous calls was that same man. The complaint form also contained the substance of her statement to the sergeant—almost identical to the account Larsen had just given the jury.

"Did Miss Voorhees sign this in your presence?" Quinn said, holding up Exhibit 3.

"She did," Larsen replied, sitting straight and tall, like a dancer.

"What, if anything, did you tell her?"

"Well, under the circumstances there wasn't much we could do. I mean, she didn't know his last name, where he lived, or anything about him. I told her to change her phone to an unpublished number. I felt that was the simplest and most practical solution," the sergeant told the jury in a gentle but authoritative

95

tone that engendered confidence. "I explained that ninety-nine times out of a hundred these type of calls are made just to frighten with no intention of following through. 'I know it's scary,' I told her, 'but I don't believe you're in any real danger.' " Larsen looked down at the checkerboard-tiled floor in front of the witness stand, shook her head, and muttered, "I didn't want her to worry herself sick."

A cop with compassion, Bastone thought, as Larsen looked up again and told the jury, "I gave her a number where she could reach me—a direct line so she didn't have to waste time going through the switchboard."

Joanna Voorhees didn't use the hot line, but two weeks later she was back at the Sixth Precinct. "I did what you suggested—I got an unlisted number," she reported to Larsen, "and last night, he called again. He's got my new number!"

The sergeant detailed the rest of her April 9th meeting with Joanna Voorhees: "She told me that, as soon as he said, 'Hello, sweetie' in that deep, muffled voice, she hung up and kept the phone off the hook for the remainder of the evening.

"I asked Joanna if she had given the unpublished number to anyone, and she said she'd given it to a few close friends, but none of them would do such a thing. I got a list of their names and addresses anyway."

Larsen had Joanna Voorhees view mug shots but none matched "Mark"—the young man she had met on the street. The sergeant then ordered an "in-house" tap on Joanna's phone along with a tracer, making it possible to trace the origin of any call lasting more than three minutes. "I told her a Detective Feldstein would come by her apartment on Monday to install the equipment and show her how to use it. 'If this guy calls again,' I instructed her, 'keep him on the line as long as possible.' "

Although the threatening calls which followed were recorded, none lasted more than the required three minutes, so none could be traced. Joanna Voorhees didn't come to the precinct again, but she did telephone Larsen several times right after receiving another call from him. On one occasion, Joanna requested police protection. "She sounded very frightened," Larsen testified. "I told her . . ." The witness hesitated, then said, as if apologizing to the jury, "We can't . . . we just don't have the manpower. I also suggested she change her phone number again, and not give it out to anyone this time . . . at least for a while, but she said, 'He'll just get it again like he did the last time.' "

Just as Quinn began his next question, the court stenographer announced that her machine needed to be reloaded with paper. Judge Warren thought this a convenient time for a ten-minute recess. He excused the witness, instructing her not to discuss the case with anyone. Sergeant Larsen stepped down from the witness stand and marched down the center aisle toward the rear door. As she passed by Tom Bastone, without conscious thought, he turned his head to hide from her view.

As soon as the judge left the bench, Bastone pushed through the crowd of exiting spectators and made his way to the front of the courtroom. Roselli and Cantor were still seated at the defense table.

"Cleveland Johnson is in San Francisco," Bastone whispered to them, without exchanging greetings. "I'm sending Brian out there tonight—with a subpoena."

"Good," Roselli said. "How much good I don't know, but hell it's worth a shot. Have you found out if he was porking the Voorhees girl?"

The question took the wind out of the investigator's sails. "No, I can't establish any romantic link between them," he said sullenly. "None of the neighbors ever saw them together, and her friends won't say."

Roselli tried to raise his spirits: "Well, we still might catch a break if you find Johnson, and San Francisco's really a small town."

"It'll be easy if he's working," Cantor added.

"Yeah, we'll get him," Bastone said, trying to sound confident. "So how's it goin' here?" he asked Mark's lawyer.

Roselli just shrugged.

Bastone patted him on the back. "Well, good luck. I better get going." He started to leave, but after taking a few steps, he returned. "Oh, by the way: Joanna's from lower-middle-class Lincoln Park, Michigan—not Grosse Pointe."

Mark smiled and shook his head. "She lied to me about that. . . . What a girl!"

When court resumed, Sergeant Judith Larsen testified about her questioning of Cantor at the Sixth Precinct. She asked him

97

where he had been between the hours of ten and eleven P.M. on April 29.

"At first he said, 'You must be kidding—that was weeks ago!' Trying to refresh his memory, I told him it was a Thursday." The witness reported that after a moment Cantor recalled April twenty-eighth, the preceding day, as the date he'd been scheduled to begin prosecution of the Orchard Beach rapist. That trial was adjourned, he told Larsen, because he came down with the flu the night before and spent the next few days in bed.

"I asked him if he'd seen a doctor and he said no. Then I asked, 'Did you have any visitors that Thursday night?' and his answer was, 'I don't think so.' "

Quinn's head was bobbing up and down. "So he told you he was home on the night of April twenty-ninth?"

"Yes," the witness said.

Cantor and Roselli looked at each other, both of them perplexed. Since being home alone is certainly no alibi, Mark's statements about his whereabouts on the twenty-ninth would seem to be without significance. Why then had Quinn underscored this testimony? Cantor and his lawyer would soon find out.

The obviously damaging part of Larsen's testimony came next. Quinn began in a casual tone: "Now before you arrested him, before you took him to the Sixth Precinct, did you have an earlier conversation with Mr. Cantor?"

"Yes, I asked him some questions when we first met in Mr. Capellini's office."

"That would be Mr. Paul Capellini—the District Attorney of Bronx County?" Larsen nodded and Quinn asked, "Was Mr. Capellini present at the time?"

"He was."

"What did the defendant tell you then?"

Larsen paused, waiting for everyone's complete attention. "He admitted threatening Joanna Voorhees over the telephone." Almost in unison the twelve jurors leaned forward in their seats, each intently staring at the witness. Only a few took their eyes off her when Roselli, his thumb tucked in his vest pocket, stood and calmly addressed the judge. "Your Honor, can we have the actual conversation rather than this witness's conclusion as to what was said."

"Yes," Warren agreed, smacking his lips. He swiveled his high-backed chair and leaned over the bench to face Larsen.

"Sergeant, tell us, as best you can, what you said to the defendant, and what he said to you."

She nodded, then turned to the jury. "I asked him if he'd threatened Joanna Voorhees over the telephone, and he said he had but that it was just a joke."

You could have heard a pin drop in the courtroom and several jurors glanced at Mark as he stirred uncomfortably in his chair. Although this had to be one of the high points of his case, Quinn refrained from gloating. Instead, he marked the moment with a somber expression and a long pause before his last question: "Did you ask Mr. Cantor how he'd obtained Miss Voorhees's unpublished telephone number?"

"No, I never asked him that."

Larsen's answer didn't surprise the prosecutor. His purpose in asking the question was merely to remind the jury that Cantor had gone to great lengths in obtaining Voorhees's unpublished number from the telephone company.

Quinn sat down slowly, as if to savor the moment. By the time he said "Your witness," Roselli was already on his feet, his baggy pants almost touching the floor. The Bald Beagle wasted no time picking up where the prosecutor had left off: "Sergeant Larsen, did Mr. Cantor ever say that he'd threatened Miss Voorhees *after* she changed to an unlisted number?"

"No," Larsen said, "I never asked him that."

Leaning over the defense table, Roselli reached into his beat-up attaché case and removed a stapled set of papers. He read from the transcript without expression: " 'It comes back. It all comes back. That's Karma. Good or bad, it all comes back.' " Roselli straightened up. "Did you ask Mr. Cantor if he'd made that call?"

"No, I didn't," the witness said without apology.

Roselli buried his head in the transcript again as he read the next recorded conversation. Still bent over, he looked up. "Did you ask him about that call?"

"No," Larsen said impatiently. "I didn't ask him specifically about *any* of the calls on the tape."

"Including the last call on April twenty-ninth—you never asked him about that one, did you?"

Larsen's face reddened as she raised her voice. "I never got the chance . . . he refused—"

Roselli cut her off with a loud "Objection!" as he straight-

99

ened up and turned to the judge: "Would Your Honor please instruct this witness to just answer my question—it requires a simple yes or no."

Warren shook his head. "I'm not so sure. While it would have been highly improper to go into this before, I think you've opened the door, Mr. Roselli. I'll permit the witness to finish her answer."

Unable to hold back a pleased smile, Larsen continued, "After Mr. Cantor told me it was just a joke, he refused to answer any more questions."

Judge Warren immediately leaned over his bench and instructed the jury that they "should not consider the defendant's refusal to continue as any evidence of guilt, whatsoever."

Tossing the transcript onto the defense table, Roselli focused his angry eyes on Larsen again: "So you never asked my client if he ever made any anonymous call—if he ever telephoned Joanna Voorhees without identifying himself?"

"No, I didn't," she responded quickly.

Roselli wandered across the courtroom along the rail until he reached the jury box and delivered his next question in a condescending tone. "Well, let me ask you this, Miss Sergeant, did Mr. Cantor ever tell you that he threatened Joanna Voorhees more than *once?*"

The lady cop shook her head without uttering a word. Roselli moved closer to her and, cupping his ear, made a mock apology. "I'm sorry, I don't hear so good any more. What did you say?"

Her eyes narrowed as she stared at him. "No," she shouted.

Roselli stared back and crossed his arms in front of his chest. "Miss Witness, did the defendant ever tell you that when he, quote—threatened—Joanna Voorhees, it was a threat *to kill* her?"

"No, I don't think he ever told me exactly what the threat was."

The Bald Beagle shuffled away from the witness and shouted while facing the jury, "And so for all you know he may have been speaking about a threat to spit in her eye, or post her telephone number in a men's room, or nail her cat to the wall." He then turned quickly to Larsen and, lowering his voice, tacked on the question, "Isn't that right?" When she hesitatingly answered, "I suppose," what Quinn had billed in his opening statement as "an admission by the defendant" didn't seem quite so devastating.

Roselli then began a line of inquiry concerning the list of persons to whom the Voorhees girl had given her unlisted number. Larsen testified that immediately after receiving their names and addresses, she ran a check to see if any had a criminal record. None did. She subsequently interviewed each of them, but that was after April twenty-ninth, when it had become a homicide investigation. Roselli demanded that the prosecution provide a copy of the list and all reports relating to this part of the police investigation. Pounding his fist on the defense table, he shouted, "And let the record show that I haven't received any of these documents before, nor was I even told of their existence!" This was mere theatrics. Under the law, the defense wasn't entitled to see that material prior to trial. Nevertheless, Roselli succeeded in embarrassing Quinn, who nervously fumbled through his file looking for the reports and then banged his knee against a chair as he turned quickly to hand them to his adversary.

With Mark reading over his shoulder and the entire courtroom waiting patiently, Roselli sat down to peruse the documents. Five minutes later he got up, papers in hand, and resumed the questioning. "Sergeant Larsen," he began, "how much time would you say your interview with William Kyle took?"

She glanced down at her copy of the same records. "Ten minutes."

"Could you tell me whether, other than checking for a criminal record and this brief interview, there was any other investigation conducted by you or your department concerning Mr. Kyle?"

"There was not," she answered.

Roselli started pacing toward the side of the courtroom farthest from both the witness and the jury. He stopped near the court clerk's rolltop desk and, with a smirk on his face, asked Larsen if she was able to verify that Kyle was an unemployed bartender who had lived in New York for only a few months. "Did you ask Mr. Kyle if he'd ever threatened Joanna Voorhees on the telephone?"

"Yes, I did."

"I'll bet he denied it, didn't he, Miss Larsen?"

Realizing that whatever answer she gave to that question

would make her look silly, the witness hesitated and half-yawned when she replied, "Yes, he denied it."

Roselli paused for a few seconds, gazing out of one of the huge windows lining the high-ceilinged courtroom, then turned to face the sergeant and in a loud voice posed his next question: "So based on his denial and a ten-minute interview, you excluded that unemployed, transient bartender as a suspect; is that right?"

Larsen didn't answer right away. A faint smile on her face, her eyes followed Roselli as he walked back to the defense table with no apparent interest in her answer. "Well, not exactly," she finally said, "but I certainly had no reason to conclude that he was the one."

If Judith Larsen found this chess game amusing, her mood changed quickly when the Bald Beagle scowled, "Did you ever record Mr. Kyle's voice and compare it to the anonymous caller?"

"No," she said, a worried look on her face.

"And you didn't do any further investigation of him?"

"No."

Pretending a random selection, though more likely each was carefully chosen, Roselli picked out three more men's names from the list of eight and, taking one at a time, he repeated the same questions he'd asked about Kyle. The officer hadn't spent more than fifteen minutes with any of them and had not done anything to verify the information they'd provided. One was an actor, another an unpublished author, and the third a salesman in the garment center. Of course, each had denied making the anonymous calls.

"Did you ask all of these people where they'd originally met Joanna Voorhees?"

"I believe I did."

"Any of them tell you she'd picked them up on the street?"

"No."

"In a bar?"

"No."

"Of course, Miss Larsen, you wouldn't know if this list is complete, would you?"

"What do you mean?"

"I mean you wouldn't know if she'd given her unlisted number to anyone whose name isn't on the list?"

"I told her to put down everyone—I can only assume that's what she did."

Roselli lowered his voice as he moved closer to the witness. "But if she had given her unlisted number to some fella she'd just met and didn't know his last name or where he lived, she couldn't very well put him on the list, could she?"

"No, of course not, but I think that by the time she'd gotten it unlisted, she'd learned her lesson about giving her number out to strangers."

Roselli nodded as if he were almost tempted to agree. "You think so?"

"Yes, I do," she said softly.

Roselli muttered, "Maybe . . . but, maybe not. A smart girl wouldn't, would she?"

"A smart girl definitely wouldn't."

Lulled by the informal, almost conversational tone of the last few questions and answers, Quinn had failed to object to the patently improper cross-examination, but he woke up when Roselli in a louder voice and lower cadence asked, "Did Joanna Voorhees ever mention to you that she'd gone to bed with this young man named Mark only hours after they'd met on the street?"

Quinn shot up from his chair, pounded his fist on the table, and with veins popping out of his forehead, screamed, "Objection!" But after getting the defense lawyer's assurance that he had a "good-faith basis" for asking the question, Judge Warren overruled the objection and instructed the witness to answer.

"No, she never told me that," Larsen responded.

"A smart girl wouldn't sleep with a man she didn't know anything about, including his last name, would she, Miss Larsen?" Roselli continued. Before the witness could answer, Quinn was on his feet again. "Objection! Objection!" he yelled, his lips quivering with anger.

Almost immediately Roselli calmly announced, "I'll withdraw my question," and, with a smirk on his face, stared the prosecutor back down into his seat.

Inferring that Joanna Voorhees had had sex with Mark was a gamble—a sword that cut both ways. On the one hand it portrayed her not only as a "fast" girl but also someone who wasn't very cautious. Roselli wanted the jury to ask themselves: If she'd go to bed with a stranger, to how many others would she give her telephone number? On the other hand, if Joanna and Mark had been intimate, it would be easier for the jury to believe that

Cantor was devastated and infuriated when she subsequently rejected him.

The last part of Roselli's cross-examination dealt with Larsen's activities and observations at the scene of the crime right after the murder. The purpose of this line of questioning was to gather information which may have been omitted from the police reports, in the hope that something beneficial to the defense might surface. Roselli also wanted to take the sting out of Sylvia Rosen's forthcoming testimony concerning her grisly discovery. The jury knew that Joanna Voorhees had been decapitated—now they would learn exactly how.

Sergeant Judith Larsen arrived at 69 East Tenth Street at one A.M. on the morning after Joanna Voorhees's death, accompanied by Detective Feldstein. They came in response to Detective Harrison's call to the Sixth Precinct after he'd discovered recording equipment in the victim's apartment. In the midst of interviewing one of the tenants, Harrison directed Feldstein and Larsen to apartment 5-B: "No one's touched the machine," he told them. "I'd like to know what it's all about. I'll be up in a few minutes."

Harrison returned to the Voorhees apartment just as Larsen and Feldstein were listening to the killer's last call: "I have your keys and I'm coming up. In a few minutes you'll be dead." Feldstein informed Harrison of the pen register and told him that this call had come at 10:14 that very night. "Let me hear it again, please," Harrison ordered, as he jotted down the time figure in his memo pad. Feldstein pressed a few buttons and the last call played again.

"Thanks," Harrison said. "Now what's the story with that machine?"

Sergeant Larsen told the homicide detective all she knew about Joanna Voorhees and the problem she was having with threatening phone calls. "There are five more on this tape, received in the last two weeks. No direct threats like the one she got tonight. They're just very ominous. Wanna hear them?"

"Later," Harrison said. "Maybe you'll make an extra copy for me." Feldstein agreed before excusing himself to bring the tape and equipment back to the precinct.

"Have you taken a look at the deceased?" Harrison asked Larsen.

"Not yet."

"Well, maybe we should make sure it's the same girl who came to see you. Mind making an ID for me before they take her away?"

"Of course not."

Harrison warned Larsen about the state of the victim, then briefed her on his preliminary investigation. "The way I figure it, that call must have sent her into the hallway screaming for help. When he got into her apartment she screamed again before he silenced her. The lady in 1-B says she called police as soon as she found the remains. The uniformed men picked up the radio run at 10:28—that's only fourteen minutes after the last call on the tape. It didn't take him long, did it?"

As they headed down the stairs, Harrison asked Larsen, "Are you any relation to Sean Larsen?"

"He's my uncle," she told him.

"Good man—we worked together up in Harlem for a while. Send him my regards."

Larsen turned around with a smile: "I will."

When they reached the first floor, Harrison got back to business: "We haven't found the murder weapon, yet. The thing I can't understand is why there's no blood in the girl's apartment. I've also been in every other apartment in the building—went up to the roof, too—no sign of blood anywhere. How is that possible?" he said, staring off into space, as if he were thinking aloud rather than talking to Larsen. "I guess he could've cleaned it up. Maybe he threw her out the window before the blood started flowing heavy. But still, you'd expect a trace.... Your uncle would've figured it out by now."

The detective and the sergeant walked through Mrs. Rosen's apartment into the backyard. After leading Larsen to the spot where the girl's head lay, Harrison switched on his flashlight and removed the towel.

"That's her," Larsen said, her voice unshaken but her face turning a ghostly white. She turned away, then took a few steps toward the white tablecloth. "Is that the rest of her?" she asked, staring at it. Harrison came over, put his arm around the lady cop in a fatherly way, and nodded. As they stood over the body, his eyes suddenly focused on a tiny pool of half-dried blood in the center of the tablecloth. "What the hell is that?" Harrison exclaimed, shining the flashlight on it.

Larsen gave Harrison a quizzical look, then shrugged her shoulders: "Must be bleeding through."

"Her neck is up there," Harrison said, moving the beam of light to one end of the covering that was still clean and white. "Besides, this tablecloth is made of plastic!"

Harrison did a deep knee-bend and slowly lifted the covering just high enough to let him stick the flashlight under and take a look at the part of the body lying directly under the red spot. He could see no sign of blood or wound there. He lowered the tablecloth, stood up, and stared at the blood. A few drops had now run down the other side. Suddenly his head shot back and he looked straight up. He shone the flashlight at the blue Chinese lantern hanging to the left and then at the green lantern a few yards to the right. Between them, and directly above, was a wire, which held up the lanterns and attached at either end to a second-story fire escape. "Get me a ladder," Harrison shouted to a uniformed officer standing nearby, "and make it quick." A few minutes later, the detective was balancing his large body atop a paint-spotted wooden ladder. He shone the flashlight up and down along the wire and then ran his index finger across a two-inch section of it. "Well, what do you know," he snickered, examining his red-stained finger. Descending the ladder with a big self-satisfied smile, he said to Larsen: "See, he wasn't such a bad guy—he only meant to kill her, not chop her head off!"

"The wire doesn't have to be taut, as long as it's secured well on either end," Michael Delaney told the jury. "Falling from that height, if she hits the wire just right, it certainly could take her head off." But there was no need to speculate, for, as he testified,

106

traces of blood found on the wire matched perfectly with a sample taken from Joanna Voorhees.

Delaney had been the medical examiner in New York County for over fifteen years. His red nose appeared swollen from drink as well as age. But with a full head of snow-white, wavy hair and dark eyes topped by bushy white brows, he looked distinguished nonetheless. Although he spoke dispassionately, Delaney's vivid description of the physiology of a decapitation made a few jurors nauseous and faint. Afterward the ME noted: "The area in the backyard where she fell was concrete, so even if she had missed hitting the wire, she would never have survived."

In addition to the skull and seven of her twelve ribs, Delaney found fractures of her right arm and leg, pelvis, and a few other smaller bones. Several organs, including her lungs, were lacerated. This was all in the autopsy report given to Roselli before trial, but it sounded even more horrible when Delaney translated the medical terms for the jury.

Asked about contusions, he defined the term as "an injury from a blow without breaking the skin," and then, for the first time, Delaney read directly from the report which described each bruise as to exact location, shape, size, and color—from "faint blue" to "bluish purple" to "brownish black." They were all over the right side of her body.

Prosecutor Quinn narrowed his steel-gray eyes as he asked: "Were any of her injuries inflicted *before* she plunged five stories?"

"Well, more than likely the *body* fractures—all of them being on the *right* side—occurred when she hit the yard," Delaney began. "As for the contusions, it's hard to say: she certainly could have sustained multiple contusions from such a fall. Of course, one or more of those bruises might have resulted from an earlier blow or blows." Delaney leaned forward in his chair. "However, at least one of her injuries *was* definitely inflicted *before* the fall." He paused a moment and turned from Quinn to the jury. "Her skull was broken in *two* different places. The fracture of the occipital bone—that's in the *back* of the head," he explained, putting his hand there, "I'm sure resulted from the fall: not only was it a nondepressed, linear fracture—the type of break you find when the skull hits a flat surface—I also found particles of gravel in her hair and in the wound. But the other fracture was on the left side of the frontal bone," Delaney said, moving his hand to the area above the temple. "Her head didn't bounce up after it hit the pavement and fracture again! *Both* head injuries were definitely *not* caused by the fall. Besides, the fracture in the front of the head was a depressed skull fracture, with a laceration," he said, tapping the spot with his stubby fingers. "I'd say she'd been hit with a heavy, blunt instrument like a metal rod." He paused before adding: "And judging by the angle, her assailant was right-handed."

Moments later, Delaney raised the possibility that Joanna Voorhees may have fought with her killer for the weapon. He testified that he scraped a brownish powder from her palm and inside portion of the fingers of her left hand. An analysis of the substance showed it to be rust.

Under cross-examination, the medical examiner had an explanation for the absence of any blood in the Voorhees apartment: "A blow to the head with a blunt object wouldn't necessarily cause blood to spurt all over the place," he told the jury, "and, at first, her hair might absorb the blood."

Roselli took him over the coals on this and several of his other conclusions, but in the end, the Irishman would not alter any of his opinions, or even temper his certainty.

Delaney had been taken "out of turn" to accommodate his busy schedule. In the afternoon session, some of Joanna's neighbors testified. Annette Rio, the elderly lady too afraid to open her door for the screaming girl, was on the witness stand for only a few minutes. Phillip Klagsbrun's testimony didn't take much longer. Having merely heard a single scream from his second-floor apartment, he had little to contribute.

Wearing a gaudy purple dress that strained to accommodate her ample figure, Patricia Nolan seemed well rehearsed, relating to the jury exactly what she'd told Detective Harrison the night of the murder: Joanna banging on all the doors and yelling for help; crying when she got no response; starting down the stairs then running back up when she heard heavy footsteps; the man whose face Nolan couldn't see, as he walked past her slightly opened door on the way up to Joanna's floor; the commotion that followed, and, of course, the "muffled cry."

Curiously, Quinn never asked the coffee-shop waitress any questions about what happened afterward. The omission seemed to play right into Roselli's hand. After only a few questions relating to her direct testimony, the defense attorney asked: "Did you stay by your door after you heard that 'muffled cry'?"

Nolan nodded.

"For how long?"

"A few minutes," she answered.

"You told Police Detective Harrison that you remained at the door for five to ten minutes. Is that correct?"

"Yeah, well that's a few minutes, ain't it?"

Nolan's hostility made Roselli suspect that she'd been prepared on this issue. "Did anybody go *down* the stairs after you heard the muffled cry?"

"I don't know—my door was closed."

Roselli knew he'd have to pull it out of her: "Did you *hear* anyone go down the stairs?"

"No, I didn't *hear* no one," she said, mimicking the emphasis he'd placed on the word.

"The steps are made of wood, aren't they?"

She nodded.

"And they creak, don't they?"

"Yeah."

Roselli repeated the technique he'd used a moment before to ensure the desired response: "You told Detective Harrison that if someone had *tiptoed* down those stairs, you would have heard him. Did you say that?"

"I don't really remember telling him that."

"But is it true—that you would have heard someone going down the stairs?"

"Yeah, I would've," she reluctantly admitted.

"And you did not hear anyone?" he shouted to punctuate his point.

"No, I didn't."

Satisfied with this victory, Roselli announced, "No further questions!" Although at that moment none of the jurors could have realized his purpose, the Bald Beagle had planted the first seed in raising next-door neighbor Cleveland Johnson as a suspect.

Bad news greeted Phil Roselli when he returned to his office after a long day in court: "Delta Airlines can only give me the *scheduled* time of departure and arrival on their flights back in

April," his secretary reported. "But as far as the time a particular plane *actually* took off and landed—they couldn't tell me that; something about not storing that information on their computer after ninety days."

"That can't be," Roselli scowled.

Nellie Rodriguez shrugged her shoulders and continued: "Not only that, they won't honor your subpoena for the passenger list or the reservation records. They claim it's 'con-fi-den-tial.' "

"What?" Roselli screamed. "Who the hell did you speak to?"

"I worked my way up to some vice president—a Mr. Muller," she said, checking her notes.

"Wonderful!" Roselli muttered sarcastically, as he pushed some papers around on the desk to make room for his attaché case.

"Can't the court hold them in contempt or something?" Miss Rodriguez asked, a pained expression on her chubby face.

Roselli shook his head. "I don't know. This judge would probably say my subpoena has no relevance to the case!"

Phil Roselli had hoped this airline information would reveal some discrepancy in the statement Cleveland Johnson gave to police. The defense couldn't prove that Johnson was the real killer, but if the jurors' suspicions were aroused, they might find a reasonable doubt as to Cantor's guilt.

In addition to the fact that Patricia Nolan had heard no one coming down the stairs after the murder, there were other circumstances suggesting Johnson's possible involvement. How could he have slept through the commotion that preceded Joanna's murder? Why did he leave town afterward without leaving a forwarding address?

But Roselli needed more. He knew that the best, and perhaps only way to get more, was to put Cleveland Johnson on the witness stand. And the best way to discredit the jazz musician was to catch him in a clear lie.

Johnson had told Detective Harrison that, on the night of the murder, he flew in from New Orleans. He'd expected to return in time to meet friends at 8:30 P.M., but his flight had been delayed and he hadn't gotten home until 9:20. No one had ever checked out Johnson's story. What if he'd lied to Detective Harrison? It was a long shot, but, Roselli decided, definitely worth a try.

He'd already ascertained that only two airlines flew direct from New Orleans to New York on April 29. Eastern had two afternoon flights, one arriving Kennedy Airport at 4:12 P.M. and a later one scheduled for La Guardia at 9:40 P.M. Delta had three flights from New Orleans that Thursday: arriving Kennedy at 2:30 P.M., La Guardia at 7:30 P.M., and Newark Airport at midnight. In light of Johnson's statement to the police, Delta's flight to La Guardia, number 1101, seemed the only possibility. But to verify Johnson's entire story, Roselli had to know the actual time of arrival and whether or not the man was on that flight.

From his desk drawer, the Bald Beagle retrieved a small cigar butt, and began chomping on it as he leaned way back in his chair. Suddenly, his face lit up. "Nellie," he yelled, "look in our closed files—either two or three years ago—case of *People* v. *Michael Harrington* and get me the phone number for *Carl* Harrington. Right away, please."

Roselli had suddenly remembered that he knew someone who held a top-level post with Delta Airlines. Carl Harrington's son had been arrested for selling drugs and Roselli had convinced the judge to put the young man in a rehabilitation program instead of prison. Carl had been extremely grateful and would surely help him cut through the red tape.

Within fifteen minutes, Nellie Rodriguez returned with Harrington's phone number. "I hope he works late," Roselli muttered while dialing.

"How've you been?" Roselli began after announcing himself. "And how's Mike?" he asked, to remind Harrington.

"He's fine, just fine—thanks to you."

After a few minutes of small talk, Roselli gave Harrington the details of his problem.

"Like most of the domestic airlines, we don't keep passenger manifests any more. I'd probably be able to find out if your Mr. Johnson had a reservation in his name and if a ticket was purchased on that reservation, but that's about all."

"Well, that would be some evidence," Roselli responded, thinking out loud, "but not really absolute proof."

"I see what you mean."

"But it would certainly help."

Then Harrington addressed the other part of the problem: "As far as the actual times of departure and arrival—the information you were given is accurate: FAA regulations require we keep these records for only ninety days." He paused, then added, "There *may* be another way to find out . . . but it won't be easy. Is this very important?"

"I wouldn't be botherin' you if it weren't," Roselli said firmly.

"Of course," Harrington responded, embarrassed that he'd questioned the need for his assistance. "If the information is available, I'll get it," he said resolutely. "How soon do you want this?"

"Well, the trial's already started . . . ASAP—isn't that what you corporate guys say?"

"Yeah," Harrington chuckled. "It may take a few days—I'll phone you as soon as I have something."

"Take my home number . . . just in case."

On the following day another neighbor—Sylvia Rosen—described to cringing jurors the gruesome discovery in her backyard: the head without a body, the open eyes, and the stream of blood she'd mistaken for an animal's tail. "I still have nightmares . . ." she broke down crying.

Quinn never called Jeremy Pakula—the homosexual living on the third floor, deciding that he was not necessary and far too "controversial" to be associated with the state's case. The married man who'd been visiting Pakula that night had subsequently given a statement to police, but he didn't hear much either, so Quinn spared him the embarrassment of coming to court.

After Patrolman Gilmore testified that there were "no signs of forced entry" on the door of apartment 5-B when he arrived, Judge Warren recessed for the rest of the day.

That night Cantor phoned Bastone and, after the unusually brief report of the day's events, told him: "I think Harrison will be on the stand tomorrow morning."

"How do you know?" the investigator wondered.

"He was waiting outside the courtroom today to go on next. Phil recognized him."

Lost in thought, Bastone mumbled, "Gee, I'd like to hear Harrison's testimony." When he realized his schedule could easily be rearranged, permitting him to attend, he added, "I'll try to be over there by eleven."

Detective Fred Harrison was already on the witness stand when Bastone arrived at court. In response to a question about "evidence of a struggle," he described a "dumped ashtray," a rocking chair "facing the wrong way," a table lying on its side, and a shattered vase. Despite his massive size, Harrison exuded warmth and gentleness from his pudgy eyes.

A three-year stint with the Queens burglary squad (before his assignment to the Homicide Bureau) qualified him as an expert on locks, and Judge Warren permitted him to testify in detail about the two separate locks on the door to the Voorhees apartment. His inspection revealed that both were engaged when he arrived. The bottom one, a standard mortise, was set so the outside doorknob didn't turn without a key. The upper lock, a sturdy Segal rim latch, commonly known as a slam-lock, was also self-locking, meaning it engaged automatically by simply closing the door. There was no chain-lock or any other device that required operation from within. To make sure the significance of his testimony didn't escape anyone, Quinn spelled it out: "Detective Harrison, could these locks have been engaged as they were when you saw them, if the last person to leave the apartment had simply closed the door even though no one was there to lock up after him?"

"Definitely," the witness answered.

Harrison found the keys to the door atop the small round table near the kitchenette. On the same silver chain were three other keys: one opened the front door to the building, another opened Joanna's mailbox, and the third fit snugly into the lock for the window gate, but the detective couldn't get it to turn.

His investigation ultimately led him to the roof of 69 East Tenth and its adjacent buildings. A thorough search failed to turn up a blunt instrument, or any other clues. Since no one had heard the killer coming down the stairs after the last scream, Harrison also checked the roof as a possible means of escape. The adjoining apartment houses were all approximately the same height as Joanna's. There were no alleyways between them, he testified, and each was separated by only a short wall. "They were all low enough for me to climb over easy—even with this excess baggage," he said, holding his gut. "That means they were pretty low!" Skin as dark as mahogany made his teeth sparkle when he smiled. Although the roof doors leading into 65, 67, and 71 East Tenth were locked from the outside when Harrison tried them, they could have been open earlier. The roof door at 73 East Tenth was closed but unlocked, while the one for 75 East Tenth was wide open. "He could've fled into any of those buildings," the detective concluded, his soft brown eyes scanning the jury.

In his opening statement at the start of the case, Kevin Quinn had likened a trial to a jigsaw puzzle. "The witnesses will provide the pieces," he'd told the jury. "You will put them together and by the end, a clear picture will emerge." The prosecution had done well in reconstructing the murder of Joanna Voorhees, and Harrison's testimony answered some important questions, including a possible reason why Nolan didn't hear footsteps going down the stairs after the murder. But at least one remained— one "piece" didn't fit. The man who killed Joanna announced in his last phone call that he had the keys to her apartment. Indeed, the person Nolan heard walking slowly to the fifth floor apparently did use a key to open the door, and this was consistent with the fact that there were "no signs of forced entry." But if Mark Cantor was the anonymous caller and the cold-blooded killer, how did *he* get those keys?

Convinced that this was the fatal flaw in the state's case, Tom Bastone discussed the issue with Cantor and Roselli during the luncheon recess. "It makes no sense," he pointed out as they sat in a booth at the Delmar Kitchen. "Look, Joanna tells Larsen that she met Mark on the street, gave him her number, and later refused to go out with him when he called. Okay, that made him angry and there's his motive. Now even if the truth comes out— they'd been intimate, made a date, and she stood him up—then that's his motive. But either way, the motive comes *later—not* when they're together, not when he has any possible access to her keys!"

Mark's eyes lit up. "That's right," he said, "the only time I could get those keys was when I was with her. But everything was fine then. I had no reason—"

"Besides," Bastone interrupted with the enthusiasm of a crapshooter on a roll, "if you'd stolen her keys, if they disap-

114

peared the night you were there, she'd have definitely gotten her locks changed as soon as the calls started."

Mark and Tom looked toward Roselli for a response. He was staring into his coffee as he stirred it with a spoon. Finally, the Bald Beagle looked up at Bastone. "Very rational approach. Sherlock Holmes couldn't have done better," he said, making the young detective feel proud. "Simple logic!" Then he summarized Bastone's theory in a sing-song voice: "He wouldn't steal the keys *unless* he was angry. Therefore, he wouldn't steal 'em *until* he was angry. He wasn't angry when he had the opportunity, so he didn't steal the keys." Waving the teaspoon for punctuation, he quickly exposed the fallacy in that argument: "That would all be true—*if* he was rational! But if he was *rational*, would he belt a girl over the head then throw her out the window just because she stood him up or didn't want to see him? Don't you understand? If you take *their* view of this case, Mark Cantor is a Dr. Jekyll–Mr. Hyde: by day—an upstanding assistant DA, by night—a masher, a madman. He doesn't need a *reason* to steal her keys." His eyes bulging, Roselli sounded like the *prosecutor* summing up to the jury: "The psychopath anticipates betrayal before it occurs. He steals her keys to be ready when she does cross him, and it may not take much to cross him!"

After his convincing performance, Roselli took a sip of coffee and, in a more relaxed tone, said to Bastone, "Your argument, young man, is based on logic. But there's often no logic to murder." Cantor nodded as his lawyer concluded. "Anyway that's one possible explanation."

But Kevin Quinn had another.

Under the law the prosecution is not required to prove *how* a crime was committed—only that it was committed by the accused. If a man is caught red-handed leaving a bank at three A.M. carrying a satchel filled with crisp one-hundred-dollar bills, the prosecution needn't show how he broke into the vault. Of course, the bank would like to know and the jury would certainly be curious. However, if that information is never supplied at the trial, in all likelihood he'll still be convicted.

But Mark Cantor wasn't caught red-handed. Since the case against him was based solely on circumstantial evidence, the prosecution could not hope for a conviction if too many questions were left unanswered. Apparently Kevin Quinn had reached the same conclusion. Yet *his* theory to account for Cantor's possession of the keys was not exactly what Roselli had anticipated.

Angel Ortega, the building superintendent at 69 East Tenth Street, was the state's next witness. Although he spoke with a heavy Puerto Rican accent, Ortega refused the judge's offer of a Spanish interpreter. He told the jury that, five days before the death of Joanna Voorhees, his apartment had been burglarized.

"Did you report this to the police when it happened?" Quinn asked.

"No sir, I don't."

"Would you tell the court *why* you didn't report it?"

Ortega's answer was barely audible. "I teenk my son do eet."

"Why did you believe it was your son who broke into your apartment on April twenty-fourth?"

Ortega slumped in the chair and his face tightened. "He do eet before. Hees a junkie—he cannot help heeself."

"How old is your son?" Quinn asked sympathetically.

"Nineteen, hees only nineteen."

"And he does not live with you?"

"No. I trrow him out. Always he steal an' act crazy. I try but ees too much. I leev alone." Ortega looked like a tough man, with greasy hair, pockmarked face, and beady eyes, but you could hear the heartbreak in his soft, fragile voice.

"And when did he stop living with you, when did you throw him out?"

"A year ago, I teenk . . . maybe more now."

"And since then your apartment has been burglarized several times, is that right?"

116

"Burgled?"

"Broken into—robbed."

"Oh . . . yes—a few times."

"And it was your son who broke in those times?"

Ortega nodded and Quinn continued. "How did you know it was your son who broke in those times?"

"He tell me later—days, weeks, whenebber I see him. He say he sorry, he cry, but he don't stop doing eet."

"Those times when he told you he did it, what did he take?"

"He take ebberyteeng. Trree telebisions he steal from me. He take, I buy, he take. A stereo too."

Quinn soon returned to the subject in which he was most interested—the April 24 burglary. Ortega didn't recall the exact date, but he knew it was the Saturday before Joanna Voorhees's death.

"What time did you return home that day?"

"Eet wuss een dee morning—nine o'clock een dee morning."

"Where had you been?"

"I wuss at work een dee factory."

"Where do you work?"

"Ees een New Yersey—we make plastic cups."

"What are your hours?"

"Dey got trree shifts, but mostly I work from midnight to eight, like I do dat night."

"And what did you find when you got home that morning?"

"Dee place ees a mess—dee drawers empty, you know stuff all ober dee floor."

"Was the lock broken?"

"No, dee lock's okay. Dee weendow ees busted."

"Your apartment is on the ground floor?"

"Yessir."

"Did you have a gate on the window?"

Ortega gave a short laugh. "Yeah, I got a gate—each time my son break een, he pulls gate off. Two times I fix—what for I fix again?"

"So there was no gate on the window on April twenty-fourth?"

"No gate."

"And what was taken?"

"At first I don't teenk nuteeng wuss taken. Dare is nuteeng to take!"

"Did you later discover something missing from your apartment?"

"Oh yes, yessir."

"What was that, what was missing?"

"Dee keys, dee keys wuss missing!"

"What keys, Mr. Ortega, were missing?" said Quinn, getting impatient now that they were coming to the important part of the testimony.

"Dee keys to dat girl's apartment!" Ortega shouted back. Several of the jurors leaned forward in their seats and, after a buzzing from different parts of the gallery, the courtroom suddenly became very quiet.

"Which girl?" Quinn asked, as if everyone didn't already know.

"The new girl, dee one in 5-B."

"Joanna Voorhees?"

"Yes, Joanna Boorhees."

"You had her keys?"

"I had an estra set of dose keys."

"Tell me, Mr. Ortega, when did you discover or find out that the set of keys you had were stolen from your apartment?"

"When dee police come. Dat night dey find her body in dee courtjard. Dey want to get eento her apartment. Dey come to me. I go to get keys but dey not dare."

"Where did you keep her keys?"

"Een a yar under my seenk weet dee udder keys."

"What other keys were in the jar?"

"For dee udder tenants een my building."

"Mr. Ortega, why did you have these keys?"

"Let me esplain to you: When you are dee superintendent one of dee teengs you do ees keep an estra set of keys for dee tenants een case dey lose dares or lock out demselves by meestake. I am around the building most of dee time, so I can let dem een."

"You had the keys for all the apartments?"

"Oh, no sir. Dees I do only for dee tenants dat want me to do eet. Some people don't like udder people to hab dare keys."

Of the fifteen units in the building, Ortega testified that he had the keys to a little less than half the apartments. He put a label with the apartment number on each key ring so he'd know which was which.

"And Joanna Voorhees was one of the tenants who gave you a set of her keys?"

"Yessir."

"And *those* were taken on April twenty-fourth when your apartment was broken into?"

"Yessir."

"Were anyone else's keys taken from your apartment?"

"No, sir."

"Just the keys to Miss Voorhees's apartment?"

"Dass right."

"After the burglary, did you have the window repaired?"

"I am the superintendent—I feest ect myself."

"When did you fix it?"

"Dee same day."

"And had anyone been in your apartment between that day and April the twenty-ninth when the police asked you for the keys to 5-B?"

"Only me."

"Had you seen those keys, the keys to 5-B, between April twenty-fourth and April twenty-ninth?"

"No, sir."

"When was the last time you saw those keys?"

"About two weeks before she get killed, she lock herself out. She ring my bell. I let her een and geeb her dee keys."

"And did she find her keys once she got inside her apartment?"

"I guess she do."

"Did she give you back the set of keys you had lent her to get in?"

"Yes sir, she geeb dem back to me."

"You're sure?"

"Yes, I'm sure."

Quinn paused for a moment as he glanced down at his notes and then looked up again. "Now, Mr. Ortega, you told us that when someone broke into your apartment on April twenty-fourth, you didn't report it to the police because you thought your son was the one who did it. Did you ever learn who did do

119

it?" Quinn asked in an undramatic tone so that the negative response which followed was not a disappointment. The prosecutor then inquired, "Did your *son* ever admit to breaking in *that* time?"

Roselli objected as Quinn was finishing the question, but Ortega had shaken his head before the judge yelled, "Sustained!" When he instructed the witness not to answer, the prosecutor couldn't hide a smile. Regarding his adversary, Quinn invited the cross-examination: "You may inquire."

Roselli was already on his feet. "Hello, Mr. Ortega," he began like a spider greeting a fly. After eliciting background information concerning Ortega's marital status and employment history, the lawyer asked the witness how long he'd been the super at 69 East Tenth, and how long he'd been keeping tenants' keys under the sink. "For more den fibe years," was the answer to both questions, so Roselli wanted to know if his addict son knew of the hiding place. The witness told the court that he kept that a secret. Neither his son nor anyone else knew where the keys were kept, and he added that it wouldn't matter if his son had known: "He steal from me—dass one teeng. But he know eef he steal from my tenants, I break hees arms and legs!"

Having disposed of these preliminary matters, Roselli vigorously rubbed his hands together, signaling that it was time to go to work. "Mr. Ortega, how long did Joanna Voorhees live at 69 East Tenth Street?" he asked, regarding the witness more intensely than before.

"Two munts, I teenk . . . maybe a leetle more."

"So that would be the end of February, beginning of March, when she moved in?"

"Yessir, somewhere like dat."

"And when did she first give you a set of keys to her apartment?"

"Een dee begeening. I change dee cyleenders for her when she move een. I geeb her dee keys and I ask her eef she want me to keep one set. First she say no, ees not necessary. But a few days later she geeb dem to me. I teenk she talk to one of dee udder tenants and dey say, ees okay, you can trust Mr. Ortega!"

"And you told us that the reason you keep the keys for some of the tenants is in case they lose them or lock themselves out, is that right?"

"Yessir, dass right."

"And you told us that this happened to Miss Voorhees a few weeks before she died, is that right?"

Ortega nodded.

"Was that the only time she locked herself out or lost her keys and had to borrow the set she gave you?"

"No. She lock herself out more den one time."

"How many times?"

"Two or trree," he said, sliding his hand over his hair from front to back.

"You're not sure?"

"No—two or trree."

"And she was only living in the building for a little over two months?"

"Dass right." Ortega smiled and added, "She wuss a leetle flakey, you know, confused sometimes. She never *lose* her keys— she leave dem eenside her apartment. I teenk eet's because of dee locks she got. You don't need no key to lock dee door. I tell her, I don't like dees kind, but . . ."

Although the witness was offering an opinion and his testimony wasn't responsive to the question, Roselli didn't object or interrupt. He just smiled and Ortega stopped himself.

"When was the very *first* time she locked herself out?"

"I teenk eet wuss right after she moob een, only a coupla days after she geeb me her keys. I remember I say to her—'See eet wuss good you geeb me dem.' "

More relaxed now that he'd been on the witness stand for a while, Ortega was getting a bit chatty, and his answers less concise.

"Did you open her apartment door for her, or did you just give her the keys?"

"She leeb on dee fift floor, and dare ees no elebator een my building. You know. I just geeb her dee keys."

"And did she return them to you?"

"Yessir."

"This first time you gave her the keys, *when* did she give them back to you?"

"Dat same night."

"Where were you when she returned the keys?"

"Een my apartment."

Roselli had the witness recount every occasion on which

Joanna Voorhees borrowed the extra set of keys. He questioned Ortega on all the particulars surrounding each instance: the time of day and what he was doing at that moment. On almost all these details, the super's memory was admittedly poor. Not having any special significance when the exchanges took place, the facts sought were minutiae, which *most* people would be unable to recall months later.

On the other hand, his failure to remember the surrounding circumstances may have created doubts regarding his insistence that Voorhees *always* returned the keys to him. In rehashing the events during cross-examination, Ortega became certain that she'd locked herself out on *three* occasions. The second time was only a week or so prior to the last incident, about which Quinn had just inquired. Roselli's design was to show that with the keys going back and forth so frequently in such a short span, the witness might be confused. To the question, "When did she return the keys?" Ortega had given the identical response for both the second and third occasions: "Dee nest day or dee day after."

Roselli asked, "Is it possible that she returned the keys the first and *second* times, but never gave them back to you the last time?"

Though it was perhaps an improper question, Quinn never objected and Ortega, confused initially, answered, "Eef eets posseebull? Dis I don't know, but she geeb dem back ebbery time. Dis I'm sure."

After Roselli had completed his cross-examination of the superintendent, he moved to strike his entire testimony from the record on the grounds that "none of this evidence connects the defendant Cantor with the burglary of Ortega's apartment."

"Will you be presenting additional proofs on this issue?" Judge Warren asked the prosecutor.

"No, your honor," Quinn replied, "but I submit that Mr. Ortega's testimony is relevant nonetheless. In this case we have a recorded conversation during which the perpetrator claimed to have keys to the victim's apartment and testimony indicating that he gained entry that way. Therefore, the theft of those keys prior to the murder is certainly relevant even though it may not shed any light on the *identity* of the perpetrator."

"Yes, I see your point," Judge Warren said, chewing on his

fountain pen. "I'll permit Mr. Ortega's testimony to remain."

Despite the court's decision, at day's end Cantor seemed relaxed and pleased. "They're reaching for straws," he said to his lawyer with a smile. "When a prosecutor has to rely on that kind of evidence, you know he's got a lousy case!"

"We'll see," Roselli interjected, rubbing his tired eyes. "Quinn marched out of the courtroom this afternoon like he couldn't wait for tomorrow. He may be showing only a pair of deuces right now, but I've got a sneakin' suspicion he's got an ace in the hole!"

We all have them. In fact, we all have our very own. We are born with them and we die with them and they never change. No two are exactly alike. Since antiquity they have been used as seals and in lieu of signatures. They stamp us all so definitively that we can never completely disguise ourselves. Surgeons are able to transform our facial features and even change our sex, but neither modern medicine nor space-age technology has yet devised a way to alter a fingerprint without destroying it.

On the night of the murder, Detective Larry Luzinski, assigned to the Crime Scene Unit, went through the Voorhees apartment "dusting" what he called "areas of interest" with a fine powder to develop visible prints from latent impressions. A lean, almost frail man in his mid-forties with coarse, gray hair and a flat face, Luzinski told the jury: "It has to be a hard, smooth surface and you've got to be very careful so you don't destroy what you're trying to preserve. I did the door, the opened living room window and parts of the wall near that window. She didn't have much furniture there—a stereo, a wooden table—I did those. There were a few glasses lying around and . . ."

With fifteen years of experience in the field, Luzinski was an old hand in this special kind of magic. He described the relatively simple technique. On dark surfaces he applied a white powder, on light surfaces a black powder. On glass, gray powder gave the best results, and on porous surfaces like raw wood or paper, a magnetic powder was sprayed on. The dusted areas were examined carefully. Wherever he saw a possible print, he applied a cellophanelike adhesive tape, took a photograph in case it didn't lift cleanly, and then pulled off the tape. He placed it on a glossy-surfaced card opposite in color to the powder used. Each card was numbered and a corresponding record kept of exactly where each print was found.

As is usually the case, many of the latent impressions developed by Luzinski, including those from the doorknobs, were badly blurred or smudged. Others were rendered useless through superimposition of other fingers.

Luzinski wound up with twenty-one possible prints, which he forwarded to the Latent Fingerprint Section for identification. There, Kim Iwata, a civilian working for the police department, analyzed the evidence.

The telephone company records showing requisition of the unpublished number by Bronx Assistant DA Mark Cantor, in combination with Joanna Voorhees's own suspicions that a man named Mark was responsible for the telephoned threats, had made Cantor a prime suspect. The deceased had never told Larsen that the Mark she met on Eighth Street had been to her apartment. In fact, she'd given the sergeant the impression that this was not the case. Logically, if he'd visited her *after* Joanna Voorhees came to the precinct, she would have notified the police. If Mark Cantor's fingerprints were found in Joanna Voorhees's apartment, the police assumed he had to have been there the night she was murdered.

Because Cantor was employed by the government, his fingerprints were on record providing a sample for Iwata's use.

After a series of preliminary questions concerning his special training and experience in fingerprint identification, Iwata was accepted by the court as an "expert witness." Unlike the ordinary witness, the expert's opinions and conclusions are admissible as evidence.

Iwata told the jury that six of the twenty-one prints he

examined were "of no value." This meant they lacked significant characteristics, which he called "points" for reliable comparison. "It used to be a rule of thumb that at least eight concordances were necessary to make a positive identification," Iwata noted, as if everyone understood what he was saying, "but it depends. There really are no hard-and-fast rules."

Kim Iwata didn't appear to be a day over thirty, but he'd been analyzing fingerprints for more than a decade. Neatly dressed in a gray chalk-stripe suit, blue shirt, and silk tie, he looked like a young Wall Street executive rather than a civil servant who spent his days in a cubbyhole staring through a magnifying glass. He was a short but handsome man, his straight, blue-black hair neatly trimmed and as shiny as his highly polished Oxford shoes. Born and raised in Japan, he'd been living in the United States for fifteen years and spoke that perfect English of foreigners educated in American schools.

To identify the fifteen remaining prints "of value," Iwata first compared them to inked impressions of known origin provided by Detective Harrison. These were of two types: elimination prints—the fingerprints of persons known to have been in the apartment, including police officers who arrived at the scene before Luzinski, and suspect prints—the fingerprints of those considered by the investigating team as the possible perpetrator. This list included the prints of Mark Cantor and the persons to whom the deceased had given her unlisted number, but only those who'd denied "recent presence" in the Voorhees apartment.

As expected, the majority of the "latents," nine to be exact, corresponded to the impressions taken of the deceased at the morgue. A single print on the outside of the door, Iwata concluded, belonged to Patrolman Gilmore.

Comparing the remaining five with the suspect prints, Iwata discovered that two matched the Mark Cantor sample.

The remaining three were classified as "unidentified": they did not correspond to any of the suspect prints Harrison had provided. Nor did they match with any in the Recidivist Offenders File, the police department's collection of chronic criminals. FBI fingerprint records were never checked; that type of search was "not part of regular police procedure," according to Iwata.

"Where had print number 8 been taken from?" Quinn asked,

referring to one of the two latents the expert had matched with Cantor's prints.

The witness looked down at his records and read, "According to the card, 8 was lifted from the 'living room window—underside of lower sash.' "

Next, the prosecutor focused Iwata's attention on the other match. Speaking more deliberately, he began: "You testified that latent fingerprint number 19 also was made by the defendant, is that right?"

"Yes, but that wasn't a *finger*print, that was a *palm* print—actually, what we call a partial palm . . . you rarely get the whole palm."

Quinn glanced at the jury as he asked, "Where was print 19 lifted from?"

Again Iwata read from his records: "The roof door," he answered.

Both Cantor and Roselli remained poker-faced.

Quinn asked: "That would be the print Detective Luzinski testified he'd taken from 'the door leading to the roof, a few inches above the latch bar?' "

Iwata confirmed: "Must be—19 is the only latent lifted from the roof door."

The prosecution had not only placed Cantor in the victim's apartment, they'd proven his "signature" was on the window—"the gateway to death," as Quinn later called it, and the roof door—an out-of-the-way place along the killer's most probable route of escape.

But Phil Roselli seemed calm and confident when he rose for cross-examination. "Were you able to determine *how long* print number 8 had been there?" he asked the prosecution's expert.

"No," Iwata said, "you can never even estimate the age of a fingerprint."

"These prints—8 and 19—they coulda been there for days before Luzinski lifted them, isn't that so?"

"Definitely."

"For weeks? Could they've been there for weeks?"

"Yes."

"Even months?"

"That's very possible, but it depends. Under optimum conditions a print can last more than a year. Heat is its worst enemy and, of course, obliteration by physical means—rubbing it or superimposition by other prints."

Roselli nodded, then asked his next set of questions in rapid succession: "So as to print number 19—if people didn't go up to the roof very often, a partial palm print on the door might last for months, isn't that so?"

"I guess," he agreed.

"In other words, if it wasn't smudged by other prints, that print—being inside and not exposed to the elements—that print could last up to a year, couldn't it?"

"It's certainly possible."

Roselli reached for some papers from the defense table, glanced at them, and then propounded his next questions. "This print number 8 was found on the underside of the window sash, is that right?"

Iwata looked down at his records and nodded.

"In that position, at that time of year, print 8 wouldn't be ruined by heat?"

"No, but if the window were opened a few times, if it was an old print, it'd probably be superimposed by other fingerprints." Iwata relaxed for a moment, having finally scored a point, while Roselli looked down at the floor, pressing a finger against his forehead, as if he were deep in concentration. And he remained in that position when he asked:

"Mr. Iwata, didn't you say before that one of the deceased's fingerprints was found in the 'leftside finger lift' of the same living room window?" Roselli said.

Iwata flipped through his records: "Yes, number 12."

"So the type of window we're talking about did have those little pockets you stick your fingers in to get a grip on the sash for opening and closing, is that right?"

"Well, I never actually saw this window," Iwata said coolly, "but there is a reference in the records to 'finger lifts' so I assume this window had them—most conventional vertical windows do."

Finally, Roselli looked up at the witness: "And if the deceased was in the habit of using those finger lifts to open her window, it'd be *very* possible for that number 8 print to have been on the underside of the sash for months, wouldn't it?" he asked.

127

Iwata's head bobbed a few seconds before he answered reluctantly: "It's possible."

Roselli's questions were speculative in nature, and an objection by Quinn probably would have been sustained. But knowing the witness could take care of himself, the prosecutor didn't interrupt.

Iwata added: "But you're dealing here with probabilities. Most people just use the finger lifts to get the window started; then they push up on the underside of the sash. And the weather is important. If we're talking about a time of the year when it's mild and windows are opened more frequently—chances are a decent print is a *recent* one. As I recall, March was unusually mild and April was nice, too . . ."

Placing the stack of papers in his hand on the prosecutor's table, Roselli charged the witness stand. His eyes narrowed. "Are you now saying that the fingerprint on the underside of the window sash—print 8—could not have been there for months?"

Iwata backed off. "No, I'm not saying that at all. There are too many variables and not enough facts to draw any conclusions regarding the age of that fingerprint."

Roselli snickered. "Well, I agree with you about that—there certainly aren't enough facts!"

After court had recessed for the day, as the defense lawyer was packing up his beat-up attaché case, Quinn called to him, "Mr. Roselli, I believe you left these papers on my table," but he made no effort to return them.

Roselli walked over and retrieved his papers. At the top of the pile he noticed Iwata's report on the roof-door palm print. "Nice of you to give me a copy of this *now*," he said.

"What are you talking about? Iwata's reports were with all the other discovery materials I gave you months ago."

"The hell it was!" Roselli fumed. "I got the others all right, but you left out that particular one—accidentally, no doubt!"

"You're mistaken," Quinn said indignantly. "I don't play games like that. And if you were so sure . . . why didn't you protest to the judge?"

"Yeah, that woulda done a lotta good," the Bald Beagle muttered sarcastically. He glanced through the other papers to make sure nothing was missing and then engaged Quinn again: "And I hope you've got stronger evidence against my client than what you've presented so far. I hope you didn't ruin this young man's career because of a few old fingerprints that prove nothin'!"

"What they and the other evidence prove is up to the jury to determine," Quinn shot back. "I'm sure you'll find a way around the prints. They're *not* the key to *this* case! Wait another day before you accuse me of a frivolous prosecution. By this time tomorrow, you'll realize Cantor's guilty as sin."

"Oh, yeah, what happens tomorrow?"

Quinn tucked the case folder under his arm and held it tight against his side. "That's when my *star witness* testifies!" he said ominously.

That evening, Bastone had convinced Mark to meet him for an hour of indoor tennis. "It'd do you good to take your mind off the trial and relieve some tension," he'd urged.

Cantor was putting on his sneakers, when Bastone came rushing into the locker room: "Guess what?" he said, punching Cantor lightly on the arm. He didn't wait for an answer. "Brian's found Cleveland Johnson," he blurted out, oblivious to the three other men changing clothes nearby. Mark smiled and, leaving his laces undone, looked up at Bastone and waited for the details.

"He's working at a club in Sausalito called—get this—the Headless Horseman. A little irony, huh?" Bastone hung up his jacket and as he unpacked his duffel bag, he continued: "Brian hasn't served the subpoena yet. The club doesn't have live music during the week, but Johnson's playing there Friday night."

"Unless someone tips him off," Cantor worried.

"I doubt that'll happen," Bastone said. "Brian told the guy he was an old friend . . . hasn't seen him in years . . . wanted to surprise Johnson . . ."

"Hey, that was smart of Brian," Cantor muttered, impressed and somewhat surprised.

"Pretty standard, actually," Bastone informed, "but it usually works." Rushing to put on his tennis whites, he asked Mark, "What time is it?"

"We've got about five minutes before our hour begins. They'll ring a bell."

"So how'd it go in court today?" Bastone whispered, as the

last remaining guy in the locker room tied up his laces, reminding Mark to do the same.

Cantor waited a few seconds for the stranger to leave and then told Bastone about the fingerprint on the window sash and the palm print on the roof door. Just then the bell rang, signaling the start of the next hour. "We can talk about this later," Mark said.

As they hurried through the clubhouse on the way to the courts, a confused Bastone asked, "Well, you seem pretty calm about the whole thing. Shit, if I were you, I'd be enraged."

"At what?" Cantor said innocently.

"Well, obviously, the cop who lifted the prints must've deliberately mislabeled that one . . . I'll bet Harrison told him to do it. Putting you on the roof makes it all very tidy, doesn't it?" Bastone's fury reddened his face. "Those fuckin' cops'll do anything to make their case!"

Mark and Tom passed through a revolving door that led to a tennis court enclosed in a canvas bubble—a temporary structure that permitted outdoor play in summer.

"Wait a minute," Bastone resumed, not taking another step. "There was no mention of that palm print in the police reports Roselli gave me. Did *he* know about this?"

Mark put his right arm around Bastone, his racket dangling from the same hand. "Quinn pulled a fast one—he didn't give us that report. But it's no big deal. Joanna and I went up to the roof the night I stayed over—I was gonna testify to that anyway. And Roselli got the expert to admit my prints could've been there for months."

"Of course," Bastone muttered, "you can't tell the age of a fingerprint. So it's really no problem, is it?"

"None at all," Mark said emphatically. "Now listen, at the rates this place charges, we shouldn't be wasting time. Let's play."

"Whoosh" went the vacuum-packed can of tennis balls when Mark broke the seal. "Don't you love that sound?" he said.

When they'd originally made the tennis date, Mark had doubted his ability to maintain sufficient concentration to play decently. But after handily beating Tom by scores of six-love, six-one, it was apparent that *Bastone* couldn't keep his mind on the game.

"Mark, you never told me about going up to the roof with Joanna," he said as they walked off the court.

"I didn't?"

"No."

"I didn't tell you that at three in the morning we went up there to find the Big Dipper?"

"No."

Cantor shrugged. "Well, we did." He studied Tom, then chuckled, "Hey, don't tell me you're beginning to wonder about this whole thing."

"Not really," Bastone lied.

Mark shook his head and was still grinning when he said, "Listen, I don't think Quinn really believes I did it, so I don't expect my best friend to have any doubts."

Mark's casual and confident manner reassured Tom. "Don't be silly," he said, embarrassed by his momentary lack of faith. "I have no doubts about your innocence. But how come you didn't tell me that part of the story?" he asked like a whining child.

Mark smiled affectionately, and in a parentally consoling tone tried to explain, "I don't know. Look, I love you like a brother and I enjoy sharing my experiences with you, but that doesn't mean every boring detail."

"Usually it does!" Tom teased with a grin.

Mark shrugged. "Maybe I was afraid you'd think it was corny."

"But you always were corny—if you thought it would work!"

"That's probably why I was embarrassed," Mark said, "I didn't do it for that reason!"

That night Bastone was having trouble sleeping, so the midnight phone call from Phil Roselli didn't wake him.

"Can you come to court tomorrow?" the defense attorney asked. "I think an important witness is gonna testify—I'd like you to be there."

"No problem," Bastone answered. "Did you get my message today?"

"No. I didn't go back to the office after court, and Nellie was gone by the time I called. Something important?"

Bastone gave Roselli the latest news on Cleveland Johnson. "Thank God," the lawyer responded. "I was starting to worry."

"I told you we'd find him."

Roselli repeated previous instructions to make sure they

were followed: "Tell your man not to ask him any questions—just serve the subpoena. Don't scare him off—just get him here!"

"Brian knows what to do. Don't worry."

"Good. Call me as soon as you hear from him. I'll be around the house all weekend."

Judy Weisenberg, the prosecution's star witness, began her testimony confused about the most fundamental fact. After she was sworn in, the clerk of the court asked her to state her name. "Judy Barnet," she announced in a voice much grander than her size. She was very thin and, without the four-inch heels, couldn't have been taller than five feet. A few seconds later she corrected herself, "Actually it's Weisenberg, Judy Weisenberg. Barnet's my stage name and I use it a lot socially, as well. I mean I like the way it sounds and I don't have to spell it for people." She was speaking a mile a minute. "But I never changed my name legally or anything. And I still use Weisenberg on official things like credit cards—thank God for plastic! And I guess I would use Weisenberg on a driver's license and important stuff like that, only I don't have a driver's license 'cause it's really stupid to keep a car in the city anyway."

Quinn looked worried. "Now, Miss Weisenberg, I know you're a little nervous," he said, trying hard to sound calm, "so I want you to sit back in that chair, take a deep breath, and just relax."

"Oh, I'm not nervous. I'm used to big audiences—well not *big* audiences, but audiences—not to hear me talk, of course, but to hear me sing."

"And is that what you do for a living, you sing professionally?" Quinn asked.

"Yes, well I have sung professionally, but it's been a little

132

slow lately. I used to sing with the rock band—the Mother Truckers. We used to play all over the city. Nothing big, you understand, mostly little clubs in Brooklyn and on the Island. But we did do some gigs in the East Village. The band broke up about six months ago. The lead guitarist and the drummer were always at each other's throats. Anyway, that really wasn't the right band for me—they played acid, you know—hard rock, and that's not my thing . . ."

Judge Warren started to clear his throat as if to signal the prosecutor, who finally interrupted, "Miss Weisenberg, do you support yourself at the present time?"

"Well, I don't have a sugar daddy, if that's what you mean. But I'm lookin'."

Almost everyone was smiling, and Roselli had the biggest grin. But Quinn wasn't amused. He glared at the girl with a look that would have cooled hot coals.

"Oh sorry," she said, getting suddenly serious. "I work in this little boutique in the Village. I'm a salesgirl. Singing never paid the rent."

Judy Weisenberg was funny-looking but cute. Her light brown eyes were so close together they almost touched, and it was a miracle she could see past a nose that was several sizes too big for her tiny face. Her long, curly hair had been tortured by chemicals. This month she was a blonde. Rosy-cheeked, with pronounced dimples, she appeared much younger than the twenty-eight and a half years she had reported to the jury.

"What is the name of the boutique where you work?" Quinn asked.

"It's called 'André's,' named for the owner—Andy Shapiro and I'm not kidding either. I went to high school with Andy—Forest Hills High."

"Where in the Village is the store located?"

"It's on Christopher Street, just west of Seventh."

Quinn may have been surprised to get a direct, concise answer to a question because it took him more than a few seconds to pose his next:

"How long have you been working there?"

"On and off for several years. Andy lets me work there when I need money. He's got a big turnover with his help 'cause he pays lousy. That guy is so cheap . . ."

Quinn let out an exasperated sigh and it seemed to release his frustrations. His features relaxed as if he had finally resigned himself to the witness's style.

"... but he's nice," she continued, "and his stuff is really beautiful."

"Miss Weisenberg, where do you live?" Quinn asked softly, exhibiting his newfound patience.

"Seventy East Tenth Street; that's between Broadway and University Place."

"Where is it in regard to Sixty-nine East Tenth?"

"It's right across the street."

"How long have you lived there?"

"Well, I've had the apartment—it's just a studio—for almost four years, but most of 'Seventy-four I stayed with my boyfriend on Bank Street. His place was gigantic, but he was a creep."

"Were you living at Seventy East Tenth Street on April twenty-ninth, 1976?"

"Was that the night that girl across the street lost her head?"

Quinn winced. "That was the night Joanna Voorhees was murdered," he said, clenching his teeth.

"That was horrible! That poor thing," Weisenberg muttered. Despite the tasteless way she'd described the murder, there was a heartfelt sincerity in her voice when she expressed her sympathies and recalled the incident: "Yes, I was home that night." And still upset, she practically whispered, "Around ten thirty" when Quinn asked her what time she'd arrived at her apartment that evening. He had her repeat her answer and then wanted to know how she happened to remember the time.

"I'll tell ya," she said, coming to life again, "I was supposed to work that night so I schlepped all the way over to the store and Andy didn't need me. Well, I was really pissed—I mean angry.—and I went over to my friend Sasha on the way home. She's a vegetarian and she's into Yoga and she's very mellow and she calms me down when I'm upset. She had a date at ten. I remember because his name was Ben and I joked, 'Ben at ten.' Anyway, we were talking and she looked up at the clock and panicked because it was a quarter after ten and she had to meet him near Sheridan Square—way across town. She ran out and I left with her. She lives on Sixteenth Street and it takes me about ten or fifteen minutes to get home from there."

"Did anything *unusual* happen on your way home?" Quinn asked, hinting with his steel-gray eyes.

"Well nothing spectacular . . . but as I was walking down the block, this guy was running toward me and almost knocked me down."

"What block was that, Miss Weisenberg?"

"That was *my* block—Tenth Street."

"Between Broadway and University Place?"

"Yes, between Broadway and University Place."

"And were you walking east or west on Tenth Street?"

"I was going . . . toward Broadway, I guess that'd be east."

"And the fellow who 'almost knocked you down,' what direction was he going?"

"The opposite direction—toward University Place."

"West?"

"I guess that's west, yes."

"Which side of the street were you on when this happened, the north side or the south side?"

The witness looked up and started pointing her hands in the different compass directions, but before she said a word, Quinn put the question a different way to make it simpler: "Was it the side of the street where your apartment building is located?"

"No, it was the other side," she answered without hesitation.

"Now when you say he almost knocked you down, could you describe for us *in detail* exactly what happened?"

"Okay. I'll try, but it happened so quickly . . . He was running down the street looking over his shoulder—behind him. He wasn't watching where he was going. I moved out of his path but he was swerving toward me. At the last second he turned forward, saw me, and tried to sidestep. But you know how sometimes you both move out of the way to avoid each other, but you both move in the *same* direction so that you wind up colliding? Well, that's what happened, only we didn't exactly collide because he stopped short and put his hands on my arms—I'm not sure whether he did that so that I wouldn't fall or to keep his own balance.

"Anyway, he said 'Sorry' and I asked him where the fire was. He mentioned something about being very late for an appointment, then he apologized again and continued on."

135

"Did he run off or walk off?"

"Like a trot."

"Same direction?"

"Yes."

The pace slowed momentarily as Quinn strolled over toward the jury box.

"When did you first learn that a dead body was found behind 69 East Tenth?" he asked.

"Later that same night. After that guy almost knocked me down, I went home. I was only there for a little while, maybe twenty or thirty minutes, when I heard a commotion in the street. I looked out the window and saw police cars so I came down. I didn't see them bring the body out—I turned away."

"Did you know Joanna Voorhees?"

"No, I didn't."

The prosecutor took a few steps toward his witness; then, with one hand on the rail of the jury box, his body slightly bent over the foreman, he turned his head to the rock singer and asked, "The man that almost ran into you that night, did you get a look at his face?"

"Yes, I got a *good* look."

"How far from you was he the very first time you saw his face?"

"I only saw his face one time, and that wasn't until he was right on top of me—maybe a foot away."

"Did you see his whole face or just a portion of his face?"

"You mean full face or just a profile?"

"Yes."

"Oh, I saw him full face. When he stopped and we talked—it was face to face. I remember thinking he was cute—not great, I mean he was no Mick Jagger, but better than most."

Quinn straightened up, letting his long arms dangle from square, bony shoulders that made his suit look like it was on a coathanger. He upped the volume several decibels, "Miss Weisenberg, I want you to look around this courtroom and tell me if you see the man whom you saw that day on Tenth Street—the fellow who almost ran into you."

There was a dead silence as the witness scanned the courtroom. She stopped when her eyes met Cantor's. "I see him," she said firmly, pausing dramatically before pointing out Mark with a jerk of her head. "That's him, the guy in the herringbone suit."

To make certain the identification was clear, Quinn asked Cantor to stand. "Is that the man you saw?"

"Yes," she said confidently.

The ADA took another step toward her and narrowed his eyes as he asked slowly but loudly, "Are you *sure*? Are you certain that's the man?"

"I'm positive. I'm real good with faces. That's him—absolutely."

Although Mark realized that Quinn wouldn't have put Judy Weisenberg on the witness stand unless she was able to identify him, when the moment came Cantor stood there stunned. His lower lip dropped, and his eyes opened wide. He never heard Quinn announce, "No further questions!" or Judge Warren declare a fifteen-minute recess. He didn't move a muscle until Roselli nudged his arm.

The prosecution had now placed Mark Cantor in close proximity to the scene of the crime. Judy Weisenberg's testimony also contradicted Mark's statement to police that he'd been home that entire evening.

Tom Bastone, also in shock over what he'd just heard, waited just outside the courtroom for Roselli and Cantor. As the defense lawyer led his client into a stairwell off the corridor, he motioned for Bastone to join their meeting.

"She's lying!" Mark exploded the moment the door closed behind them. "I don't know why but she's lying." He strained to keep his voice down. "Somebody put her up to this," he said as they walked down a flight of steps to the next landing. He looked Roselli straight in the eye: "I wasn't on that street. I haven't been near the place since the night Joanna stood me up. She's fulla shit!"

"Does she look at all familiar to you?" Roselli asked, an unfamiliar urgency in his voice. "Do you have any idea why she'd say it?"

"I never saw her before in my life," Mark answered, shaking his head. "Listen, Phil, I'm not exactly a man without enemies. There's a hundred guys rotting away in Sing Sing who I've put there and I'm sure some of them would love to see me behind the same bars. They read about this case. They've got sisters and girlfriends. One of those cons gets a bright idea and suddenly

Quinn gets a call from Judy Weisenberg—she's somebody's something. That's the only way I can figure it."

"Could be," Roselli muttered. Both he and Cantor had been ignoring Bastone, until now. "Tom, you'll have to check her out . . . but it may be tough to find the connection. In the meantime, on cross I'll try to elicit some background information to help you, so take notes . . . I'll ask her if she knows anyone Mark prosecuted. If she's a put-up job, she's certainly not going to admit it, but it won't hurt to plant that idea in the jury's mind."

Bastone, who'd been silent, offered, "Maybe she's not related to anyone—maybe she's being paid."

"That's possible too," Roselli said without turning around. "And if that's the case it's gonna be even harder." He reached into his jacket pocket, pulled out a well-chewed cigar butt, and lit it. Smoke filled the stairwell as the Bald Beagle, lost in thought, stared at a wall, puffing away. After almost a full minute of silence, Roselli turned to Cantor. "You want to know something? I don't think she *is lying*," he said, and Mark's eyes bulged. "I think she's just mistaken. She saw someone who looked like you— maybe just a vague resemblance—but she convinced herself it was you." Roselli shrugged. "She's *spustata*—what you call *meshuggener*—a dizzy head. I really believe it's a mistake. We'll investigate her; we won't discount the possibility . . . but I don't think she's a phony!"

Throughout the cross-examination the defense lawyer spoke gently, never once raising his voice. At the outset he called her Judy, and asked if she minded. She said, "Of course not, that's my name," and from then on it was always the familiar Judy, and never Miss Weisenberg. His questions had an informal, conversational structure, as well as tone. He smiled when she smiled and never interrupted her even when she went off on one of her tangents.

It was a slow process—she was on the witness stand the entire day—but the defense did score some points. Weisenberg admitted that the "good look" she'd supposedly gotten lasted only "a few seconds." Although she had "stared right into his eyes," she was unable to recall their color. And all she remembered about his clothing was that he wore "dark pants and a dark jacket."

138

During their brief conversation, the young man—in his "late twenties," she estimated—appeared to be "extremely nervous." Yet she made no mention of him to the police who were standing around outside the building when she came back down from her apartment. As explanation she testified that someone in the crowd said it was a suicide. But a few days later, when she'd heard the woman had been murdered, she made the connection and wondered if the man she'd seen running might be involved. "Maybe that's why he stuck in my mind," she told Roselli.

"And was it then that you reported the incident to the police?" the lawyer asked, as if he didn't know the answer.

"No . . . no, it wasn't. See, I figured it was a long shot and at the time I was getting ready for my trip. This stockbroker I'd been dating invited me to Barbados. It was kinda spur-of-the-moment and I didn't have a thing to wear so I had a lot of shopping to do and then I left." A bit defensively, she added: "I mean it wasn't as if I saw him actually kill the girl or even saw them together. If it was something like that, I definitely would've gone to the cops even if it meant messing up my plans. As it turned out, it rained almost every day down there and the stockbroker was a bore!"

"So you called the police when you got back?" Roselli asked in the same innocent way. Again, he got a negative response, this time the witness explaining that she was "afraid they'd yell at me for waiting so long."

Judy Weisenberg did not contact the authorities until she saw Mark Cantor's picture in a newspaper after his arrest. She telephoned the Sixth Precinct immediately—"it wasn't a long shot any more"—and met later in the day with "a lady sergeant" whose name she couldn't recall although she did give an accurate description of Judith Larsen, adding that she looked "more like a stewardess than a cop." At the interview Weisenberg described the subject as male, white, slim build, brown, curly hair with a mustache. She said he "looked Jewish except his nose was too small and if he'd had plastic surgery, you couldn't tell, so get me the name of his doctor."

Weisenberg told Larsen the man was about six feet tall. But at the trial she testified he was five-eight or -nine. Reading from the police report, Roselli confronted her with the discrepancy.

"I may have told her that at the precinct," the witness said. "I'm so short that anyone taller than five-five looks six feet to me."

"Tell me, Judy, before you came to court, did Mr. Quinn or Sergeant Larsen or anyone mention to you that the defendant was only five feet eight inches tall?" Roselli asked in a gentle, nonaccusatory fashion.

"No, no one said anything about that. When you asked me today how tall the man was, I guess I was basing my answer on how tall Mr. Cantor looked when he stood up before."

"He didn't look six feet tall to you?"

"No."

"And I take it you haven't *grown* since April?"

Judy Weisenberg looked puzzled for a moment and then her dimples popped out as she smiled, "Oh, I get it! No. I haven't grown, but from up here lookin' down people seem shorter than when I'm down there lookin' up."

That was typical for the cross-examination. Roselli had permitted her to run off on tangents because he thought that given enough rope, she'd hang herself. But each time Roselli exposed a flaw in her story, Judy Weisenberg managed to wiggle her way out with some explanation or excuse which was often amusing and always reasonable. There was one exception near the end. Little Judy dug a small hole for herself and this time Roselli made sure he got the last word:

"Judy, you've been on the witness stand now all day yesterday and several hours today. I know this is an ordeal, but I have just a few more questions—"

"Oh, it's no ordeal," she said, "I don't mind—I'm used to this sort of thing."

"Have you testified before in a court case?" Roselli asked, as if he were just curious.

"No, this is my first time, but in the clubs I've worked, you sing for hours with only a few ten-minute breaks. That's much harder, but I love it."

"You like being in the spotlight?"

Quinn objected quickly; Roselli withdrew the question, but he'd made his point.

Although she was not what you'd call an impressive witness, Judy Weisenberg had her own special charm. Even her candor—

inappropriate and sometimes outrageous—was somehow endearing. Her response, for instance, when Roselli asked if she wore glasses: "I hate glasses—I wear contacts. My vision is better than twenty-twenty with my contacts and I never take them out until I go to bed. With some of the boyfriends I've had, it helps to be blind in the morning!"

In fact, Judy Weisenberg was so frank one got the feeling she couldn't even tell a *white* lie, so it seemed inconceivable that she'd falsely swear Mark was the man she saw. But the possibility remained that she might have been mistaken. Thus Roselli had tried to discredit her reliability. But would Weisenberg's failure to remember minor details, her mistake of a few inches in height, and the suggestion that she enjoyed attention, cause the jury to discount her testimony?

Prior to the trial, Roselli had asked Mark to avoid conferring with him while he cross-examined a witness. "When you take an active role you lose the sympathy that some jurors naturally feel for the accused," he explained. "Besides, it's very distracting! I know it'll be difficult, but you'll just have to trust me."

Mark had been following his lawyer's advice, but during the cross-examination of Judy Weisenberg, he couldn't restrain himself, tugging on Roselli's arm to whisper suggestions. The Bald Beagle hid his displeasure at the time, but as soon as the jury was excused for the day, he laced into Cantor: "God damn it, I told you not to interrupt me—you break my rhythm and it looks lousy."

But Mark was even more irate: "She's a space cadet. Why didn't you rip her apart!"

"I thought I did pretty well," Roselli said firmly.

"You were too easy on her. I would've destroyed that lying bitch."

"Listen, Mark, the jury liked that kid. If I got too rough, they would've felt sorry for her—and I'da wound up alienating them. I know what I'm doing."

Cantor shook his head, then put his face into Roselli's and spoke deliberately: "That witness buried me and you barely laid a glove on her." Then he stormed out of the courtroom, dashing right past Tom Bastone.

The investigator waited for Roselli and walked him to his car. "You did a good job on that girl," Bastone said.

Roselli smiled. "Oh yeah? Your friend doesn't think so."

Tom looked surprised. "Don't tell me that's why he rushed out of here . . ."

"That's why," Roselli shook his head. "You know the old saying: A lawyer who represents himself has a fool for a client?"

"Sure," Bastone nodded.

"Well, I got a better one: A lawyer who represents another lawyer is a fool . . . 'cause he'll never have a satisfied client!"

Bastone put his arm around Roselli. "He's just upset over that girl's testimony. He'll cool down."

They walked the next block in silence before Roselli spoke. "I still think I'm right about Weisenberg. I wish she was a bald-faced liar. That kind of witness is easy to cross-examine. Somewhere along the line they usually mess up—and give themselves away. But a witness who's mistaken—those are the tough ones." Waiting for the traffic light to signal WALK, Roselli tapped his hand nervously on a lamppost as if he were beating a drum. "She couldn't possibly be that certain," he said without even looking in Tom's direction, "but she's talked herself into it," he muttered.

"You mean it's difficult because she thinks she's telling the truth."

"That's it."

Tom tried to sound optimistic. "Well, she only saw him for a second or two—she admitted that. Anybody can make a mistake under those circumstances."

"And that, young man, is going to be my main argument. You shoulda been a lawyer." Roselli paused for a moment, to tie the laces on his scuffed brown shoes. "I'll tell ya, without that rock 'n' roller putting our friend on Tenth Street, they don't have a case," he said, straightening up. "I'm not worried—not yet, at least. Even with Weisenberg's testimony, it's pretty flimsy, don't ya think?" But he wasn't really asking.

Without any conscious plan, Bastone raised a subject that had continued to trouble him: "What about the palm print on the roof door?"

Roselli shrugged. "So! He went up to the roof—that's no crime. And it's no evidence of murder either. Not unless they can pinpoint the time." Roselli thought for a moment and added, "Or I guess if he'd told the cops he'd never been up there, we might have a problem. But they never asked."

142

"Still, you must have been a little surprised when that came out at the trial?" Bastone commented in an innocent way, though he was really searching for specific information.

"Not really. If the fingerprint on the window was still intact, I figured they might find one on the roof."

Still play-acting, Bastone casually asked the important question: "Oh, then Mark told you he went up there?"

"When I take the facts from a client, I make sure to get them *all*," Roselli said, his barrel chest puffed proudly. "Even things that may seem unimportant at the time, can turn out to be crucial. You should know that."

"I just thought Mark might've forgotten to tell you about it."

"Let me tell you something. I know *everything* that happened that night—except maybe the positions they used!" Roselli said, flashing his tobacco-stained teeth. "Your buddy is a real romantic, isn't he? Hell, I can see going up to a roof to set the mood, but after you've already screwed the broad!"

Tom Bastone left Roselli, relieved to know that, right from the start, Cantor had told his lawyer about being up on the roof. But Tom felt ashamed of himself for suspecting that his best friend might have fabricated a story to explain the palm print, and the obvious implication of that deceit—that Mark might well have been a murderer.

After visiting a sick aunt in Brooklyn, Bastone headed home, anxious to hear from Brian. Tonight was the night Cleveland Johnson was to appear at the Headless Horseman and his partner would phone him as soon as he made contact.

He entered his Upper East Side apartment pleased to note that Stella, the housecleaner, had made her biweekly visit, leaving the place clean and tidy. He hung up his coat, loosened his tie, and moved the coffee table and floor lamp back to where he'd left them before Stella rearranged the furniture as she always did. "That woman never gives up!" Tom muttered.

After eating some leftovers, he picked up a magazine, but found himself reading the same lines over and over again. He spent the rest of the night switching channels on the TV and constantly glancing at his silent telephone. Tom had dozed off when it finally rang.

"I got him," he heard Brian's excited voice announce. "Johnson returns on Monday and he'll be in your office at nine A.M. on Tuesday. He seemed a little nervous at first. I gave him that bullshit about all the neighbors testifying. He said he had to be in New York anyway. . . . I think it'll be okay, but I'll stay with him to make sure he gets on that plane."

"Good idea, Brian . . . and nice goin'. I owe you one—a big one!"

Without looking to see what time it was, Bastone phoned Cantor with the news, and Mark promised to notify Roselli.

The next morning, after his first good night's sleep in weeks, a bright autumn day greeted Bastone as he stuck his head out the bedroom window. His original plans for the day had been to visit 72 East Eleventh Street—one of the buildings behind Joanna's—trying to see the tenants he'd previously missed. But upon hearing rain forecast for Sunday, he decided that would be a better time to check those few apartments still left on his list. Besides, he hadn't taken a day off in weeks and sorely needed one.

So Bastone took the subway to the Cloisters museum. In the northernmost part of Manhattan, the Cloisters was a great place to get away from it all. Far above the noise of the city, atop a tree-covered hill on the bank of the Hudson River, the Cloisters looked like a medieval monastery. In fact, portions of such structures had been taken apart stone by stone and shipped from Europe for its construction. Tom wasn't drawn by the art and artifacts; he just found the place soothing.

As soon as he arrived, Bastone went to his favorite spot— an outdoor terrace facing the Hudson and New Jersey's Palisades. He'd brought along a new wide-angle lens for his camera and he tried it out snapping pictures of the George Washington

144

Bridge and a huge barge being tugged down the river. His mind totally free from any thoughts of the Cantor case, Tom reveled in his first relaxing moment in months.

On weekends the Cloisters staged concerts, and, from an open latticed door on the terrace, Bastone could hear chamber music. Following the sound, he walked through an arcaded passageway and came upon a patio garden where he stopped to admire a patch of golden chrysanthemums. Then, through a fountain's mist, Tom spotted a familiar face and this time recognized her immediately.

Without hesitation, he walked a slate path leading to the bench where she sat. "Hello," Tom said with uncharacteristic boldness. "Remember me?" Her blank stare momentarily embarrassed him. "The coffee shop in Foley Square . . . ," he said timidly, and to jog her memory he added, "You hate diet soda and I never eat breakfast."

A look of recognition finally crossed Judith Larsen's face. "Oh, yes—the private detective who looks like a salesman."

"Right," he smiled with great relief.

They'd never exchanged names that day at the Delmar Kitchen, so he carefully introduced himself as Tom, then asked if he could join her.

When she told him her name, Bastone pretended this was new information: "Judy? That's a happy name. Pleased to meet you, Judy." She had a firm handshake, he noted.

"Well, you certainly don't look like a salesman today," she said, glancing down at his striped sneakers and faded jeans, a neat crease down the legs being the only hint of his usual impeccable appearance. "I didn't recognize you at first because the last time we met, you looked so sharp in that double-breasted suit."

"Same sharp guy—different outfit," Tom said, rubbing his stubbled chin. "You look a little different yourself." She was wearing an antique velvet cape and a flowered silk skirt.

"Today's my day off," she explained.

"So you know about the Cloisters, too?" he asked, changing the subject.

"Yes. It's a lovely place."

"Sure is. Most people don't even know it exists."

"That's right," she exclaimed. "This is the first time I ever bumped into someone I knew."

"Me, too. Must be fate," Tom smiled, not totally convinced it really wasn't. "So when did you discover the Cloisters?"

"Oh, I've been coming here for years, since I was a kid. Grew up not far from here—Washington Heights."

"Did you go to George Washington High School?" he guessed.

"Yeah, you too?"

"No. I went to Brandeis, but I remember George Washington because they always had the prettiest cheerleaders. You must have been a cheerleader."

"No . . . no, I don't think I would have made it," she said, blushing.

"Why? You must have been real pretty—I mean, you still are pretty. I mean, I'm sure you were pretty enough. You just didn't try out."

"Well, actually, I did want to be a cheerleader, but my parents were very strict and didn't approve of my jumping around in those skimpy little dresses."

"Yeah, those skimpy little dresses were wonderful," Tom smiled. "Where do you live now?"

"I still live in Washington Heights."

"With your folks?"

"No . . . well, it's the same building but I have my own apartment. Sometimes it feels like I'm still living with them."

"They still strict?"

She smiled, and if Bastone wasn't already hooked, those dimples would have done it. "No, they've mellowed quite a bit. They're not strict, but I don't want to be a cheerleader any more!"

He laughed without taking his eyes off hers. In the bright sunlight they were even bluer than he'd remembered.

"So are you working undercover today?" she asked, glancing at the camera at his side.

"No, photography is a hobby of mine."

"Well, your equipment looks very professional."

"Unfortunately, my pictures don't! But I'm getting better."

Larsen looked at him with that half-smile given to children when they say something endearing, and the expression lingered until she asked, "Did you come for the concert?"

"No, not really. I come for the view. What about you?"

"Sometimes I just need to cool out, to be alone—with no telephone, no one knocking at my door . . . and this is my secret refuge."

146

"I'm sorry if I disturbed you," he said earnestly. "If you want to be alone, I understand—believe me—and I don't want to intrude . . ."

As Bastone started to get up, she put her hand on his knee: "Oh, no," she said, "you're not intruding. I didn't mean that I need to be alone right *now*. I like talking to you."

Tom suddenly felt at ease, and when Judy Larsen asked him how he'd become a private investigator, he answered her as honestly as he could: "I worked part-time for a detective agency while studying law; I hated school and loved the job . . . I graduated, but after failing the bar exam twice, I decided: Why go through that again? It made no sense! May sound like sour grapes, but I really enjoy being a PI."

They strolled through the park surrounding the museum, discussing photography, politics, and recent movies they'd seen. Brown leaves cracked with each step and there was a chill in the air, but to Tom Bastone, it somehow felt like spring. Although he was usually shy with women he'd just met, conversation with Judy Larsen came easy for him and even the moments of silence seemed relaxed and comfortable.

"Listen . . . um . . . if you don't have plans for the evening, maybe we could have dinner together."

"Tonight?" she asked as if caught by surprise.

"Yeah, tonight. Unless you've had enough of me for one day."

She looked at Tom with warmth in her eyes. "I think I could stand you for a *few* more hours. What about you?"

"Easy," Bastone said softly. In the silence that followed, they never took their eyes off each other. For the first time he could feel electricity from her—a sexual vibration—and it triggered a throbbing in his groin. She caught herself and suddenly turned away.

A little while later they were sitting at a checkered table in Gallagher's Steak House, his restaurant suggestion after Judy had described herself as a "meat-and-potatoes girl."

When the waiter asked if they'd like a drink before dinner, she said to Tom, "I don't know if I should. I haven't eaten all day and I get drunk very quickly on an empty stomach."

"Why don't you just have one and if you get a little sloppy, I promise not to hold it against you."

"Okay," she nodded with that sweet smile, "I'll have a gin

and tonic." Bastone ordered a screwdriver and, a few minutes later, the waiter brought the drinks.

"Your family still live in New York?" she asked.

"My folks live in Florida now."

"Any brothers and sisters?"

"I'm an only child."

"Spoiled, I'll bet."

"Very," Tom said, pretending to be serious. "Actually my parents are from 'the old country.' You know the story: My father came to this country with forty dollars in his pocket. They were so afraid I'd be spoiled, they bent over backward depriving me."

Judy feigned sympathy. "You poor thing, didn't even have a bicycle?"

"Oh, I had an old truck bike, but not an English racer like Mike Puccio had—he was my best friend in the sixth grade."

Judy grinned. "Well, have you forgiven Mom and Dad for that?" Bastone nodded and she asked, "And do you ever go down to visit them?"

"A couple of times a year. I went a few months ago. Had a very funny experience on the flight home. This lady sitting next to me on the plane was chewing my ear off about her marriage going bad. Totally unsolicited—I mean I hadn't asked a single question and hardly said a word—she tells me the lengths she went to to keep her husband, which included an experiment with swinging—you know, wife swapping. I couldn't believe she was telling me this stuff! Then she mentioned that she works nights and I asked her, 'What kind of work do you do?' And she says, 'That's none of your business!' Can you imagine?"

"Maybe she was a hooker," Judy offered as possible explanation.

"I don't know. She didn't look like one . . . I just think people differ on what they consider personal."

Just then the waiter came and took their dinner order. As soon as he left, Judy said, "How come you haven't asked me what I do for a living?"

"I did. The first time we met—at the coffee shop. You said you worked for the city."

She nodded, as if she recalled the conversation, then said, "But that doesn't tell you very much."

148

"No, it doesn't. But I figured you didn't want me to *know* very much."

"Well . . . I didn't then—you were a total stranger. But now . . . if you want to know I'll tell you."

Tom paused, trying to decide how to handle the situation. He couldn't very well say, "I don't care," and feared telling her the truth might open a Pandora's box. Tilting her head, she recaptured his attention with a long stare. Finally, Bastone said, "You don't have to, *Sergeant.*"

She squinted. "How did you know?"

"I saw you testify in court last week."

"The Cantor case?"

"Yeah," he reluctantly admitted, "the Cantor case." The dam was cracking.

"What were you doing at the Cantor trial?"

"I'm the investigator for the defense," Tom said softly, braced for the floodwaters.

Her mouth dropped and her face began to pale. "Tom . . . ," she muttered. "Tom *Bastone*—you're Tom Bastone!" He nodded. "Why, you sneaky son of a bitch," she growled with narrowed eyes. Starting to rise from her chair, she reached onto the table for her purse, but Tom prevented her from taking it by quickly placing his hand on hers.

"Please don't leave," he pleaded. She looked at him as if he were insane. "Look," he argued, "just because we're on opposite sides doesn't mean we can't have dinner together. Lawyers do it all the time."

"That's different—they know they are adversaries," she shot back, trying to remove her hand from his grasp.

"And so do you!"

Her face reddened. "Yeah, *now* I know," she said, through clenched teeth. "Maybe if you'd have been up front about this . . . ."

Tom smiled. "Oh, really? Let's face it: If I'd told you earlier, you wouldn't be here. Please sit down—just for one minute."

Uncomfortable crouching over the table, she complied with his request, sitting on the edge of her chair and still holding onto the purse.

"I'm not here as a spy. I haven't asked you anything about the Cantor case, and I don't intend to discuss it."

She looked deeply into his eyes, as if she were sizing him

up. Her face softened for an instant, then she caught herself and tensed up again. "That doesn't matter," she said. "The mere appearance of impropriety is bad."

Tom released her hand, but the purse remained on the table. "I understand," he said. "I shouldn't have asked you out until the trial was over . . . but I couldn't wait. And, of course, I should have told you who I was right away. I'm sorry . . . but I knew *this* would happen."

The ends of her mouth drooped and her sad look gave Bastone the courage to continue. "Look, as long as we're here already . . . I mean, no harm's been done, and if I'm wrong you could always say you had no idea—"

"I didn't!" she shouted, interrupting him.

"I know you didn't. What I'm trying to say is . . . there really is no reason for you to leave this *instant*. Besides, our food's going to be here any minute now, and . . ." With heartfelt sincerity Tom added, "I'd feel terrible if you ran out of here right now."

After mulling over what he'd said, she nodded, "Okay. I guess at this point it doesn't make much difference. I'll stay, but only on one condition: We don't talk about the case at all—not at all!"

"Of course," Tom agreed.

Fifteen minutes and a gin and tonic later, Judy relaxed and they were getting along fine again. Curious to know how she ever got to be a cop, Tom asked and got the whole story. Her father had been a New York City detective for ten years, after almost an equal number walking a beat in the West Bronx. Judy's Uncle Sean had also dedicated his life to fighting crime, as a homicide detective working in the busy Harlem precinct. "He was a bachelor and used to come over every Friday night for a home-cooked meal," Judy told Bastone, recalling her childhood. "He and Dad were always talking about their cases, even though it used to make Mom angry—she didn't want us kids to hear about that stuff. And we loved the stories, especially Uncle Sean's 'cause he solved murders—just like on TV."

Judy's father loved police work and always hoped that at least one of his three sons would follow in his footsteps. But her brother Bill preferred fighting fires, Michael decided the money was better in construction work, and Patrick made his mother proud by becoming a civil engineer. "Always Daddy's favorite," Judy Larsen surprised the whole family by joining the department.

"You folks care for another round?" the waiter asked as he delivered the salads and cleared away their now-empty drink glasses.

"Sure," Judy bubbled, putting caution to the wind.

Tom had never known a lady cop. Sensing his genuine interest in the subject, she told him a little about her career: "The first year or so I worked at a desk, typing and doing clerical work. I was nothing more than a secretary in a police precinct and I hated it. I didn't sweat through the academy for that! Then I worked for a few years in a radio car at the Nineteenth—that's the chic Upper East Side Precinct, but believe me, they've got plenty of crime there. It was just an experiment. In those days, they weren't sure a woman could be effective on the street. They were also afraid she'd distract her partner.

"Last year the department felt the pressure of the women's movement and decided to start these sex crimes units," Judy continued. "My uncle suggested that I take the sergeant's exam. He said they'd be looking for women to head these divisions and as an officer, I'd have a big edge—there weren't too many female sergeants around." Then she shrugged. "He was right."

When the main course arrived, Judy's eyes, now a little bloodshot, focused upon the steak knife their waiter had placed next to her plate. She gripped the fancy carved-wood handle and, with an outstretched arm, held the knife in front of her face, the long, thin blade pointing straight up. She spoke slowly, her words a bit slurred: "Is this a dagger I see before me, the handle in my hand?" Putting down the knife, she regarded Tom. "Your client, Mark Cantor, is a real poet, isn't he?"

"What do you mean?" Bastone asked, totally confused.

"That was one of the calls he made to the Voorhees girl."

"What are you talking about? That's Shakespeare!"

"Shakespeare?"

"Yeah, it's from *Macbeth*: 'Is this a dagger which I see before me, the handle toward my hand?' Macbeth says it a few minutes before he kills King Duncan," Bastone explained.

"And Cantor says it a few days before he kills Joanna Voorhees," Judy shot back. "Ha! I didn't think it was original."

"You're drunk," Tom muttered.

"A little," she answered.

Her icy stare made Bastone uncomfortable and he wanted to change the subject fast. "Listen, I thought we weren't going to talk about the Cantor case."

Her face softened. "You're right," she said. "I'm sorry."

"Your dinner's getting cold."

Judy began eating and, after putting some food in her stomach, sobered quickly and became friendly again. They were talking about health foods and she told Tom, "I can't see how anyone can prefer a plate of seaweed to a hunk of prime red beef. I've also never understood exactly why unprocessed food, organically grown vegetables and all that other stuff, should be so much more expensive . . ." She began to discourse on the health-food fad being another hoax of American business, when, still troubled by her reference to the Cantor case, Tom finally blurted out what was really on his mind: "That line about the dagger—you said that was one of the calls Joanna got a few days before her death?"

Coming out of left field, his question surprised Judy, who froze for a few seconds before nodding.

"But why wasn't it on the tape?" Tom asked.

"It was," she said.

"I heard the tape twice and I also read the transcript. I don't remember anything about a dagger."

"You don't?" Her face took on a quizzical look, then suddenly she perked up, "Oh, right—that was the call Feldstein erased by mistake. It wasn't on the tape they played in court."

"How come *you* knew about it?" he asked.

"I heard the original before Feldstein made copies."

"Oh yeah," Bastone said, recalling the testimony of the police electronics expert. "How come you never mentioned that call when you testified?"

Judy's eyes narrowed. "I was never asked about that call!" she said curtly. "I knew I should have left," she muttered to herself. "I told you I don't want to discuss the case and I certainly don't wish to be cross-examined—"

"I'm sorry," he said, interrupting her. "We've each been bad once. We're even now and you've got my word: no more talk about the Cantor case. Scout's honor," Tom said, putting his hand over his heart.

She smiled. "You've obviously never been a Boy Scout."

The rest of the evening went smoothly, but when Bastone said good night, Judy made it clear that she didn't want to see him again until the Cantor case was closed. "And I mean till he's tried *and sentenced,*" she said firmly.

"Maybe I should wait until he serves his time!" Tom said, angry that she hadn't recognized even the possibility of an acquittal.

$\mathbf{P}$hil Roselli lived in a magnificent French Tudor home in Saddle River, an exclusive New Jersey community not far from the George Washington Bridge. Exquisitely furnished by his wife with valuable antiques and expensive artwork, his home was a showplace. But Roselli felt truly comfortable only in the study—with its low, wood-beamed ceiling, small leaded glass windows, and the soft beige tones of a Sarouk oriental rug. The room resembled his Bronx office in its Dickensian clutter and the smell of Garcia y Vegas which always permeated the air.

Sinking deeply into an old leather easy chair, Phil Roselli read the Sunday *Times,* still wearing his plaid flannel bathrobe, although he'd finished breakfast hours before. As he reached to the window seat for another section of the newspaper, the phone rang. After identifying himself, Carl Harrington, his contact at Delta Airlines, began the conversation: "I think I've got that information you wanted."

Roselli leaned forward in the chair. "Great, what d'ya find out?"

"Well, first off, on April twenty-ninth a Cleveland Johnson did have a reservation on Delta's Flight 1101. The ticket was purchased with an American Express card in the same name.

Of course, as I told you before, this wouldn't prove that he was actually on the flight."

"I know, but that's fine," Roselli responded, hoping more information was forthcoming.

Harrington didn't disappoint: "As for the times—on April twenty-ninth, flight 1101 *was* delayed. Due to arrive at 7:30 P.M., it didn't land at La Guardia until 9:10."

As Roselli jotted down the figure in the margin of the newspaper, his mind flashed to Cleveland Johnson's statement to the police that he'd gotten home at 9:20. Only Superman could make it from La Guardia to Greenwich Village in ten minutes, he thought. Then he asked Harrington, "Are you sure that plane arrived in New York at 9:10 and not 8:10?"

"Yeah. 9:10's right. The aircraft had repairs done on the landing gear before takeoff. It didn't leave New Orleans until 5:36."

"But that can't be a three-and-a-half-hour flight," Roselli said after doing the simple subtraction in his head.

"No, it's two and a half hours," Harrington stated.

"Well, didn't you say it left at 5:36?"

"Right . . ."

"Well, 5:36 to 9:10 is more like *three* and a half hours," Roselli said as he nervously spun the world globe that decorated a corner near his chair.

"New Orleans is an hour behind," Harrington explained. "When the flight left New Orleans at 5:36, it was *6*:36 in New York. Get it?"

Roselli did get it now. The wheels in his mind were turning, too: If Cleveland Johnson got off the plane at 9:10, by the time he got his bags and got back to the Village it would have been closer to 10:20 than 9:20. And if he arrived at 10:20, those must have been *his* footsteps Nolan heard, he reasoned, not sharing his thinking with Harrington. And if Johnson lied about the time, he must have been covering up something. Giving the globe one last spin, he pushed so hard that it flew off the wooden stand and bounced along the floor. "Oh shit!" he yelled.

"I'm sorry if that doesn't help you," Harrington said, "but those are the facts. I got this stuff straight from the pilot's logbook."

"No, no, it does help me. It's terrific, you're terrific," Roselli gushed. "But I may need those records. Any problem?"

154

When he didn't hear an immediate response, Roselli got a little nervous until Harrington answered, "I guess we could arrange that,"

As soon as Roselli hung up, he dialed Cantor's number but there was no answer.

He tried all day but wasn't able to reach his client until that evening. "Where the hell have you been?" Roselli shouted. He didn't wait for an answer. "Never mind. I've got some important news. A friend of mine at Delta Airlines did some checking for me, and guess what: On the night of the murder, Cleveland Johnson's plane didn't land till 9:10. That means he couldn't have gotten home at 9:20 like he told police. He must've returned at about the time she started screaming." He paused to let Cantor digest this information.

"Oh, that's interesting," Mark said, unimpressed. "But I've got real news—"

"Interesting?" his lawyer exclaimed, cutting him off. "Don't you get it? Johnson *lied* to the cops. That nigger was hiding something. . . . I think your prosecutorial instincts were correct—I'd bet Cleveland Johnson killed the Voorhees girl!"

"No one killed Joanna," Mark said with authority. "You're not the only brilliant detective on this case. I just left Tom Bastone—he's been working overtime, too . . ."

Tom Bastone awoke at noon on Sunday, with Judy Larsen the first thing on his mind. Despite the sour note on which their evening ended, Tom Bastone had enjoyed being with her far more than any of the women he'd dated since Susan Lehrer walked out on him two years ago. As he lay in bed, he hugged his pillow, pretending it was the cute lady cop with those blue eyes and big dimples. He knew he couldn't see her for a while, but was sure they'd be together as soon as the Cantor case concluded. Tom Bastone was infatuated.

Anxious to share his excitement with his best friend, Tom put up some coffee and reached for the telephone to call Mark. But after dialing the first few digits, he stopped. It suddenly dawned on Bastone: He'll be furious with me for fraternizing with the enemy. And I could hardly blame him!

A little later, while in the shower, Tom began feeling guilty for not telling Mark about his encounter with Larsen. It's not right to hide it from him either, he pondered. Damned if he

155

did, and damned if he didn't, Bastone finally decided: If Judy had given me any helpful information, I'd certainly tell Mark the whole story, he rationalized. But since she didn't, why make trouble?

His problem solved, Tom dressed quickly to attend to more important business. The weather forecast had been correct for a change. The gloomy, drizzly Sunday afternoon would provide the perfect opportunity to complete his work at 72 East Eleventh Street.

Although Tom had really lost hope of finding a witness to the Voorhees murder, a thorough job required that he speak with every single person living in the two tenements on Eleventh Street, whose back apartments had a view of Joanna's window. After many previous visits to the location, at different hours of different days, he'd already checked everyone at 70 East Eleventh Street, and only three units remained on his list for 72 East Eleventh, when Bastone knocked on the door to apartment 6-E. An old man with wispy white hair and a long, gaunt face opened it a few inches.

"Good afternoon, sir. My name is Tom Bastone. I'm a private investigator," he said, flashing an ID card. "I was wondering if you'd be kind enough to give me a few minutes of your time?"

"Non capisco. Non parlo l'inglese."

Bastone repeated the introduction in his first language: *"Dicevo: Buon giorno. Mi chiamo Tom Bastone. Sono agente investigativo privato."*

"Italiano, eh," the old man said, opening the door wider.

The detective nodded. In the conversation that followed both men spoke Italian: "You are Mr. Mantucci?" Bastone asked.

"Yes, Dominick Mantucci."

"I am very pleased to meet you, Mr. Mantucci." Tom extended his arm for a handshake. "I have been here several times, but I have not found you at home."

"I am home now. Come in, please," Mantucci said, looking the well-dressed detective up and down as he entered the small, dark apartment. "You were born in Italy?"

"No, I was born in America, but my parents came from the old country."

The old man led him through a living room crammed with

156

well-worn furniture and framed photographs, into the kitchen, where they sat down at a large formica table. "Would you like some coffee?"

"No, thank you."

"You speak Italian well."

"I learned as a child. At home my folks spoke only Italian."

"They are Sicilian?"

"My father is Sicilian, my mother Calabrese."

The old man smiled, revealing rotted teeth: "That's quite a combination. My wife—God bless her soul—was half Sicilian, half Calabrese. What a temper . . . and so jealous—if I even looked at another woman, she would go crazy. Of course, such passions have their virtue." He winked at Bastone. Then, staring down into his coffee cup: "She was a good woman," he muttered, "and so beautiful." He looked up. "Forgive me, you did not come to hear about my Emilia."

"It's okay," Bastone said softly.

"What is your business with me, Officer?"

"Well, to begin, I am not a police officer—I am a *private* detective investigating a murder that occurred on the next block." A quizzical look crossed the old man's face, as Bastone turned in his chair to face the window right behind him: "You see that gray building?" he said, pointing to the rear of 69 East Tenth. "Last spring a young woman who lived there was hit over the head and thrown out her window." Mantucci winced. "I am trying to find someone who saw it happen."

The old man shook his head: "This I did not see. I am sorry, I cannot help you."

Having come with no expectations, Bastone was not disappointed. And he'd enjoyed conversing in Italian. "Well, thank you anyway," he said, rising slowly from his chair.

Mantucci remained seated, gazing out the window. "That building is cursed," he said.

"What do you mean?" Bastone asked.

"A few months ago another woman jumped off a window ledge from the same apartment house."

"During the summertime?"

"Maybe it was *before* the summer."

"Which window ledge, Mr. Mantucci, which window ledge did she jump from?"

157

"The one on the top floor," the old man said, pointing directly across the way, "just to the right of the fire escape."

Bastone's eyes opened wide and he leaned over the table. "How did you learn of this tragedy? Did someone *tell* you about it?"

"I saw the whole thing with my own eyes."

The detective exhaled. "And she committed suicide?"

"No, it did not look like she was trying to kill herself."

"Please, sir, tell me exactly what you saw," Bastone said, straightening up.

"That night, I was sitting right here watching her pace back and forth in her apartment. Then she opens the window and climbs out onto the ledge. She was standing . . . let me show you." Mantucci got up and stood facing the window, holding onto the frame at either side.

"Her back was to you?" Bastone interrupted.

"Yes. Then she moves like this." He inched both feet over to the left as his right hand joined his left on that side of the windowframe. "She kept looking over toward the fire escape and all of a sudden . . ." The old man bent his knees and jumped to the left, his feet barely leaving the floor. Then he turned around to face the detective: "I think she was trying to get to the fire escape. I do not know why she didn't just go out her other window—that leads right onto it." He paused, shaking his head.

Bastone felt tingly all over. "And she missed the fire escape?"

"No, she caught hold of it with one hand—at the side, toward the bottom—but she could not lift herself up. She hung under the fire escape for a few minutes," he said, posing like a left-handed Statue of Liberty, "then she let go." His voice cracked. "I will never forget the scream." The old man looked out the window for a few seconds before continuing. "She almost landed on the fire escape one floor below, but her head hit the railing and she bounced off it."

"Your eyesight is good, Mr. Mantucci?"

"Now to read—I must wear glasses, but other than that, I still see fine."

Bastone's heart pounded. "And you could see into her apartment?"

158

"Yes. Her lights were on. The window had no curtain, no shade."

"Did you see anyone else there besides the girl?"

"No one," Mantucci said firmly.

Bastone smiled and the old man looked at him as if he was crazy. "Forgive me," said the detective. "Do not misunderstand. I am deeply sorry for this girl, but you see, she's the same person my client is accused of murdering."

"But she was not murdered!"

"Yes, yes." Bastone grabbed the old man's arm. "That is why I am so happy."

But as he stood rechecking the view from Mantucci's window, his face suddenly took on a worried look. "Wait a minute. She is hanging by one arm and cannot hold on any more so she falls—*feet* first," he thought out loud. Then he turned to the old man and asked: "How could her *head* hit the fire escape right below?"

"Well, you see . . ." Mantucci explained that while trying to lift herself up to the fire escape, the girl had gotten a toehold on the side of the building. She fell with her body in a tilted position.

"Did you ever tell the police what you saw?" Bastone asked in an urgent tone.

"I tried. The operator connected me, but they did not speak Italian. I was on the phone with the police when she fell."

"You called *while* she was hanging from the fire escape?"

"Yes. It is right there," Mantucci said, pointing with his chin to an old-fashioned black telephone on a cupboard shelf right near the window. "Someone else must have told them, because they did not understand me, yet I saw the police in the backyard very soon after."

Bastone was beaming. He cupped the old man's gray-stubbled face in his hands and kissed him on the forehead.

23

In his attempts to find a witness months before the trial began, Phil Roselli had subpoenaed the computer printout for all police emergency calls made on April 29, 1976. He'd not learned about Mantucci at that time, because, due to the language problem, the old man's call wasn't entered into the computer. However, Mark remembered that all 911 telephone communications were recorded as a matter of normal police procedure, and to substantiate Mantucci's story, Roselli obtained a court order for the actual tapes.

In a conference room at Bastone's plush Manhattan offices, Cantor, Roselli, and the detective listened as a sleek Panasonic replayed the emergency calls police had received the night Joanna died. There was a holdup in a midtown restaurant, a burglary in an Upper East Side townhouse, and three calls for the same purse snatch in the theatre district. A hysterical woman complained that her ex-husband was breaking down her door, before another female voice calmly recited her name and address, told the police operator, "I've just been raped," then broke down and cried.

Between each call, the exact time was announced. Finally at 10:25:

"Police Emergency. Can I help you?"

"*Polizia, c'è una ragazza appesa d'una scala di sicurezza!*" Bastone turned to Roselli. "That's it!" His eyes bulged. The detective translated for Mark: " 'Police, there's a girl hanging from the fire escape!' "

"Can you speak English?"

"*In italiano, italiano—non parlo l'inglese. Dio Santo, ella non ha la forza. Si deve spedire l'aiuto.*"

Every now and then, Bastone pressed a button stopping

the machine to give him time to translate. He acknowledged obvious portions by nodding as he spoke: " 'Italian. Italian—I don't speak English. Lord Jesus, she is not strong enough. You must send help.' "

On the other end of the line, the police operator could be heard asking, "Anyone here understand Italian?" And after a pause, the answer became apparent: "Ah, shit. Sorry mister. Try it in English, in Inglesia—just try!"

Suddenly the caller gasped. When he finally spoke again, Mark stared at Bastone as he gave the words meaning: " 'She has fallen, heavenly Father, bless her soul.' "

The conversation ended seconds later with the police operator groping, "No speaka Italyano, comprendey?" It wasn't clear who hung up first.

After hearing the tape, Cantor and Roselli exchanged smiles of relief. Then Mark noted: "All fits together, doesn't it? The last scream came when Joanna couldn't hold on any more. . . . That's why the only neighbors who heard it were those in the back apartments, like Klagsbrun and Mrs. Rosen."

"Hey, you're pretty sharp." Roselli's eyes opened wide. "You must've studied Tom's chart of the building."

"I've read the whole file a hundred times." Suddenly Mark's face took on a confused look. "Wait a second. Patricia Nolan also heard that scream. How's that possible? Her apartment—4-A— faces the front."

"She said she heard a 'muffled cry.' And don't forget: Nolan stood there listening for it!"

Cantor nodded, "You're pret-ty sharp yourself."

A few minutes later they discussed whether to immediately disclose the Mantucci evidence to the prosecutor, or save the old man as a surprise witness at trial. Mark felt the jury would almost certainly acquit, but he recognized that juries were unpredictable. Roselli agreed and also feared that formal rules of evidence might bar the defense from playing the 911 tape. "If the jury doesn't hear it," he warned, "they could think the old man's a phony." Both concurred: the safer course was to tell Quinn about Mantucci *now*. Faced with such clear proof of Cantor's innocence, he'd surely drop the charges.

161

*   *   *

The conference was held in the privacy of Judge Warren's wood-paneled chambers. With the aid of an official court interpreter, Mantucci told his story. After he described how Joanna hit her head on the way down, Roselli chided Quinn: "That's how she got the *depressed* fracture—no weapon—just the side rail of the fourth-floor fire escape—a *right-handed* fire escape, no doubt." Quinn frowned, unamused by the reference to the ME's testimony. "And the rust on the girl's *left* hand," Roselli continued, "came from her hanging from the fifth-floor fire escape. Didn't that bother you a little?" he asked the prosecutor. "She was right-handed. If she got that rust stain from grabbing a 'blunt instrument,' it would've been on her right hand!"

Quinn questioned Mantucci at length, then asked him to wait in the courtroom. The others remained to hear the tape translated by the court interpreter. After it had played, Judge Warren looked over at Quinn: "Well, that confirms it—obviously Mr. Mantucci was not subsequently manufactured by the defense. This call came in while it was happening."

The prosecutor fidgeted with his pen. "No, but the call could've been part of a master plan," he said without conviction. "Maybe he paid Mantucci to phone during the murder." When the judge shook his head in disbelief bordering on disgust, Quinn added, "Well, it's possible!"

"Don't you think he would've chosen someone who spoke English?" Warren asked, glaring at the prosecutor from behind his large mahogany desk. "That way the *police* could've found Mantucci easily and the case never would've gone this far. Besides, with Mr. Cantor's background, wouldn't he know better than to add an accomplice who might blow the whistle on his 'master plan'?" he asked, mocking the prosecutor.

Quinn had a puzzled look on his face as he stared into space.

"Your Honor, there's more . . ." Roselli interjected, but he was ignored.

"So what's bothering you?" the judge asked Quinn.

"Weisenberg may have been mistaken. But there's still Mrs. Nolan's testimony—she saw a man go up there, remember?"

"I can also explain that," Roselli said, too softly for his engrossed colleagues to hear.

162

"I remember . . . ," Judge Warren answered Quinn, his eyes narrowed with sudden concern. "Well, I'll give you a week's adjournment to investigate any possible connection between the defendant and this new witness. . . . Do you want to give Mr. Mantucci a lie detector test? Give one to Mrs. Nolan, too!"

Roselli stood up from his chair to get the judge's attention. "Neither one of them is lying, Your Honor," he said loud and clear. "What I've been trying to tell you both is that Mrs. Nolan did see a man going up to the fifth floor. But he wasn't my client and he wasn't any killer. The man walking up those stairs didn't even go to her apartment. . . . Excuse me."

Quinn and Warren both had their eyes fixed on Roselli as he shuffled over to the door and opened it enough to take a quick look out into the courtroom. "Good," he muttered, letting the door close. He returned to the green vinyl-covered chair in front of the judge's desk: "It's really very simple. The girl gets that last call and thinks the guy's downstairs coming up to kill her. She bangs on her neighbors' doors, screaming for help, but no one answers. She starts down to the next floor but hears footsteps coming up, so she runs back into her apartment. Maybe she never considered going up to the roof; or maybe she thought that the door was locked—Patrolman Gilmore testified that he had to give it a *strong* push. So she's back in her apartment, scared stiff. She thinks he has the keys, so she's gotta get out of there. The window in front of the fire escape has a lock on it and her key goes in but it doesn't turn—Detective Harrison tried it and that's what he said. So she opens the *other* window and climbs out onto the ledge." Both Quinn and Warren leaned forward on the edge of their chairs as Roselli continued: "The fire escape is a bit too far away to reach, but she's panicked. Once she hears the key go into the door, death is certain, so what does she have to lose? She leaps for the fire escape."

The Bald Beagle crossed his legs. "Okay to smoke in here, Judge?" Warren nodded and Roselli searched his pockets until he'd located a cigar butt, then repeated the process to find a match.

"I thought you said the man never went into her apartment," Quinn said.

"He didn't," Mark's lawyer answered before pausing to light the cigar. "Joanna Voorhees lived in 5-B. The door to 5-C is

163

right next to hers. The fella Nolan saw going up the stairs was the man who lived in 5-C." Roselli blew smoke right into the prosecutor's face and continued: "Now I'm not sure if he was so tired or drunk that he put *his* key in *her* lock by mistake . . . Those doors are so close to each other, it's also possible he put the key into his own lock and she *thought* it was hers. I used to live in an apartment where every time my next-door neighbor came home, I thought someone was bustin' in on me!"

"What about the broken vase and all the other evidence of a struggle?" Quinn asked as he thumbed through papers in his file.

Roselli shrugged: "Joanna Voorhees ran around that apartment half-crazed. She knocked over the ashtray and the table herself. Wicker isn't very heavy. She coulda kicked it while climbing onto the window ledge. The vase fell when the table went."

A cocky grin flashed on Quinn's face as he finally found the report he'd been looking for: "You say the man she heard was the guy in 5-C, huh? Well, that's impossible: Cleveland Johnson lived in 5-C and he got home at least a half hour *before* all that happened."

"An hour," Roselli corrected, rolling the cigar with his stubby fingers. "9:20—that's what he told your man Harrison. But Johnson was mistaken. He really came home at 10:20—six minutes after Joanna Voorhees received that last threatening call, seven minutes before Mrs. Rosen heard the thud in her backyard!"

Judge Warren scratched his head. "Johnson? I don't recall any Mr. Johnson testifying," he said.

"That's because he never did testify," Roselli answered. "He's the guy who lived in the deceased's building and disappeared after her death. Before the trial, I asked you to order the DA to give me his new address."

"Ah, yes. Now I remember. I believe I denied—"

Quinn didn't wait for the judge to finish his sentence: "How do you know Johnson was mistaken about the time?" he asked.

Roselli glared at his adversary. "I spoke to him. Why don't you? He's sitting out there in the courtroom right now."

Seated between Brian Downey and Tom Bastone, in the first row of the empty courtroom, Cleveland Johnson had been waiting patiently for the signal from Roselli. A black man in his early forties, the jazz musician had conservative short-cropped hair and a pencil mustache. But the thick horn-rimmed glasses and dashiki he wore gave clues to his artistic bent. Once inside the judge's chambers, Johnson stated that he had, in fact, come home an hour later than he'd originally told the police. Having just returned from New Orleans—in a time zone one hour earlier than New York—he'd forgotten to turn his watch ahead. When Johnson realized his mistake the following morning, he phoned the Homicide Bureau and left a message for Harrison. Apparently the detective never received it. By the time the DA's office got the case, Mark Cantor had already been arrested and Quinn's only concern was to get a conviction. When he interviewed the residents of 69 East Tenth, Johnson was out of town. Not needing him as a witness, the prosecutor neglected to follow up.

After Johnson explained his error, Roselli conveyed the information he'd uncovered about the airline's flight times. That cinched it. When offered the opportunity to question the jazz musician, Quinn declined. Apparently he'd tired of fighting windmills. Roselli's interpretation of events now seemed incontrovertible.

Judge Warren was irate, and as soon as Johnson left his chambers, he let Quinn have it: "This is a disgrace," he said, shaking his head. "You never spoke to this man personally?"

"No," Quinn muttered with a sheepish look on his face.

With the prosecutor dangling on the ropes, Roselli took a shot at him. "Didn't you think it strange that the guy was home, yet didn't hear the girl screaming for help in the hallway . . . or banging on his door?" he yelled, waving a copy of Johnson's statement to the police. Then Roselli placed it on Warren's desk and, as the judge read, Quinn responded:

"Of course we wondered about that." Pointing to the second paragraph in the report, he explained. "But we figured he could have been in the shower or sound asleep by then."

"Well, good," Roselli began in his most condescending tone. "Now you won't have to ask me why Johnson didn't hear her scream when she fell."

"He was in the shower?" Quinn guessed, his meek voice barely audible.

"Probably—he did take a shower as soon as he got home. Besides, his apartment didn't face the back!"

Judge Warren stood up, and, leaning over his desk, raised an eyebrow at Quinn. "Before moving this case to trial, you should have interviewed this Johnson fella yourself!"

"We couldn't find him," the prosecutor pleaded.

With a jerk of his head toward Roselli, Warren shot back, "They were able to locate the man without the kind of resources at your disposal. There's no excuse!"

Quinn's head was bowed as the judge paced back and forth without taking his eyes off him: "I assume your office will now dismiss the indictment against Mr. Cantor so as not to waste any more of this court's time. I realize there's also a charge of aggravated harassment for making the threatening phone calls, but after all you've put this young man through, I think a complete dismissal would be the only fair thing to do."

Cantor spoke for the first time at the conference: "Besides, I didn't make any of those crazy calls—" Not wanting him to say more, Roselli squeezed his client's arm and Mark stopped. Then everyone looked at Quinn for his response to the judge's suggestion.

"I'd like to verify that flight information, and discuss this whole thing with the boss," said the assistant DA.

"Of course. Mr. Krieger should be consulted," said Judge Warren. "We'll recess until 2 P.M. tomorrow. If you need more time, let us know then."

Bastone knew the conference had gone well when he saw the frown on Quinn's face as the prosecutor tramped out of the judge's chambers. "Let's go celebrate," he suggested after getting the details from Mark.

"Why don't we wait until tomorrow," said a cautious Phil Roselli, "until after Quinn dismisses the charges."

Mark nodded. "Warren was so angry at Quinn, I got the impression *he'd* dismiss the case himself, if the DA doesn't," he said, bubbling.

"Maybe . . . but I hear this judge is afraid to stick his neck out one inch." Roselli blew his nose, then continued: "The DA will probably throw out the murder charge, but they still have a good case against you for making those phone calls. They've put too much into this to come out empty-handed, and if they get a conviction they'll save some face. Of course, that's a helluva lot better than a murder rap, but if the jury finds you guilty of aggravated harassment, you could still be disbarred."

Roselli's pessimistic analysis of the situation had taken the smile from Mark's face. "I can't believe this," he said, shaking his head. Then he cheered himself up. "Well, I've got confidence in you," he said to his lawyer, "and faith in the jury system. When the defense attorney knows what he's doing, innocent people don't get convicted!"

The next day, Quinn entered the courtroom with the bounce back in his step. After a smug glance at Roselli, he faced the judge and announced: "Based on the newly discovered evidence presented to us yesterday, the state moves to dismiss Count One of the indictment. The state does, however, intend to proceed with its prosecution of the remaining charges."

Glancing at the indictment, Judge Warren noted, "Count *Two* also charges murder. You want that one dismissed as well, don't you?"

Kevin Quinn stood straight and stiff, his cold gray eyes fixed on the judge. "No, Your Honor, along with Count Three, charging aggravated harassment, we intend to continue the trial on Count Two—murder in the second degree!"

Count Two:

The Grand Jury of the County of New York accuses the defendant Mark Cantor of the crime of Murder in the Second Degree, committed as follows:

The defendant, on or about April 29, 1976, under circumstances evincing a depraved indifference to human life, recklessly engaged in

*conduct which created a grave risk of death to one Joanna Voorhees,
and thereby caused the death of Joanna Voorhees.*

The words of the indictment were taken directly from the
New York State Penal Law. "Reckless" murder, as this crime is
called, does not require the *intention* to kill. More surprisingly,
the Penal Law sections for murder speak in terms of *conduct* that
causes death, rather than a physical *assault* that *results* in death.

When the indictment was originally drawn, the prosecution's case against Mark Cantor was based on an intentional,
premeditated murder (Count One), but alternative legal theories
are commonly included in all indictments in the event that the
proofs at trial turned out differently than expected.

After Quinn's dramatic announcement, Roselli asked to approach the bench even though the jury wasn't present.

"You can't be serious!" he said to the prosecutor in a strained
whisper, loud enough for spectators in the gallery to hear.

Quinn spoke more softly: "Why? Your client threatened to
kill that girl 'in just a few minutes.' It put her in a state of panic
that led directly to her death. The situation is no different than
those cases where a robber points a gun at someone who becomes
scared stiff and has a heart attack. If the victim dies, the thief
is guilty of murder, as well as robbery. And the appellate courts
have consistently upheld those convictions."

"That's a lot different," Roselli countered. "The robber is
present when it happens. Can a person commit murder when
he's not even there?"

Quinn responded quickly: "Of course! I put poison in your
food and leave; later you eat it and die. Am I not guilty of
murder?"

Clearly defeated on that argument, Roselli went on to his
next: "In those heart-attack cases, the victim doesn't do anything
to cause his own death—his heart just gives out. But in our
situation, there's an intervening act that causes death: she jumped
from a window ledge. If she hadn't, she'd be alive today."

"Your client's call *made* her leap for the fire escape," the
prosecutor shot back. "His reckless conduct caused her death.
Under our laws, that's murder!"

"He didn't make those calls! But even *assuming* he did, and
assuming, for argument's sake, that you could prove it beyond

a reasonable doubt," Roselli shouted, enunciating each word slowly, "making a threatening call doesn't constitute 'a depraved indifference to human life,' " he said, quoting from the Penal Law.

"Well, I disagree," Quinn yelled back.

Roselli waved him away with his hand and regarded the judge: "In light of the ridiculous position being taken by the DA, I'd ask Your Honor to dismiss Count Two."

Warren rubbed his eyes and scratched his head, looking as if he didn't know what to do. Finally, he spoke, softly and slowly: "I, personally, agree with Mr. Roselli that the connection between the phone call and her death is not direct enough to constitute the crime of murder." He cleared his throat and continued: "However, I believe that's a question of fact, not law, and therefore, the jury should make the decision—not the court." The gutless judge was unable to look Roselli in the eye when he concluded, "Your motion to dismiss is denied. The trial will continue."

The jury was brought into the courtroom and Judge Warren told them that the state had dismissed Count One of the indictment because of "newly discovered evidence." "In order to avoid confusion," as he put it, the judge also explained the new legal theory under which the prosecution was now proceeding. He then permitted Quinn to call Mantucci to the stand, followed by Johnson, as part of *the state's* case. The assistant DA made no attempt to deceive the jury into thinking he'd found these witnesses. In fact, his first few questions to both the old man and the jazz musician brought out their discovery by *Roselli's* investigators. Although the dramatic impact would have been even greater had the two surprise witnesses been presented to the jury by the defense, because they testified for the prosecution their credibility was never an issue. Furthermore, judging by the glares and raised eyebrows several jurors gave Quinn, he'd definitely lost some of their trust.

The prosecutor had to win back the jury's sympathy. In a murder case, the state must establish the identity of the deceased. This formality is usually accomplished by the testimony of a relative. The timing was perfect for Helen Voorhees to take the stand. Although she had no first-hand knowledge of how her daughter died or the threatening calls that led to the death, Mrs. Voorhees provided emotional appeal to the prosecution's case just when it was needed.

A handsome woman with chiseled features, she wore no makeup, not even lipstick, making her look washed-out and sad. "A prosecutor's ploy," Mark later commented, noting that her nails were well manicured and her jet-black hair, pulled back into a bun, was obviously dyed. She wore a black polyester suit, as if still in mourning.

"When was the last time you saw Joanna alive?" Quinn asked.

"Around Christmastime. I try to get to New York twice a year—I live in Lincoln Park, Michigan—just outside Detroit. We spent a few days together during the holidays . . ." Her voice trailed off.

"And when was the last time you spoke with your daughter?"

"A few days before"—she tried to find the words—"it happened. I used to phone her at least once a week. The last time we talked she seemed disturbed. I asked, but she said, 'Nothing's wrong.' She never wanted to worry me." As Mrs. Voorhees spoke, she stared straight ahead, hardly even blinking, like in a trance.

"What did you two talk about? Can you remember?"

"Talk about? Yes. She had an audition later in the week. She'd been studying to be an actress. She had a lot of talent and when she set her mind to something . . . Even as a little girl . . . She was to audition for a TV movie, but she didn't seem very excited about it."

The prosecutor walked closer to the witness stand until he was only a few feet away. "I know this is difficult," he said, "but I'm going to ask you to please keep your voice up." Quinn glanced at the jury and then, regarding Mrs. Voorhees again: "Did there come a time when you were asked to come to New York City, to the county morgue?"

Tears welled in her eyes and she started to tremble. She tried to speak but broke down sobbing.

"Take your time, madam," Judge Warren said in a gentle tone. "Would you like a drink of water?"

She shook her head, removed a handkerchief from her handbag, and blew her nose in a ladylike way. After a deep

170

breath, she mustered the strength to say, "Yes, I got on the first plane out and went straight to . . . the morgue."

"Do you recall the date?"

"April the thirtieth," she muttered.

"And were you asked to identify a young woman's remains?"

Again Helen Voorhees began to sob, but this time held herself together just long enough to scream out, "It was my Joey, my darling Joey!"

Helen Voorhees left the impression that she and her daughter had been very close. Mark knew this wasn't the case, but as Roselli put it: "How can I cross-examine her about that? The jury will hate me if I try to discredit her, and despise me if I succeed. It's a no-win situation!"

After Joanna's mother testified, the prosecution rested. Roselli then renewed his motion to dismiss, and to no one's surprise, Judge Warren again denied it.

On the way out of the courtroom, Quinn collared the defense lawyer, inviting him to his office for a conference.

Located in the courthouse, Quinn's working quarters were drab and cramped. He shared the twelve-by-fifteen-foot room with another assistant DA—a young man with glasses much too large for his tiny face—whom Quinn didn't bother to introduce when he entered with Roselli.

Seated behind a gray metal desk, with thumb in vest pocket, Quinn began, "I've got good news for you, Phil." Roselli's eyes focused over Quinn's shoulder to a windowsill covered by at least thirty empty soda cans, neatly stacked in rows. "My office has reconsidered its position on this case," the prosecutor said with a friendly smile. "Of course, we still believe your man is technically guilty of murder. Unfortunately, as you know, under the law, the *minimum* sentence for murder in the second degree is fifteen years to life imprisonment. If the jury convicts, the judge has no discretion to give him anything less." Quinn loosened his tie. "We think that's pretty harsh under these circumstances."

His eyes now fixed on his adversary, Roselli sat and listened, his face expressionless.

"I may have a solution that will satisfy everyone," Quinn declared. "We're willing to accept a plea to manslaughter in the second degree. You can ask for probation, we won't object, and I'm sure Judge Warren will go along with it." He winked as if it had already been arranged. "There'll be a promise on the record."

Seated at a desk on the other side of the room, Quinn's officemate had been eavesdropping on their conversation and peered over the book in his hand to see Roselli's reaction. The Bald Beagle had a sneer on his face, but said nothing.

Quinn leaned forward and urged: "Look, Phil, I know you think you've got a winner here, but if you're wrong and Cantor's convicted . . . at least this way he doesn't go to jail."

Roselli rose slowly. "If you'd offered a plea to aggravated harassment with probation, we'd have something to think about." He shook his head and said sharply, "But manslaughter—the man will never practice law again, and with that on his record, he won't be able to get any kinda decent job!"

"I can't go any lower. There's too much pressure: the mother, the news media, the whole community! The girl's dead, and it's because of those telephone calls."

"He didn't make those damn calls!"

As Roselli reached for his beat-up attaché case, Quinn stared down at him: "Fifteen to life—is it worth the risk?" And when the defense lawyer headed for the door, he shouted after him, "At least ask your client!"

Roselli stopped and turned to face Quinn. "It's my duty to inform him—" his eyes narrowed—"but I cannot, in good conscience, recommend this deal."

Mark was waiting in the lobby of the courthouse when Roselli arrived with a troubled look. As soon as he began telling him about the "plea bargain" Quinn had offered, Cantor shook his head. "I'm not pleading guilty to something I didn't do!"

The defense began its case on the following day with three *character* witnesses testifying on Cantor's behalf. They were an impressive group: U.S. Congressman Sam Bellamy had been a friend of the family for years; Judge Gaynor Fitzgerald had taken an almost fatherly interest in Mark while presiding over several trials in which Cantor was the prosecutor; and Mark's former boss, Bronx DA Paul Capellini, must have surprised his Manhattan counterpart by taking the stand to praise the defendant's good name.

What impact would they have? Cantor felt that character witnesses rarely altered the outcome of a trial: "You always read about those homicidal maniacs whose neighbors couldn't believe that the polite, gentle man next door ate babies for breakfast." Roselli didn't exactly disagree, but thought that having such dignitaries stand up for Mark "certainly couldn't hurt."

At day's end, a much more important question remained: Should Cantor testify?

Roselli met with his client at the lawyer's Bronx storefront to resolve the issue. To Mark's surprise, Tom Bastone had been invited to join the discussion.

"No. There's no point. It's too risky!" Roselli paced back and forth, shaking his head as he spoke.

In contrast, Cantor was the picture of calm, leaning way back in the oil-stained, plaid chair, his feet up on the edge of Roselli's desk. "What are you so worried about, Phil? Quinn's not going to rattle me."

"Don't be too sure, smart guy. You may know your way around a courtroom, but you've never been a witness before. It's not so easy, especially when you're the accused!"

"Look, I'm not a dumb thug like your other clients. I can handle—"

His face red with anger, Roselli cut Mark off: "I don't just represent 'thugs.' " He reached up to the bookshelf and pulled out a five-inch-thick trial transcript and started waving it in Mark's face. "Remember Klein, the assemblyman from Pelham Parkway who got caught taking kickbacks? I had an acquittal in that case, till the prick insisted on testifying—thought he could charm the pants off the jury. But he blew it and got convicted!" Roselli slammed the transcript on his cluttered desk and papers went flying all over the place, but he just continued: "I got a reversal on appeal and at the second trial, Klein listens to me and doesn't take the stand—the jury acquits after only two hours of deliberation.

"You know it yourself—as a prosecutor, how many weak cases did you win because the defendant took the stand and you ripped him apart?"

Mark smiled. "Kevin Quinn isn't Mark Cantor," he said.

"Don't sell Quinn short!" Roselli yelled back. "He may not be Mr. Personality, but he's no dope. He was assigned your case because he's *good*, very good! He's been pretty sharp so far and from what I hear, he's an excellent cross-examiner."

"He's not that sharp—poor preparation—Didn't even *speak* to Johnson before trial."

"He didn't *want* to speak to Johnson," Roselli said in a stage whisper, "and he never expected us to find him."

"So he's already made one big mistake . . ."

The Bald Beagle cleared his throat, looked down at the floor as if he were gathering patience, and finally tried again: "A defendant shouldn't testify unless he has to. The evidence against you is so flimsy . . . Why do you think Quinn tried to make that plea-bargain deal? 'Probation.' He knows he's got problems. By the time I'm through, he won't have a case!" Roselli caught his breath and concluded: "All you can say on the witness stand is, 'I didn't make those threatening calls.' It's not necessary. On summation, I'll remind the jury that by going to trial you've already denied your guilt. And Quinn can't cross-examine me!"

Mark leaned forward slowly until the chair's front legs touched down, and his feet were back on the ground. With eyes narrowed and jaw tensed, he told his lawyer: "The jury wants to hear that denial from my lips, not yours!"

In a softer voice, Roselli tried to reason with Mark: "Sure they'd like to hear what you have to say, but that doesn't mean they'll find you guilty if you don't take the stand."

Mark stared at the Klein trial transcript for a moment, then shook his head. "The stakes are too high. I can't take any chances—I've got to testify."

His patience exhausted, Roselli turned to Bastone: "Would you please talk some sense into your mule-headed friend."

Tom didn't know what to say. Like Mark, he feared the jury might equate his silence with guilt. On the other hand, such an ardent plea, from a man with Roselli's reputation and experience, could not be ignored. Bastone told Mark: "It seems to me you hired Phil because you respect his judgment as well as his talents and I think it's very difficult for you to be objective about this—"

"I'm being objective. This is a matter of trial strategy. You're out of your field—you don't understand the problem!" Mark snapped. Then he got up and walked over to where Roselli stood by the window, gazing out onto the street. "I've got to tell the jury that getting her unlisted number was no big deal," he said talking to his lawyer's back, "and what I meant when Sergeant Larsen questioned me. I've got to explain all that."

Roselli wheeled around to face Mark and yelled, "Your explanations stink! Are you gonna tell this jury that you made only one anonymous, threatening phone call, instead of *six?*"

"Well . . . it's, it's true," Mark stammered. "I have to tell the truth."

"You do and it's all over—they'll never believe you didn't make those other calls, too."

An embarrassed look crossed Roselli's face when he suddenly noticed Bastone, as if he'd forgotten the investigator was there. Without uttering a word, Tom's eyes assured the lawyer he could be trusted just as Mark underscored the problem by saying, "You want me to give false testimony—to lie under oath?"

"I don't want you to give any testimony!" Roselli shot back. Then, no longer concerned by the presence of a witness to his subornation of perjury, he put it directly: "But if you insist on taking the stand, you cannot admit making *any* anonymous calls."

"Then what on earth was I referring to when Larsen asked me if I ever threatened Joanna on the telephone, and I said, 'That was just a joke'?"

"The first time you called her, when she offered no excuse for standing you up and lied about trying to phone you, didn't you say something like, 'Someone ought to teach you a lesson'?"

"Yes."

"Well, that's the threat you were talking about," Roselli said, slamming his fist on the desk.

"That's a joke? It doesn't make any sense," Cantor responded.

Roselli stared down at the floor massaging his temples with those stubby fingers, then shook his head. "You're right—it doesn't make sense."

"That's why I must testify," Mark said in a soft, calm voice. "That's why I've got to tell the truth."

Torrential rains delayed proceedings almost an hour waiting for two jurors who'd been late because of the storm, but, as usual, the courtroom was crowded with spectators when the burly court clerk began the day with his "Hear ye, hear ye, all rise. Part Twenty-two of the Supreme Court in and for the County of New York is now in session. Give your attendance and ye shall be heard. The Honorable Linford Warren presiding."

After taking his seat at the bench, the judge motioned with his hand for everyone to be seated and asked Roselli if he was ready to proceed.

"We are, Your Honor," the Bald Beagle answered.

"Then call your next witness," Warren ordered.

Roselli stood and in a soft monotone announced: "At this time, the defendant will take the stand." With the gallery buzzing in waves from front to back, Cantor rose and, holding his head high, walked briskly to the witness box. After being sworn, he sat down and his soft brown eyes gazed across the length and breadth of the courtroom like a toddler confronted by his first flight of stairs.

Roselli told him to "sit back, relax," and after fielding a series of preliminary questions about his educational and professional background, Mark appeared more at ease.

"Did you know a young woman named Joanna Voorhees?" Roselli asked, getting to the point.

Mark Cantor related the entire story. Although Roselli wanted him to "downplay his infatuation for a girl he hardly knew," and perhaps omit some of the embarrassing details, Mark gave an accurate and complete account. He acknowledged being overwhelmed by her good looks and charm their first evening together. Like a true gentleman, he didn't mention having sexual relations with her until Roselli specifically asked. Mark told the jury how much he looked forward to his next date with Joanna and noted his disappointment when she stood him up. He even described how he used the credit card to gain entry into the building and ran up the stairs to knock on her apartment door

176

after not getting any response on the intercom. When he testified concerning his phone conversation with Joanna a week later, he included her comment about being "high and horny," and his closing remark—"Someday, somebody is gonna teach you a lesson." "I didn't mean *me!*" he told the jury softly but emphatically.

Up until this point, Mark had remained calm and cool, conveying the impression of a normal, feeling person. But then came the tough part.

"At first I was shocked by her attitude," he began. "After I thought about what she'd said, I became angry and I wanted to tell her off. So I decided to call her again, but as I dialed I realized that she'd hang up if I tried to scold her. When she answered the phone"—Mark winced—"I just blurted out, 'Someday you'll pay' or something like that, then I hung up." After glancing over at the jury, Rosclli asked Mark, "And is this the call you had in mind when Sergeant Larsen questioned you about threatening Joanna Voorhees on the telephone?"

Cantor nodded and his lawyer said, "But you told Miss Larsen that it was just a joke."

"I didn't mean a ha-ha joke—I meant . . . a sort of . . . practical joke. Only it wasn't planned—it just came out that way."

All twelve jurors stared at Mark, their faces giving no indication of their thoughts. Roselli shuffled around the counsel table toward the jury box, and with eyes narrowed and voice raised, he asked Mark, "After that call, did you ever phone Joanna Voorhees again?"

"I tried, but the number had been changed—and it was unlisted."

"Why did you try to call her?"

"I wanted to give her another chance. I hoped that perhaps she was just in a terrible mood when she said those things."

Roselli could feel his insides churning, but he spoke calmly when he asked, "And did you, in fact, obtain Joanna Voorhees's unpublished number from the phone company by claiming that she was a witness in the Jenkin's case?"

Mark admitted his wrongdoing, exhibiting remorse, while at the same time explaining that this particular abuse of authority was not unusual among his colleagues. "But after I requisitioned the new number," Cantor told the jury, "I realized that it would be foolish to pursue Joanna and I never called her."

Roselli positioned himself only seven or eight feet from the witness stand. "In other words, Mr. Cantor, after that one 'practical joke' call, you never spoke to Joanna Voorhees again; is that correct?"

Sitting tall in his chair, Mark answered loud and clear, "That's correct."

Roselli moved even closer to his client, but turned his body to face the jury. "Mr. Cantor, you heard that tape the prosecutor played for this court—a series of threatening phone calls Joanna Voorhees received?" Mark nodded and his lawyer clutched both hands on the witness stand railing. "Tell the jury, Mr. Cantor: Did you make those calls?" he shouted.

Mark faced them. "I did not!" he said in a steady voice.

Roselli waited for a few seconds as Mark let the jurors look into his eyes. Then the Bald Beagle took a few steps back, leaned against the defense table, and spoke more softly: "And you heard that April twenty-ninth call, the last one on the tape, where the voice said he was downstairs and coming up to kill her? Did you make that call?"

"No, sir."

As they left the courthouse for the luncheon recess, Roselli asked Mark, "You hungry, kid?"

"No, not really," Cantor said.

"Well, you oughta put something in your stomach. Let's take a little walk and maybe you'll build up an appetite."

The rain had let up and the sun was trying to break through. Joined by Tom Bastone, they strolled through the concrete park behind the courthouse. The benches were still wet, keeping away the elderly Chinese people who were usually there playing checkers and reading newspapers.

"You did good, real good," Roselli said. Mark just nodded. "In fact, I'm almost glad you insisted on testifying. What'd you think, Tom?"

"Not guilty!" the private investigator said with a smile. He opened the buttons of his trenchcoat to reveal a diamond stickpin in his silk tie. "He sounded pretty good to me—straightforward, sincere, and totally credible."

"Well, I agree—you were great, just great," Roselli repeated.

"Thanks," Mark said softly, "it's not hard when you're telling the truth."

"Now just keep cool, think before you answer, and don't let Quinn bait you. If you do only half as good on cross as you did on direct . . . I'm not worried at all." Roselli's confidence brightened Bastone's mood, but Mark stared off into space, lost in his own thoughts.

They entered an old Italian restaurant on the other side of the park. While waiting for the hostess, Bastone recognized Detective Harrison and Sargeant Larsen seated in a side booth. "Maybe we should eat someplace else," he said, pointing with his eyes.

Judy Larsen looked up at Tom as if she wanted to speak. He stared back, his heart beating and his body frozen. After glancing at Mark, she turned her attention back to her luncheon companion and Bastone breathed a sigh of relief.

Bastone led them to a Chinese restaurant a block away, but only Roselli ate more than a few bites. On the way back to the courthouse, Mark led the pack, moving so quickly that his lawyer yelled, "Slow down. I'm an old man—don't want to have a heart attack just when I'm about to win a murder case." Then Roselli turned to Bastone: "First time I ever saw a defendant in a rush to be cross-examined!"

Most of Quinn's questions were expected, like: "When she stood you up, were you angry?"

"Disappointed, not angry. I was almost sure she had a reason . . ."

"And when you phoned her a week later and she offered no real explanation, were you angry then?"

"Sure."

"And when she told you that you were making a big deal out of nothing, because she was just 'high and horny,' did this make you more angry?"

Mark paused before answering. "Actually, I was very surprised."

"And angry?" Quinn shot back.

"And hurt," Mark corrected.

A smirk covered the prosecutor's face. "And when she told

you that she'd tried to phone and you knew that was a lie, were you angry, Mr. Cantor, or were you 'hurt'?"

"I guess that part made me angry. It's hard to separate my emotional reactions. I'd say, by the time that conversation was over, I was both angry and hurt."

"You were furious, weren't you?" Quinn baited.

Mark recognized the prosecutor's style and gave a knowing smile. "Look, I've dated a great deal and this wasn't the first time I'd ever been stood up. I've done it myself . . ."

Walking toward Mark, Quinn asked his next question: "Prior to your evening with Joanna Voorhees, when was the last date you'd had, Mr. Cantor?" He'd obviously done his homework.

"Quite a while . . . maybe months before. After I broke up with my girlfriend, I didn't go out with anyone for a while."

"About a *year*, wasn't it?"

"Maybe a year," Mark said, squeezing the arm of his chair.

Standing almost on top of the witness, Quinn raised his voice. "So Joanna Voorhees was your first date in a year and she stands you up, then puts you down, and lies to top it off. Weren't you furious, Mr. Cantor?"

With daggers in his eyes, Mark stared at the prosecutor. Roselli rose. "Would Your Honor please ask the prosecutor to step back and stop yelling in the witness's face."

Judge Warren told Quinn, "Move away from him," then turned to Mark and instructed him to answer.

The interruption seemed to calm Mark down. "I thought that she could've, at least, called to break the date. That part made me very angry."

"So angry that you wanted to get even, isn't that true?" asked Quinn, standing between the jury box and the prosecutor's table with a scowl on his face.

"No, I wasn't looking for revenge," Mark said softly.

"Then you phoned her, and without identifying yourself"—he paused and glanced at the jury—"you said 'Someday you'll pay,' or words to that effect, is that correct?"

"Yes."

"Well, Mr. Cantor"—Quinn marched toward the witness stand again, pointing his index finger—"didn't you make that anonymous, threatening phone call because you were furious at her and wanted to get even?"

Mark stared at Quinn for a few seconds, then gazed around the courtroom at the jurors, and the faces in the gallery. His eyes met Bastone's for an instant and then looked away. Finally, he took a deep breath and spoke slowly: "I didn't make that call 'to get even.' As I've already said—it wasn't planned. It turned into a childish practical joke, but I didn't make the call intending to do that. I phoned to scold her and make her aware . . . If she were standing in the room with me, I would've held her by the shoulders and shaken her—as you might to wake someone from a deep sleep. You see, Joanna Voorhees was unconscious—I honestly believe she didn't realize what a horrible thing she'd done." Although Mark regarded Quinn, his eyes kept wandering around the courtroom. "Of course, she knew it was wrong, but in her mind, she committed no crime; that kind of thing happens all the time," he said in a casual way as if he was mimicking her thought process. Then suddenly his face reddened and he turned up the volume: "That's why what she did to me was so bad— because it does happen all the time! This is the 'Me Generation'— nobody gives a damn about the other person. It's a disease . . . only the stricken don't suffer—just the people who come in contact with them!" Mark ran his fingers across his forehead to calm himself and resumed in a softer voice: "It may be worse in the singles world, where men and women frequently interact with people they hardly know, but you encounter this type of callousness everywhere these days.

"Most of us don't usually get very upset. We try not to let ourselves feel emotional pain—at the first sign, we brush it aside pretending it's not important." He leaned forward and continued. "But these experiences leave scars inside, making us suspicious and distrustful, afraid to be honest, afraid to connect with another human being. Before long," he raised his voice, "we've got the disease—do unto others before they do it to you! This disease is contagious," he warned, holding up his index finger, "and we've already got a plague on our hands.

"So many are afflicted . . . You can't tell by looking at them or talking to them—they seem okay," he said, his eyes blinking rapidly. "You don't know who they are, until you get burned."

Roselli started to rise, but changed his mind and sat back down as Mark resumed: "Most of them are basically good people. If they only realized what they were doing, they'd be cured.

That's why I phoned Joanna Voorhees—to shake her and say, 'You can't treat people like objects. People have feelings and feelings are fragile. You don't have to go out of your way for anyone, but at least be civil.' " Mark caught his breath. "I wanted her to know she'd hurt me."

Quinn jumped in: "So why did you disguise your voice, when you made the threatening phone calls?" he yelled.

"I made only one call, and I did not disguise my voice," Mark said calmly.

Slouched in his chair, Cantor looked exhausted, but relieved—the tension around his eyes for months suddenly gone. Everyone in the crowded courtroom sat silently staring at him. Finally, Judge Warren cleared his throat. Kevin Quinn shook his head, announced "No further questions," and returned to the prosecutor's table.

Late for an appointment with a client, Bastone rushed out of the courthouse after telling Mark he'd speak to him later. As Tom walked to the corner he noticed Judy Larsen leaving the building through a side door. Confident that Cantor's testimony had made his innocence apparent, he trotted to catch up to her.

"Hello," Bastone said, giving her a start. "Still think he's guilty?"

She looked up at him as if he were weird, then nodded. "Now I'm convinced."

Tom stepped back. "Do you honestly think he's the type of person who could have made those calls? Didn't you hear him today?"

Her cold blue eyes narrowed. "Yes, I did. And he sounded like a real nut job. They all think everyone *else* is crazy," she continued.

Bastone couldn't believe his ears: "No, no. You don't understand," he yelled, competing with the rumble of a delivery truck barreling down the narrow street. "He was talking about callousness—that's all. And Mark would be the first to admit that he's also been guilty of it. And what he said was so true."

"That there's a 'disease' sweeping the country—a 'plague,' " she mimicked with a sarcastic twang in her voice. "Come on, isn't that a bit much?"

"Oh, he was just being dramatic. As an assistant DA, his summations were always like that. It's his style."

"How do you know what his summations were like?" Larsen said with a raised eyebrow.

"I've seen Cantor in court many times," Bastone answered carefully.

But Larsen had begun to sense his emotional involvement in the case. "You've seen him in the course of your detective work?" she probed.

"No, I've known Mark for years." Tom looked straight into Judy's eyes. "He's my best friend."

Judy Larsen was furious. "You're a deceitful bastard and your friend's a lunatic!"

She turned and started to walk away, and Bastone grabbed her arm. "If Mark's guilty, why'd he offer to take a lie detector test?"

"Back then, he was being accused of pushing her out the window, remember?" she said in a condescending tone.

"But he still would've been asked about the calls."

"Maybe, maybe not."

Bastone didn't buy her answer, but another question troubled him: "Why wouldn't Quinn agree to give him the lie detector?" he asked. "And don't tell me that the DA didn't want to be accused of a whitewash—that's bullshit."

"They were afraid Cantor might beat the test," she blurted out. "He was very friendly with the guy who did the polygraphs for the Bronx DA's office and he knew a great deal about it." With a sneer on her face, Judy pushed Tom's hand from her arm. "Now leave me alone." She swept a golden strand of hair from her eyes, then marched off. After a few steps she stopped and turned back to Bastone. "And don't call me," she yelled.

"Oh, you don't have to worry about that!" Bastone shot back.

Summing up first, Phil Roselli came out blasting. He chastised the prosecution for changing the theory of its case in the middle of trial: "Quinn told you in his opening statement that he'd prove the defendant hit that girl over the head and threw her out the window." With a contemptuous glance at his adversary, he yelled, "And he'd still be trying to sell *that* bill of goods if *my* investigator hadn't found Dominick Mantucci." The Bald Beagle smiled. "Now he's gonna tell you my client murdered Joanna Voorhees by making a bunch of phone calls." He paused, shaking his head.

"But what proof is there that Mark Cantor made those phone calls?" Roselli reviewed the evidence of Mark's guilt, calling it "circumstantial," "flimsy," and "with more holes than Swiss cheese."

"Sure Cantor had her unlisted number, but was he the only one? No," he screamed, holding up the piece of paper with the list of names and addresses. "At least twelve others had that number. And these are only the people Joanna Voorhees told Larsen about. Who knows how many more?" he railed. "Who knows if she gave it to another stranger after a meeting on the street or in a bar?"

Judy Larsen was Roselli's next target. He waved the list in front of the jury. "The police investigated these people," he said with a sarcastic twang in his voice. "The lady sergeant asked them all if they did it. And guess what: each of them denied making the calls. End of that investigation." He tossed the list onto the prosecutor's table. "Very thorough," he said sarcastically. "That Larsen's a regular Columbo." Several jurors grinned and the defense lawyer responded immediately: "Yeah, it would be funny if an innocent man wasn't being tried for this thing."

Roselli stepped back with his hands in his jacket pockets.

"When asked if he had ever threatened Joanna Voorhees, Mark Cantor did not deny it. He made an implied admission when he said, 'That was just a joke.' But he was referring to *one* call— which wasn't even on the tape. '*That* was just a joke,' not—'*Those* were a joke.' One call, not several." Bent over, clasped hands bobbing as if in prayer, the Bald Beagle asked: "If Cantor had threatened to kill that girl, wouldn't he deny making *any* of those phone calls?"

Roselli then noted that Joanna recognized his client's voice during the first call—the one Mark admitted making. He recalled Larsen's testimony: "In the calls that followed—the recorded calls and one other—the voice was 'muffled' and 'much deeper.' Joanna Voorhees *assumed* they were made by the same person trying to disguise his voice. But if this were true, why didn't he disguise his voice the first time, too?" Not only were the voices different, Roselli pointed out, but also the "style" of the recorded calls differed drastically from that first one. Cantor's call was "short and simple," the others were "much longer, weird and sinister, subtle but not *too* subtle."

The defense lawyer sauntered away from the jury and leaned his rump against the rail fronting the first row of the gallery. "On the tape you heard Joanna say during one of the calls, 'I know it's you, Mark.' But did she really *know* or was she just guessing? No one can answer that. That's why the judge has told you not to consider it as any evidence against the defendant."

Roselli loosened his tie. "And there's another recorded conversation that you cannot consider as evidence." His face got redder and redder as he continued. "I am speaking about the April twenty-sixth call—she answers, 'Hello,' and for the next twenty seconds the tape is *silent,* then we hear only a few words: 'toward my hand,' the voice says. And how is this twenty-second gap explained? Detective Feldstein, supposedly an electronics *expert,* tells us he ac-ci-dentally erased part of that conversation. Evidence that might have shed new light on this case was *destroyed* by the police!" he shouted, walking to the defense table. "And if it was ac-ci-dental, and not de-liberate, then why does the transcript say 'inaudible'?" Roselli held it up as he marched toward the jury box, his jowls bouncing. " 'Inaudible,' " he screamed, "not 'erased.' Why did that cop lie when he made this transcript?" His eyes narrowed. "What are they covering up here?"

Quoting the character witness, Roselli told the jury that

his client is a "fine man, who'd dedicated his career to fighting crime." He noted Mark's willingness to testify, and the embarrassing admissions he'd frankly volunteered. But not wanting to remind the jury, the defense lawyer never mentioned Cantor's "sermon."

"One last thing," Roselli said, as if it were an afterthought: "Whoever did make those calls was a sick man who committed a mean, vile crime. But the crime was *not* murder. That last phone call may have been very frightening—but it was not the direct *cause* of Joanna Voorhees's death. She didn't die of a heart attack. She died because she jumped to the fire escape and didn't quite make it." Roselli bowed his head and spoke softly. "Her own act caused her death.

"Now, Mr. Quinn will tell you that this never would have happened if she hadn't received those phone calls. And, of course, he's right. But by the same token, if one of Miss Voorhees's neighbors—just one—had opened their door while she was screaming for help . . ."—his voice grew steadily louder—"if one of them had given her refuge . . . if one of them had just called the police *before* it was too late . . . that girl never would've tried that dangerous leap. Are the neighbors guilty of murder, too?"

Roselli paused for a moment, calmed himself, and resumed speaking softly. "Whoever made those calls should be found and punished. But not for murder, because under our law, he did not commit the crime of murder."

Roselli's summation was like a shotgun—loud and dramatic, spraying arguments everywhere to create a reasonable doubt somewhere. Kevin Quinn's closing remarks were more like a laser—quiet and methodically cool, but sharp and to the point.

He began where Roselli left off, addressing the issue of causation: "Let me pose a hypothetical set of facts which will clearly illustrate the proposition. Suppose I were to approach Phil Roselli on the street and at gunpoint force him into the rear seat of a chauffeured limousine. As the driver heads north on the parkway, I tell Mr. Roselli that we are going to a deserted area upstate where I intend to kill him. Fearing for his life, he decides to jump from the car. He may realize the danger in exiting a vehicle going fifty miles an hour, but, facing certain death if he remains, Roselli is willing to take the risk. When the opportunity presents itself, he opens the door and makes his escape. Unfortunately, his head strikes the pavement and he dies as a result." Quinn stood erect, his eyes moving from one juror to the next. "I submit to you, ladies and gentlemen, that if this had happened I would be guilty of murder. For even if I had not really *intended* to kill Mr. Roselli, even if it was just a bad joke, my reckless conduct caused his death.

"In the same exact way, those threatening phone calls put Joanna Voorhees in a state of fear. And the last convinced her that she faced imminent death."

Reading from the transcript, Quinn deepened his voice: " 'Now I want you to listen carefully to me—you know who this is. I'm downstairs, in the corner phone booth. In the last half hour, I've made a dozen bogus calls to the Sixth Precinct. Every available patrol car in the area will be tied up for at least the next twenty minutes. You can try the cops but they'll never get there in time.'

"At this point, you'll recall, Miss Voorhees said: 'Why are you doing this to me? Why don't—'

"And then he cut her off, saying: 'I have your keys and I'm coming up. In a few minutes you'll be dead.' "

"So she tries Larsen's hot line and it's busy, or maybe she can't find the number. She screams for help. . . ." Quinn reenacted the probable sequence of events, a version identical to the one Roselli had proposed a few days before in the judge's chambers. "The fire escape is her only hope and the only way she can get to it is by leaping from the adjoining window. She may well have realized the danger, but Joanna Voorhees had no choice." Quinn stared down at the floor as if the girl's decapitated body lay there. After the pause, he added, "Yes, her neighbors might have *prevented* her death, but they certainly didn't *cause* it. The man who made that phone call killed her—as surely as if he'd pushed her out the window. And the man who made that phone call," Quinn raised his voice for the first time, "the man who made *all* those threatening calls, was that man," he yelled, turning and pointing, "the defendant—Mark Cantor!" Roselli couldn't hold back a smile, thinking Quinn had copied his client's "*j'accuse* position."

The prosecutor also argued persuasively that Cantor made the calls, countering Roselli's main points as he highlighted the evidence: "The defendant made false statements on an official form to obtain her unpublished telephone number. And he would have you believe that he went to all *that* trouble and never dialed the number! Absolutely unbelievable.

"By his own testimony, the defendant was angry at Miss Voorhees—angry and *hurt!* She'd made him suffer and he wanted to get even. He needed that phone number to execute his plan for *revenge*—a scheme to terrorize this young woman with a series of anonymous, threatening calls, each more frightening than the last, and the final one—the scariest of them all. A coward's revenge," Quinn called it, in a voice sharp with anger.

Never roaming from a centered position in front of the jury, he continued: "This case might have been difficult, but Mr. Cantor made it easy for you. When asked if he'd threatened her over the phone, he told Sergeant Larsen, 'That was just a joke'— an *admission* that he'd made those calls. Now he claims to have done it only *once*. But he admits he phoned and, without identifying himself, threatened her. The defense asks you to believe that there was *another* man who did the *same* thing to the *same* person, at about the *same* time. What a coincidence!" Quinn grinned before pausing to sip from a cup of water.

" 'If Cantor made all the calls,' Mr. Roselli asks, 'why didn't he disguise his voice for the first one?' The answer is obvious: after the first, he became more cautious. A novice when he began, he merely 'improved' his technique. And for the same reason, the calls got longer and more diabolical. It's that simple," he declared.

Since the prosecution had abandoned their claim that Mark had entered Joanna's building and pushed her out the window, Judy Weisenberg's testimony no longer seemed significant. But Kevin Quinn never conceded that she'd been mistaken and proposed that evidence as further proof of Mark's guilt: "If the defendant didn't make that last call, what was he doing on Joanna's block moments later?" he asked rhetorically. "You'll recall, Miss Weisenberg positively identified him as the man who almost knocked her down as she returned home on that tragic night. She saw Cantor close up and even spoke to him briefly. Another coincidence? Or was he hoping to get a glimpse at the havoc he'd wrought? After all, revenge is so much sweeter when you can actually *see* the results. And if Mr. Cantor just happened to be there, why did he tell Sergeant Larsen that he was definitely home all evening on April twenty-ninth? If he hadn't made that call, he'd have no reason to lie."

During the prosecution's one-hour summation, Joanna's mother sat in the first row dabbing her teary eyes with a lace handkerchief. Roselli had expected Quinn to conclude with a mournful eulogy and an impassioned plea for justice. Instead, he merely turned to the defense table and calmly said, "According to Mr. Roselli, the man who made these calls was 'sick.'" Then, regarding the jury with a cold stare: "The defendant testified. You saw him, you *heard* him. You decide."

From the moment the jury enters the courtroom to deliver its verdict until it's announced, the world stops. You can't think about women, sports, personal problems, or anything else. There's an intense silence, disturbed only by the pounding of your heart, as if it were your *life on the line.*
Mark Cantor, 1974
describing to Tom Bastone
the thrill of being an Assistant DA

On the first day of the jury's deliberation, Roselli and Cantor camped out in the courthouse hallway. Bastone stopped later in the afternoon to join the pacing. At six P.M., Judge Warren sent the jurors out for dinner and at eleven P.M. when the jury still hadn't reached a verdict, he ordered them sequestered at a hotel.

On the following day, Roselli and Cantor were given permission to wait at Bastone's office, since it wasn't far from the courthouse. Phil had brought a pile of paperwork with him, but was unable to concentrate on that and passed the time cursing over the *New York Times* crossword puzzle. Bastone moved in and out of the office, handled an occasional phone call, and, trying to be a good host, offered his guests tea, coffee, and soda. Cantor couldn't sit still and spent most of the morning circling the office, with frequent stops at the window where he stared out in an almost catatonic way.

Well past noon, Bastone broke one of the long periods of silence when he said, with a note of optimism: "The longer the jury's out, the better it is for the defense—isn't that what they say, Mark?"

When Cantor didn't respond, Tom called to him and repeated the remark. Mark turned away from the window to face his friend. "Usually that's right," he said, "but not in this case. If the jury believed I didn't make those crazy calls, they would've been back in less than an hour. But if they think I did, they've got to decide the issue of causation . . . and that could be taking all this time."

An eavesdropping Roselli, amused by Cantor's dogmatic tone, looked up and smiled but said nothing. Bastone noticed the grin and asked, "What do you think, Phil?"

"I don't play that game any more!" he answered, puffing on his third cigar of the morning. "It's ridiculous. They're out for a day and a half—so what does that mean? Eleven jurors could've voted for acquittal on the first ballot and they're all waiting for one blockhead to come around. Who the hell knows! You can never tell what's goin' on in there." He flicked a long ash in a paper coffee cup rather than dirty the pewter dish Bastone had provided for that purpose. "A few months ago I tried a case where the jury had been deliberating for days. The foreman comes in with a note: 'Could the judge explain again the difference between robbery in the first degree and robbery in the second degree?' Sure he's got a winner, the prosecutor is grinning from ear to ear. The judge rereads that part of his instructions to the jury and a half hour later they come in with a verdict—not guilty on every count! You figure it out."

Just then the intercom in the office buzzed. "Judge Warren's clerk is calling for Mr. Roselli," came the voice of Bastone's secretary. "Pick up on three."

Roselli lifted the receiver to his ear. He listened for a moment, then answered, "We'll be right over." Cantor didn't know whether they were being summoned because the jury had reached its decision, or if they merely had a question. He stared at his lawyer, waiting for the answer. Roselli picked up his attaché case and announced: "Gentlemen, they've got a verdict."

By the time the three of them arrived at the courtroom, it was already packed. Judy Larsen sat next to Joanna Voorhees's mother in the front row, alongside Detective Harrison. The press corps had swelled during the last days of the trial and, pads in hand, occupied almost the entire second row. As the elderly court buffs fought curious lawyers for places to sit, Kevin Quinn arrived through a side door, his necktie loose and his hair uncharacteristically mussed.

The court clerk tried to quiet the buzzing crowd by pounding a book on his desk. "All rise," he yelled as Judge Warren entered, his robe slightly askew because he'd skipped a button. Throughout the trial, the judge had always *followed* the jurors into the courtroom, but now he *preceded* them as if recognizing that today their act had top billing. In a conversational tone he said, "Bring in the jury," and his words silenced all chatter.

Mark's heartbeat quickened, as it always did at this part of a trial, but this time *his* life was on the line. Cantor had always claimed he could anticipate a verdict by watching the jurors as they entered the courtroom. If they looked at the defendant, it meant acquittal, but if they avoided his eyes—a conviction. But as the jury walked in through the side door, Mark stared straight ahead.

At the judge's instruction, the foreman stood. "Has the jury reached a verdict?" he was asked by Warren.

A slightly built man in his late fifties with a bent nose and an obvious toupee, the foreman cleared his throat before answering. "We have, Your Honor." The world stopped.

"As to Count Two, charging murder in the second degree, how do you find—guilty or not guilty?"

The long, dank room, filled with
fifty or more formica tables, looked like an old mess hall. Fluorescent lights hung from the thirty-foot ceiling, and yellow paint
brightened cinderblock walls, but the cloudy day, through wire-
screened windows, overwhelmed the cavernous space. Cantor
and Bastone sat on hard, wooden chairs among a sea of faces—
mostly black and Hispanic. The stench of ammonia permeated
the air.

"I guess they just cleaned the place," Tom said, sniffing hard.

"They're *always* cleaning around here," Mark snickered.
"That's because they don't have to pay their help."

Mark Cantor had been convicted of murder in the second
degree. He'd become dazed when the jury announced its verdict
and hadn't even heard Roselli on his feet asking to have the jury
polled. After the last juror stood to confirm the vote, two court
officers led Mark out in handcuffs.

Three days later, Bastone visited him at the men's house
of detention on Rikers Island. His eyes looked glassy and his
face was pale and drawn.

"Are you okay?" Tom asked.

He nodded. "I'm fine."

"Are you sure? You don't look so good. Do they have a
doctor you can see?"

"I'm all right—just a little constipated. The last time I took
a shit was when the foreman said 'Guilty.' I can't go to the bathroom here—the stalls don't have any fuckin' doors."

"It's like the army. You'll get used to it."

"I better."

Cantor's parents still knew nothing about his arrest and
prosecution. Tom offered to help, but Mark replied, "Thanks,
but I've got to take care of this myself."

At first, Bastone strained to hear him amid the din of forty other "private" conversations in the same room, but he soon grew accustomed to the background noise. Hoping to raise his friend's spirits, Tom told him that Roselli had already hired a specialist to handle the appeal. "The lawyer's name is Meltzer and he's supposed to be excellent."

Mark spoke in a monotone. "I know—Phil was here yesterday. . . . Meltzer's one of the best."

"They've already discussed the case and Meltzer thinks you've got a good shot at a reversal."

"Yeah, Phil told me." Mark's voice trailed off. "But even if we win the appeal, everyone will still think I made the phone calls."

"Not after you're vindicated," Tom urged.

Lost in thought, Mark ignored his friend's optimism: "Those calls were so weird . . ."

"They sure were," Bastone responded. "I never thought there were so many different ways to threaten someone."

"Yeah, he certainly was more creative than me!"

"And more literary—he quotes from Shakespeare," Tom joked, forgetting for a second that the line from *Macbeth* was in the call *erased* from the tape before Mark heard it.

"Well, I know 'Friends, Romans, and countrymen, lend me your ears,' " Cantor grinned, "but I never even read *Mac—
. . . beth.*" He swallowed the second syllable, suddenly realizing his slip, and his mouth dropped open.

Immediately, Bastone realized that Mark couldn't have known about that call unless he'd made it. A lead weight lay in Tom's stomach and the clamor around them became a faint hum. Mark stared at his friend with wounded eyes as if Tom had intended to trap him. Bastone, too, felt betrayed. "Is this a dagger which I see before me—the handle toward *your* hand?" he paraphrased.

A nervous smile crossed Cantor's face. "How did *you* know what was said during that call?"

"It's a long story," Tom answered, not wanting to digress with the tale of his encounters with Judy Larsen. "I guess I don't have to ask you that same question."

"I'm sorry," Mark said softly, tears welling in his eyes. "I couldn't admit it to anyone—not even you."

Leaning over the table, Tom whispered, "Why? Why did you do it?"

"I've already answered that question—on the witness stand. I told the truth, except . . ." Mark looked at him without blinking, "One call wasn't enough—you made me realize that."

"I encouraged you to make those calls?" Bastone asked, trying to keep his voice down.

"Not deliberately," Mark smiled. "Remember when I phoned you after I'd made the first call? You told me it was no big deal, that she'd think it was a prankster or a wrong number, and that she'd soon forget all about it."

"So?"

"So that was no good. I wanted her to worry about it—I wanted to shake her up. Of course, I never expected . . ." Mark's head fell into his hands and he clutched it, beginning to weep.

Then one of the guards approached the table, his muscled arms bulging from a short-sleeved blue uniform. The shiny black face with cold eyes looked down at Mark and Tom. "Time's up."

Epilogue

On December 1, 1976, Mark Cantor was sentenced to a prison term of not less than fifteen years and not more than life. "Sometimes the law seems unduly harsh," Judge Warren began. "I daresay that if the jurors could have been told the consequences of their verdict, they may well have reached a different result. But they have found you guilty of murder in the second degree and the law mandates no lesser punishment than I have imposed."

On December 3, 1976, Mark was taken to Sing Sing Prison in Ossining, New York, to serve his time. Among the inmate population were at least two dozen convicted felons who'd been prosecuted by Cantor. To insure his safety, he was immediately placed in "protective isolation."

On March 17, 1977, the Appellate Division for the First

Department decided to reverse the conviction of Mark Cantor. In addition to citing errors in evidentiary rulings by the trial judge, the court held: "The causal connection between the defendant's conduct and the death was insufficient, as a matter of law, since the intervening actions by the deceased could not reasonably be foreseen." A new trial was ordered for the crime of aggravated harassment. The court's decision was not typed and filed until March 24, 1977.

On March 19, 1977, Mark Cantor's body was found in a canvas vat in the prison laundry. The medical examiner found ten stab wounds inflicted by at least three different "sharp instruments." No one was ever charged with his murder.